PLEADING
the Fish

SEASIDE CAFÉ MYSTERIES, BOOK 7

BREE BAKER

Poisoned Pen
PRESS

Published by Poisoned Pen Press, an imprint of Sourcebooks
P.O. Box 4410, Naperville, Illinois 60567-4410
(630) 961-3900
sourcebooks.com

Library of Congress Cataloging-in-Publication Data

Names: Baker, Bree, author.
Title: Pleading the fish / Bree Baker.
Description: Naperville, Illinois : Poisoned Pen Press, [2022] | Series:
  Seaside cafe mysteries; book 7
Identifiers: LCCN 2021037080 (print) | LCCN
2021037081 (ebook) | (paperback) | (epub)
Classification: LCC PS3602.A5847 P54 2022 (print) | LCC PS3602.A5847
  (ebook) | DDC 813/.6--dc23
LC record available at https://lccn.loc.gov/2021037080
LC ebook record available at https://lccn.loc.gov/2021037081

Printed and bound in Canada.
MBP 10 9 8 7 6 5 4 3 2 1

ALSO BY BREE BAKER

SEASIDE CAFÉ MYSTERIES

Live and Let Chai

No Good Tea Goes Unpunished

Tide and Punishment

A Call for Kelp

Closely Harbored Secrets

Partners in Lime

To my sweet mama and her unending love of the sea

PROLOGUE

APRIL

I didn't believe in my family's curses until I met Grady Hays. Even then, it had taken a couple of years and plenty of dangerous situations for me to come around. According to my great-aunts, Swan women were cursed in two specific ways. One, we couldn't leave the island; if we did, bad things would happen. Two, we couldn't fall in love, lest the object of our affection surely die. The amount of evidence in support of both curses was astounding.

Still, I used to believe folks made their own luck with level heads, determination, and good decisions. I'd mastered the former two at a young age, but I'd been working on the latter all my life. Which explained the occasional life-threatening situation I wound up in. Curiosity gone awry, not a curse in action. At least, that was what I'd thought until my most recent bad choice landed Grady (not me) in the hospital only days after I'd realized I was no longer falling for him—I'd already completed the trip and landed hard. Before I'd dared voice the truth to anyone, the curse had struck, and I'd almost lost him. I couldn't let that happen again.

So like the level-headed, determined woman I was, I'd been actively avoiding Grady ever since. For his safety.

And like the strong-willed, intelligent, kind, protective, perfect man he was, he'd given me the space I'd needed. Until ten minutes ago, when he'd materialized in my gardens, at the gazebo where I sat, alone in the dark, wishing he was there.

"Can we talk?" Grady asked, pleading with ethereal gray eyes. He'd traded his usual detective uniform for a suit and tie. The jacket hung, folded, over one crooked arm. He looked gorgeous and slightly tormented. The long sleeves of his dress shirt had been rolled up to his elbows. His sleek black tie hung loose and askew. The top button undone at his throat. He'd clearly dressed for my best friend, Amelia's, massive birthday party happening inside my home.

"I don't think that's a good idea," I admitted. "I miss you, and I hate the way things have been, but they'll get easier with time." At least, I hoped they would.

He stuffed something small and dark into his pocket, a gift for Amelia, perhaps, but his eyes never left mine. "How've you been?"

Awful, terrible, and miserable came to mind. "Okay," I said instead, looking away. In truth, I'd felt as if half of myself had gone missing in the weeks since I'd last seen him. And I hated the bland, awkward way my future seemed to roll out before me with an obvious missing piece. Like living the rest of my days under hazy skies when I knew the sun was just on the other side.

"I haven't been okay," he said. "My body's healed, but I'm not whole."

My eyes snapped back to him, his words so closely echoing my thoughts. "What if my family is really cursed?" I whispered. The hearty spring breeze picked up around us when I voiced the concern, throwing my wild brown curls against my cheeks. The scents of freshly bloomed flowers and the sea mixed with Grady's signature cologne, and my resolve weakened by a fraction.

He moved closer, raising both hands to push the hair from my face, then cupped my cheeks in big warm palms, holding the curls at bay. Withstanding the wind for me. Shielding me from it. Forever my protector in all things great and small. "I told you, I don't believe in curses," he said, caressing my chilled skin with his thumbs. "I meant that."

"Everyone else believes," I said. "How can this entire community be wrong for two centuries running?"

My family's legends and lore were practically historical fact in my hometown of Charm, North Carolina, a small seaside village on a set of barrier islands known to most as the Outer Banks. My ancestors had settled the town more than three hundred years ago, so to the Swans, Charm had always simply been home.

Grady's eyes searched mine. Determination slowly

changed the hope in his expression to resolve. As if he'd just realized whatever he was up to would be harder than he'd planned, and he was rising to the challenge. "People thought the earth was flat for a lot longer than that, and plenty still do. It doesn't make it true."

I frowned. "Are you comparing me to a flat earther? Because this is not the same. If they're wrong, you won't die an untimely death and orphan your son." I pressed my lips and wrapped my arms around my middle, sickened by the thought of poor Denver losing another parent. He'd already lost his mother to cancer while he was still in preschool. I'd never take any risk so selfish that it would leave him fatherless too.

Grady pinched the bridge of his nose. "Flat earthers are wrong," he said. "There's no possibility they're right. Just like there is no possibility that you are cursed. Look." He dropped his hands to his sides and fixed me with that determined stare once more. "I should've probably led with this, or told you about two years sooner, but I love you, Everly Swan. Deeply and without condition. That won't change, and your family folklore won't stop me."

I gasped, eyes misting and mind reeling. I stepped back on instinct, checking the sky for stray bolts of lightning, and one flashed. "Oh!" I scurried further away. "No, no, no," I hissed. "You can't say that." I covered my mouth before I recanted and begged to hear him say those words again.

Grady scowled and stalked forward. "Your family isn't cursed. You aren't cursed."

Thunder rolled.

"Grady, don't," I warned.

"I came here to ask you something," he said. "I wavered a while. Partially because I knew you'd react this way and partially because this isn't how I'd planned to ask. But that's on me, because I fell in love with a nut." He smiled and reached into his pocket.

I shook my head and backed out of the gazebo at the opening on the opposite side. My heart couldn't afford to hear whatever it was he wanted to ask. Because whatever it was, I would agree. Grady Hays had a hold on me like none other. He was my weakness, even though he was my strength. Which made zero sense, and my thoughts began to coil like a corkscrew.

And holy tea cakes! He loved me too? My heart skittered, then took off at a sprint.

The night sky darkened formidably, as if hearing my thoughts. Thick clouds raced over the moon, plunging us into darkness. It wasn't uncommon for storms to brew and hit quickly on the island, but typically they were predicted by local weather reports. Tonight was supposed to be a perfect night.

Laughter and voices spilled from my home, reminding me of the party going on inside. Bright, smiling faces were visible through the windows, each lit with the merriment and hoopla of the theatrical magic-library-themed event, arranged by Amelia's boyfriend, Ryan.

Outside, the raging winds and Grady's confession threatened to blow me into the sea.

He pulled out his hand and produced a small dark box.

My heart rate grew loud, pounding wildly in my gut, throat, and head. "What is that?"

He snaked a long arm out and caught me as I tripped over a cluster of newly bloomed daffodils. "Hey," he said gently, broad hand spreading over my back as he hauled me to him. The frown I loved was plastered on his handsome face. His concentration face. "Stop running from me."

"Stop chasing me," I said, unintentionally breathless and utterly without conviction.

"Never."

I smiled, and his frown deepened.

Waves broke and crashed against the beach, only yards from my home. Lightning flashed brightly, sending streaks of gleaming white against an inky sky. Electricity raised the hairs on my neck and arms.

"If I let you go, are you going to try to escape again?" he asked. "Or can I please do what I came here to do?"

"Depends," I said, pulling masses of windblown hair away from my face once more. "If you're here to say love is enough to save you from my curse, you're wrong. My dad and every other man unfortunate enough to be loved by a Swan woman is proof of that. Plenty of them dropped dead much younger than you," I said, projecting my voice against the storm.

Grady's jaw set.

"You would do the same thing I'm doing if the tides were turned. And you know it," I accused. "So don't ask me to risk a single second of your life, Grady Hays. I won't."

Grady stuffed the box back into his pocket and wedged his big hands over narrow hips. The thin material of his shirt and pants beat roughly in the ferocious wind. He cocked his head and eyed me. "What if there's proof the curse is fake, or at least blown out of proportion?"

My brows raised. "Proof?"

"Yes. What if the truth is documented somewhere?" he pressed. "At one of the island historical societies, in a library or your family's archives? What if we pinpoint where this rumor started and track it to the present? Including all the reasonable explanations for things everyone around here accepts as mystical mojo?"

"Really bad mystical mojo," I muttered. *The deadly kind.*

But I'd never considered seeking specific details before.

I looked out to sea and wondered if what he'd suggested was possible. My family kept an extensive archive at the homestead, with tomes from almost as far back as we'd been on the island. Could there be documentation to support Grady's theory?

Was it possible I wasn't cursed?

My gaze snapped back to Grady, ready to set a research plan into action, but his determined face was no longer posed six inches above mine.

He was on one knee before me, wobbling slightly in the relentless wind. The small box in his hand. "Everly," he said, speaking my name with pure adoration and reverence. "I love you. I have loved you for a long while now. In various little ways from the start, then in every possible way, until I couldn't deny or ignore the truth any longer."

Wind howled through nearby trees, and rain began to fall as I struggled for breath.

"I admire your tenacity of spirit, your wicked laugh, and your lemon cake." He grinned. Fat drops of rain slid over his cheeks and forehead as he looked into my eyes. "I aspire to be like you, to be more trusting and less jaded. To have your big heart and to love others the way you do, selflessly and with abandon. Most of all, I love the way you love me, despite myself, and the way you love my son. I don't deserve you. I know that, but it doesn't change the fact I want to be by your side, in all things, whatever comes. Always."

Tears burned my eyes, blurring my vision as he opened the box.

A beautiful diamond, sapphire, and emerald ring sat inside.

"I found this in an antique jewelry store," he said. "It sounds crazy, but it spoke to me, and it said it belonged to you." He rose and removed the ring from the box, putting the case back into his pocket. "This diamond reminded me of you, brilliant and mighty, delicate in appearance, but stronger than any other stone. The sapphires and emeralds reminded me of this place, the plants and the sea. A golden band to represent the sand." He lifted my hands in his, the ring pinched between his thumb and first finger. His Adam's apple bobbed. "Do you trust me?"

I nodded, speechless and unprecedentedly peaceful in the midst of a bellowing storm.

"Do you love me?" he asked, flipping his gaze from one

of my eyes to the other. Seeking truth and undoubtedly finding it.

"Yes."

"Marry me," he said. "And I promise you I will outlive everyone you know out of sheer hardheadedness and the compulsive need to please you."

I laughed, and more tears began to fall.

"Trust me," he implored. "You are not cursed. You are the embodiment of life and love and goodness. You don't deserve to live in fear of loving me or of being loved by me, and you can't stop it anyway. It's too late. I'm already yours, heart and soul."

I threw my arms around his neck without answer, beaten and battered by stinging wind and rain. And I cried against his collar. The choice he asked me to make was impossible, excruciating. Gutting. If I chose wrong, he would pay the ultimate price.

Grady drew back, resting his forehead to mine. "What if *I'm* right?" he asked, echoing the path my thoughts had been on. "What if I'm right, and we miss out on fifty or sixty years of life together. On countless epic adventures, on children and grandchildren. What if we don't get to grow old and gray and wrinkly together because we were afraid."

He tilted his head and kissed me slowly. "Everly," he whispered against my lips. "Don't be afraid."

I exhaled a lifetime of fear and kissed him back.

The storm faded behind my closed lids. And I saw a vision of myself in white, walking the aisle in his direction, then another of me heavy with his child. I saw myself at Denver's graduation, and with Grady years after that, cradling grandbabies in our arms.

I slid my fingers into his wet hair and pressed myself against him, despite the storm trying to tear us apart.

My future had always been and would always be Grady Hays.

There was never a decision to make.

So I said yes.

CHAPTER

ONE

"How do you feel about sand sculptures?" Amelia asked. Her cheery voice rang through my cell phone speaker as I motored along Bay Street in my golf cart, Blue.

I smiled, enjoying the stifling July heat. Summers in Charm were hot and humid, the brilliant southern sun oppressive and relentless. Determined rays brought color to everything in sight, from pinked cheeks and tanned skin to the endless bouquets of beautiful flowers and native greenery. I loved it all.

"I like sandcastles," I said. "Are you thinking of hitting the beach after work and looking for company?" A drop of sweat fell from my brow, and I nudged my large, white-rimmed sunglasses higher on my sweaty nose.

"Everly," she scolded. "You know exactly why I'm asking."

I did, and that fact only made my stomach clench. She was trying to sort out the details for my beach wedding. "The beach is pretty perfect already. Don't you think?"

"I do," she said. "I just want to make sure we've thought of everything, and you get the wedding day you've always dreamed of, you know? Ice sculptures are popular at indoor venues. I thought sandcastles could be a fun seaside twist."

"Simple is probably better," I said. "I'd get married in cutoffs and flip-flops if you'd let me."

"Everly," she said again, this time breaking my name into syllables. "This is your wedding, not a high school bonfire."

I smiled at the little phone screen attached to my dashboard, where her thin, freckled face frowned back.

"Fine. I'll mark sandcastles off the list, but you are wearing a wedding gown." She tightened her sleek blond ponytail, then raised a pen.

I put my eyes back on the road.

Amelia had appointed herself my personal wedding coordinator the moment Grady and I had announced our engagement. I'd easily agreed. Both because I was intimidated by the thought of organizing such a large-scale event and because until I found the answers I needed about my family's alleged love curse, I wouldn't be able to think of much else.

So far, the loosely laid wedding day plans included a small beach ceremony, followed by a massive town-wide reception at the Swan family homestead. Grady's old friends from DC and the U.S. Marshal Service would likely attend the party as well.

"Welcome to Charming Reads," Amelia called, flicking her gaze away from the camera.

Amelia owned and operated the town's only bookshop, and she rarely had more than a minute or two between customers. Which meant I was about to be off the hook.

"Gotta go?" I asked, shamefully crossing one set of fingers on the steering wheel. I was excited to marry Grady, thrilled even, but our quest to disprove my family curse was off to a pathetic start, and we'd been looking for three months. It was getting difficult to emotionally separate phrases like "wedding day" from others like "Grady's untimely demise." Nothing about the latter made me happy, so getting amped up about the former was basically a nonstarter.

"In a minute," she said. "Do you want to meet for lunch and go over options for the guests' swag bags?"

"Can't," I said, taking the final turn toward my destination. "I'm meeting Aunt Clara at Northrop Manor now. Are you attending the fish fry tonight?" I parked Blue beside my great-aunt's Prius.

"That's the plan," she said. "And if Ryan's flight isn't delayed, he'll be with me. I'm expecting to pick him up at the airport this afternoon."

I smiled despite myself. The nosy Manhattan reporter-turned-friend made Amelia happy, and that made me happy. "Sounds like this is shaping up to be a great day."

Amelia squealed. "Okay. I'd better go check on my customers," she said. "See you tonight!"

"Bye," I told the phone, already back to my home screen following the disconnected call.

I climbed down from the cart, then collected my purse and picnic basket.

Before me, the historic Northrop property extended as far as the eye could see, eventually spilling into the sound on the other side of an extensive manicured lawn. The home was yellow with a maroon roof, black shutters, and matching door. The structure had been commissioned at the turn of the last century by a mega-wealthy industrialist. Since then, the place had been bought and sold by other incomprehensibly wealthy families. Most recently, Grady's mother-in-law. Thankfully, she'd sold the place to the town historical society before returning to DC last year.

Now, after months of preparation, the property would soon open as a living museum. Tonight, locals would celebrate the victory with a fish fry. The party was a thank you gift to the countless volunteers, donators, and workers who had made the transformation from private home to public museum possible. There were few things Charmers loved more than preserving and honoring history, especially island history, and the lineup of guest speakers, historians, and actors in period costumes already on board for the season was remarkable.

I squinted at the glint of sunshine off distant waters as I hurried toward the front door. Even my favorite sunglasses weren't enough to dim that shine.

As president of Charm's Society for the Preservation and Retelling of Unrecorded History, my great-aunt Clara had been given an office inside the manor. Her society was dedicated to preserving and passing on stories of our land, culture, and people that no one had ever bothered to write down. I'd suggested the group take a few minutes to properly document the tales now, but she said that wasn't the point. Storytelling was apparently an art.

The whole thing seemed like an excuse to spread really old gossip to me, and it probably amounted to the longest-running game of telephone on record, but it made a lot of people happy, Aunt Clara included, so who was I to argue?

Last night the museum had offered Aunt Clara a reoccurring role, telling the unrecorded stories to visitors and guests, and she'd eagerly agreed. I was bringing lunch from my café to celebrate.

I waved at the elderly security guard seated on a stool in the entryway. "Hey, Oscar," I said, setting my sunglasses on my head and smiling. I fished inside my basket and retrieved a jar of mint iced tea, then set it on the welcome table at his side. I added half of a paper-wrapped pita I'd stuffed with grilled tomatoes, peppers, and pesto at its side, then set a thin stack of napkins on top. "Aunt Clara says you eat junk from the vending machine at lunch," I explained. "She also says you need to watch your blood sugar, so she asked me to bring you something more nutritious."

He smiled at the delivery. "She did?"

I nodded, and his smile widened. "Your aunt's a good woman," he said, eagerly unwrapping the sandwich. "Always worrying about everyone else."

"It's in our DNA," I said, appreciating that he hadn't assumed she was nosy or meddlesome. Aunt Clara genuinely cared. About everyone. And everything. "I brought her lunch too. You're welcome to join us if you want."

"Oh, no," he said, raising bushy caterpillar brows. "I

wouldn't think of interrupting Clara's quality time with her favorite great niece. I'm trying to stay on her good side. If I play my cards right, she might eventually accept my offer to buy her ice cream." He stage winked. "Put in a good word for me?"

"Absolutely." I took a step away before turning back. "Any chance Susan Thames is here today?"

Oscar set the pita down and checked a clipboard on the desk. He ran a thin finger over the grid of names, dates, and times. "Yes, ma'am," he said. "Looks like she's here until one o'clock today."

I checked the time on my bossy fitness bracelet. 12:10. I could eat with Aunt Clara and still catch Susan before she left. "Perfect. Thank you!"

I hurried down the long hall to my aunt's office. Oil paintings of the estate's previous owners lined the walls in large, gilded frames. Little lights illuminated the subjects' faces and the small plaques engraved with their names and life spans. I smirked at the fact Senator Denver hadn't sat for a painting during her short stint as a Northrop owner. Denver's grandma had spent some time in Charm, supposedly to be near her grandson, though she'd also wanted Grady to do her an enormous favor. I wasn't clear which was her true motivation, but I supposed it was a mix of the two. Regardless, she'd never really made Charm her home, and it would've felt wrong to see her among the portraits now.

"Knock knock," I called, rapping my knuckles against the wooden trim around Aunt Clara's door.

"Goodness!" She straightened sharply in her chair, positioned behind a large cherry desk. "You nearly scared the honey out of me," she accused, rising and smiling as she hustled in my direction. Her long silver and blond hair flowed over narrow shoulders, nearly to her waist, a style she'd worn faithfully for the thirty years I'd known her. She kissed my cheek, then peeked into the hallway before closing the door behind me. "Did you see anyone out there?"

I frowned. "Just Oscar."

Aunt Clara pressed her lips together, then turned away, hurrying back to her seat.

I set the picnic basket on the desk and fixed my attention on her. "What's gotten into you?" Aunt Clara was normally the calm, easygoing one. I was the uptight nervous nelly.

She took a steadying breath, then fixed a polite expression into place, but tension coiled visibly through her small frame, betraying her feigned cool. "There's a man in town who's been asking about me, and it's put me on edge. He came into Blessed Bee yesterday while I was here and asked Pearl a lot of questions before spending the afternoon at the café across the street."

Pearl was one of a handful of seniors living at the Crooked Oaks Retirement Community, who called themselves Corkers, based on the initials and phonetics. Their little group was always in search of ways to stay entertained and busy, so they'd picked up some shifts at Blessed Bee, my aunts' shop in town. The new situation was a triple win. The Corkers had something extra to do, Aunt Clara could spend more time at the museum, and her sister and business partner, Aunt Fran, could concentrate on being the town mayor.

Aunt Clara peered up at me, unsettled and vulnerable. "What do you think he's up to?"

"I don't know," I said, setting two jars of pomegranate white iced tea on the desk between us. "Didn't Pearl ask him?"

She shook her head, then screwed the lid off one jar. "He didn't introduce himself or leave a card. Am I wrong to worry?"

"You're never wrong to feel what you feel, but I'm sure his interest isn't nefarious," I told her. "I'll see what I can find out. Did Pearl give you a description?"

Aunt Clara pried the lid from her strawberry soup next and stirred the pale pink mixture. "She guessed him to be in his forties. Fair skin, balding, and dressed in nice slacks with loafers, so he probably wasn't local. Traveling business-man, maybe. A lawyer?" She covered her mouth. "Do you think I'm in trouble?"

I raised my eyebrows. Aunt Clara was seventy-two years old. She co-owned a shop with her older sister, where they sold products made from honey produced by their bees and flowers grown in their gardens. She was the definition of innocent and wholesome. "What could you be in trouble for?"

Her shoulders climbed to her ears.

I took the seat opposite her, then spread a napkin across my knees. "I'll find him and ask how I can help," I said. "If I don't like what he has to say, I'll point Grady in his direction. He doesn't get to throw his weight around much living here. He'd appreciate the opportunity."

Aunt Clara patted my hand. "Thank you. Now, let's talk about you. When will you be coming over to look at the family wedding gowns?"

I froze, a pickle poised before my lips. "Soon." I bit into the spear, crunching and avoiding eye contact. "Maybe the next time I come by to read in the archives."

"And when will that be?"

I moved on to the hummus and flatbread triangles. "There's no rush. I still have three months to choose a dress," I said. Not to mention the fact I wasn't sure I could go through with the wedding if the curse wasn't disproven soon.

The mean little voice in my head reminded me that the vows didn't matter. Swans didn't have to marry a man to set him on a course for destruction. A nice voice never piped up to set him straight.

I set the pita aside, rubbing the spot on my chest where an invisible vise had tightened. "I'm actually hoping to catch Susan Thames before she leaves today," I said, wiping my mouth and fingers with a napkin. "I'm hoping she's had some luck looking into things for me."

Aunt Clara's smile fell a bit. "Oh, sweetie," she said. "It's a long shot. You know that."

"I know," I said. "But I have to try."

I'd contacted Susan the morning after Grady's proposal because she was unequivocally the island's best researcher and she specialized in local lore. She had a special interest in my family's alleged curses, and as a result, she'd given me a drastic discount on her usual fees.

If anyone could dig up the facts about our alleged family curses, or evidence against them, it was her.

Aunt Clara nodded. "Of course."

My great-aunts were firm believers who'd each lost a lover in their youth. Aunt Clara's gentleman was a fisherman lost at sea. Aunt Fran's had a motorcycle accident near the cape. Having both loved and lost, my aunts waffled between cautious joy for my big day and preemptive grief for Grady's imminent demise.

The whole thing was a struggle.

"Tell you what," she said, squaring her shoulders and refreshing her smile. "How about you go see Susan, and I'll have lunch with Oscar. I'm not ready for him to buy me ice cream, but I can carry my lunch out there and share my mealtime with him. You brought him something too?" she asked.

I smiled. "I told him it was from you."

Her jaw dropped. "Snitch."

"I'll catch you later and we can trade stories," I said. "I'll let you know if Susan learned anything new, and you can tell me all about your lunch date."

"It's not a date," she said, hurriedly gathering her meal.

I took a long pull on my iced tea, then returned the jar to her desk. "Whatever you say."

We parted ways in the hall, and I hurried to Susan's office.

The room was filled to the brim with books, maps, and

documentation piled on endless overflowing shelves. The strap of her handbag poked out of her desk drawer, but Susan was nowhere to be seen.

I groaned at my terrible luck, then resolved to find her. She hadn't gone home without her purse, so she had to be on the premises somewhere. I started with the ladies' room, then worked my way through the building, checking every interior nook and cranny before heading outside.

Twelve minutes later, I had sweat circles under my arms, a stitch in my side, and eyes on my target. "Susan!" I called, one hand gripping my ribs and the other hand waving above my head.

"Everly?" She smiled and waved in return. Her tan dress pants and white blouse were neat as a pin, accented by a beautiful sea glass necklace and navy blue flats. Her chin-length brown bob was tucked behind her ears. Red-rimmed glasses roosted on her nose, coordinating nicely with the color on her lips. "What are you doing here?"

I slowed to a walking pace and attempted to catch my breath.

She waited beside an old well outside a small, reno-vated stable, which had been transformed into a costume closet for museum staff. The well appeared to be a work in progress.

"I was just looking for you," I said, still panting slightly when I arrived.

"Here I am," she said. "I try to get out here every time I'm on the property. It's a routine I've adopted. Do you know about this well?" she asked.

I gave the structure a more thorough look. The wooden frame, rope, and bucket over its brick and mortar base was new. The brick and mortar were crumbling.

"I don't think so," I said, stopping to catch my breath and eyeball the structure. "There's a story?" I guessed.

She nodded, eyes bright. Susan was probably in her fifties, but when she spoke about island legends and history, she looked and sounded like an awestruck youth. "This well is very special." She ran a hand along the new wooden frame. "It's fed by an underground lake. The water level is at a historic low, and we were able to get a look at its depths."

"Find anything good?" I asked, curiosity piqued.

Her smile was wry. "Quite a bit of moss and duckweed. And about a thousand old coins."

I gaped, my gaze swinging to the well. "Wow."

"Legend has it, the water from this well kept many souls alive during the building of the home. There was a horrific drought throughout the islands that year, but this well provided. People came from all around to get water for their families and livestock. It was considered a miracle by many."

"How were you able to see what's down there?" I asked. The stone frame seemed unstable. I couldn't imagine leaning over for a better view was the method of choice.

"Tunnels." She raised a smile and her brows. "When the original owners wanted to know what happened to the water following the drought, they went looking. Teams of men dug in this direction from the basement below the manor. It took a few failed tries and false starts, but eventually they made it. I recently had the opportunity to take a look as well."

I turned wide eyes to the distant home, then back to my friend. "What's it like down there?"

She shrugged. "Dark and dirty, but also amazing. The place where the lake existed is now a hollowed-out cavern. In places, the water is shallow enough to see all the coins from years gone by."

"Why do you think people started tossing money in there?" I tried again to see into the depths, careful to keep my distance from the ancient bricks.

"After the drought ended and the well stopped being used for water, folks remembered the miracle and started asking for other things. Hoping to receive their hearts' desires," she said softly. "I drop a penny in here every day before I head home, and I ask for the preservation of this lovely island tradition. Do you want to know why?"

"Because you value traditions?" I guessed.

"Because I believe in the power of hope." She smiled warmly as she fished a pair of coins from her pocket. "Would you like to join me?"

"Absolutely," I agreed, accepting the offered coin.

"What will you hope for?" she asked.

"Won't that ruin the wish?"

She shrugged. "I think that sometimes giving voice to what we need helps the universe answer."

"Like prayer," I said.

"Exactly."

I closed my eyes and tossed in the coin, not ready to speak my wish aloud. There was a long silence before the hint of a splash far below.

Susan held her coin over the well and fingered the beads of sea glass on her necklace with the other hand. "I hope this tradition never ends," she said. Then she let the penny fall. "We need to understand our past if we want to improve our futures." She turned back to me with a sigh. "Time is so important. None of us have enough of it, and not enough people appreciate the time they have."

I nodded, fully in agreement. I'd lost my grandma, the woman who'd raised me, far too soon and without warning. I wasn't over it, and most days, I missed her so much it hurt. I didn't want to lose anyone else before their time. And I wanted to make the most of mine, preferably surrounded by the people I loved. "Any luck digging into my family's past?" I asked.

"Some," she said. "You?"

"There are a lot of books to go through in the family archives, but my aunts are working on it. So are Grady and I, when we have the time," I said. The problem was that the family archives were an extensive hodgepodge of journals, songbooks, cookbooks, and ledgers. The ink was often faded or illegible on delicate, discolored paper. Fully exploring a single book took hours, and there were hundreds. Legal documents were scarce, and I suspected Susan was much more likely to locate any official documents than we were.

"Keep plugging away. Most families can't trace their lineage back three or four hundred years the way you can," she said.

"It's quite fascinating. You have nothing to lose and a deeper understanding of your ancestry and legacy to gain. That is absolutely priceless."

I smiled, absorbing her contagious energy.

"Meanwhile," she went on. "I'm compiling all the legal documents and newspaper articles I can find regarding the births, deaths, and general doings of your family throughout the years. The file's in my office."

"Are you headed back there now?" I asked, certain it was past the time Oscar said she was leaving.

"No." She frowned. "I got suckered into a meeting I hadn't planned for. I won't be available this afternoon, but I'll be back for the fish fry tonight. Will you be here?"

"Yes."

She nodded. "I'll get the file to you tonight."

Her gaze lifted over my shoulders and seemed to catch on something in the distance. Her frown deepened, the wind clearly gone from her sails. "I'll see you then." She stepped around me with a rigid back and marched toward the home's front entry.

A tall, slender man stood near the manor's door. His jet-black hair fluttered in the balmy breeze, and he fiddled with the button on one cuff of his dress shirt as she approached.

My phone buzzed in my pocket, reminding me it was time to get to work at the café, before my friend and helper, Denise, had to leave.

I gave the man a closer look as I headed toward Blue.

He trailed me briefly with his gaze, until Susan arrived and ushered him inside.

I couldn't help wondering who he was and why someone as kind and happy as Susan had been so clearly displeased to meet with him. And why she'd felt she had to.

But I had plenty of things that were my own business to look into, and a stranger, who was allegedly following Aunt Clara, to locate and question. So I adjusted my sunglasses on my nose and climbed behind Blue's wheel with a grin.

Tonight, I would get a file of details to help me prove I wasn't cursed.

CHAPTER

TWO

My insides fluttered a moment before the doorbell rang, and I knew Grady had arrived. My ability to sense his nearness was uncanny and a little surreal, but true nonetheless. I hurried down the interior stairwell from my private second-floor living quarters to the first floor of my historic Victorian home. My favorite flowy, aqua, A-line tank top fluttered over the hips of my most comfortable jean shorts. My favorite accessory, the unspeakably beautiful engagement ring on my left hand, was a constant reminder of Grady, and it twinkled as I opened the door.

He drank me in with cool gray eyes, and my already racing pulse spiked. His strong, stubbled jaw and confident, capable posture curled my toes inside my sneakers. The Charm P.D. T-shirt and jeans told me he'd just gotten off work and hadn't had time to go home and change.

"Hey," I said. "Thanks for picking me up."

"No problem," he said. "I've been waiting for this all day."

"The fish fry?"

He stepped forward, a small look of amusement on his handsome face. "You."

"Oh." I melted into his kiss, and my brain went a little fuzzy.

Too soon, he rested his forehead against mine and peeled partially away.

I struggled to stay upright and collect my marbles. The buzzing of my bossy fitness bracelet drew our collective attention to my wrist.

Digital fireworks shot across the tiny screen, congratulating me on my workout. "Look at what you did," I panted. "You got me all worked up again, and this thing thinks I was exercising."

Grady chuckled. "I like your bracelet."

"Because it feeds your ego." I tried to scoff, but a head full of dopamine and serotonin from our kiss made it impossible. "This thing is mean when you aren't around. And all these falsely recorded workouts are skewing my progress charts."

He released me with a broad smile. "Hungry?"

"You have to ask?" I rolled my eyes. "It's as if you don't know me at all, Grady Hays." I locked the front door and let him lead me to his truck. "Community fish fries are the best." I'd offered to contribute side dishes from my café, but the historical society had it covered. So tonight, I was just a girl on a date.

Grady opened the passenger door and helped me inside, then circled back to the driver's side and climbed behind the wheel. A moment later, we were off.

Riding in Grady's truck was the best. The soft leather

interior was always warm from long days in the sun, and it smelled like all my favorite things: Grady's signature shampoo and cologne, mingled with scents from an open pack of spearmint gum in the cupholder and the beloved salty sea air. A small baseball mitt lay on the seat between us.

"How'd baseball camp go today?" I asked, stroking the glove with my fingers.

Grady shot me a proud daddy grin. "They're teaching Denver to pitch, and he's loving it. Denise took him home to shower and change, then they'll meet us at the manor."

I turned my eyes to the road, imagining our little man in action, pitching his first game. I couldn't wait to ask him for details.

We picked up speed outside the downtown area. Warm night air rushed through the open windows, cocooning us as we traveled. Darkness dimmed our views of the ocean and sound, one on each side of the road, while simultaneously illuminating the sea of stars overhead.

"How was your day?" Grady asked.

"Good," I said. "And it's about to get better. I ran into Susan Thames at Northrop Manor around lunchtime. She has a file of information about my family, and she's giving it to me tonight."

He reached for my hand, twining our fingers on the seat between us.

I smiled. Hope had been bubbling in me all day as I'd daydreamed between customers about what Susan might've found. I was nearing my limit for contained anticipation. Any minute I'd surely burst.

"Just remember," Grady said. "There's always a reasonable explanation, even for the most unreasonable things." He glanced at me when I didn't respond. "And no matter what's in the folder, we're going to figure this out. We'll get you the peace you need. Whatever it takes."

His thumb blazed a trail across my knuckles to the ring he'd placed on my finger a few short months ago. "Okay?" he prompted.

I fought the familiar wave of emotions that always came with the reminder my love could hurt him. "Okay."

Grady's gaze warmed my cheek a long moment before he turned his attention back to the road. "You think this is an impossible quest, but it's not. Curses aren't real, and I'm going to convince you I'm right. I just have to disprove the centuries-old rumor, then grow old at your side."

I laughed at the enormity of his goals. "No problem then."

"Not for us," he said, lifting our joined hands to his lips. "Of all the things you and your unusual town have taught me, the fact nothing is impossible has been my favorite."

I rested my head against the seat back and turned my eyes to the stars, treasuring the time alone with my fiancé. Two busy schedules, a well-meaning, but nosy, community, and his absolute angel of a son, Denver, made these quiet moments few and sometimes far between. So I did my best to absorb them, to be present and not to let worry steal any of the joy. Not easy for a natural worrier.

Thankfully, my mind was a busy place, and it didn't take long to push the worry aside. A happy thought turned my attention back to Grady. "I made some progress on the third floor," I said proudly. I'd been avoiding it for months due to the sheer scope of work, but I'd discovered a few minutes each morning after my first cup of coffee and the sunrise made a big difference at the week's end.

My home was large and filled with endless nooks and crannies. The house had once been used as a boarding school, and later as apartments during the Great Depression. There was more than enough square footage for my café on the first floor, and Grady, Denver, and me on the second, but I wanted more than "good enough" for them. I wanted them to feel truly at home.

It had only been a couple of years since they'd moved to Charm from the mainland after Grady's wife's death. So my house would be Denver's third in five years. That was a lot for anyone, and I wanted him to know this move would be his last.

Grady had offered for me to move into their home after the wedding, but I couldn't fathom leaving my place. It didn't make sense for me to commute to work every day when I could continue to live right upstairs. Plus, I was attached to my home. Grady had to commute for work, regardless of where he lived, and Denver did the same for school. So logically, their move made sense, not mine.

Both Hays men would miss their stables and horses, but I had the beach outside my back door. Not to mention a part-time cat and peculiar seagull who liked to haunt the place. Maggie and Lou were just as good as any horses. And I loved horses.

"Do you have a plan in mind for the third floor?" Grady asked. "Are you thinking elbow grease and a coat of paint, or should I call a construction company?"

"Probably both," I admitted. The top floor of my home was used like an attic. An unfinished place to store things and collect dust. But it was also a blank slate with endless opportunities. "I moved some things left by previous owners to an unused bedroom that I'm now considering storage space. I'll figure out what to do with all that later. My aunts will take anything I want to keep, but not necessarily store, back to the homestead, and the historical society will take any antiques I want to donate. I'm planning a yard sale for the rest. Once the space is empty, I thought we could hire an interior designer to make an official plan."

"For a playroom?" Grady asked.

"Maybe a couple of rooms or a suite," I said. "The whole floor could be Denver's personal domain. Bedroom, playroom, possible home theatre, game room, whatever you think. And he can choose the colors and theme."

The expression on Grady's face softened, turning from interest to awe. And I felt the tug on my heartstrings. "You don't have to do all that," he said.

"I want to. This can be our first family project." I squeezed his fingers and smiled. "We are going to be amazing together and raise the happiest, most adored and well-adjusted child on this planet."

Grady's Adam's apple bobbed and he nodded.

Our short drive ended far too soon, and Grady piloted the behemoth truck into a field designated for parking.

We hopped out and made our way into the mix of happy Charmers and their guests, hand in hand. Rows of bistro lights bobbed and danced in the breeze off the sound, illuminating a large area lined in buffet tables that smelled like my best dreams. My stomach cheered in response.

Piles of fish, grilled, pan-seared, and battered, filled shiny silver trays, accompanied by a variety of steamed veggies, cornbread, shrimp and crab.

My great-aunts were haunting the dessert table, small plates piled high, because Swans knew how to party.

I lifted my fingers in a wave as we headed in their direction. Aunt Clara and Aunt Fran were half sisters who shared a mother but had different fathers. They also shared a passion for old-fashioned clothing and both preferred monochromatic looks. Aunt Clara leaned on whites, creams, and silvers, all beautiful accompaniments to her light skin, eyes, and hair. Aunt Fran stuck almost exclusively to black, which accented her olive skin, dark eyes, and salt-and-pepper hair. More often than not, the color choices reflected their personalities.

I might've looked like Aunt Fran, but the similarities dwindled there. Most significantly, she was tough and fearless. I was a marshmallow.

Grady leaned close to my ear as we walked. "Clara looks uncomfortable. Did something happen?"

I frowned, having nearly forgotten what she'd told me earlier, and loving that Grady was nearly as attuned to my aunts as he was to me. "She thinks she's being followed by a balding, middle-aged man from out of town," I said, rushing to tell the story before arriving at my aunts' sides. "Apparently, he came into Blessed Bee while the Corkers were covering her shift, and he asked a lot of questions. Then he sat outside the rest of the afternoon."

"Waiting for her?" Grady guessed.

"Maybe, but regardless, the news weirded her out." I frowned because it was probably my fault she'd assumed the worst of the stranger. I'd spent eight years away from the island and seemed to have brought a string of bad luck home with me. There'd been six murders in about three years, and a historic number of associated crimes, including several abductions and attempted murders starring me as the victim. I doubted an inquiring customer, even an especially curious one, would've worried Aunt Clara a few short years ago.

Grady wrapped an arm around my waist. "Let me know if you need my help," he whispered.

I beamed. "I love that you don't ask me to leave things alone anymore," I said. "And that you're willing to help if I come up short."

"I quit asking because you never listened," he grouched. "And I've always been helpful, you were just too stubborn to ask."

I sighed, overcome with pleasure once more. "You totally get me."

Grady snorted, and I felt him shake with silent laughter as we cut through the crowd.

A couple I recognized, but didn't personally know, smiled cautiously at me as they passed. The man fixed

Grady with a remorseful expression, then whispered to the woman as they walked away.

I gaped after them, dragging my eyes back to Grady on a pang of sorrow and indignation. "Did you see the look they gave you?" I whispered. They were probably thinking about how sad it was that Grady would soon marry me, then drop dead.

Grady tugged me against his side. "Most folks look at me that way. You forget I'm a cop in a small town. And not a people person. You can't make a whole town like me."

"Challenge accepted," I said, hoping he'd survive long enough for me to make good on the promise.

"Then you're going to have to petition to raise the speed limits," he said. "Because I gave that guy two tickets on Main Street this month. Most recently, while he was on his way to church with his family in the car."

I looked over my shoulder at the disappearing couple behind us. "He's upset about getting speeding tickets?"

"I assume," Grady said, "but I don't worry about what everyone else is thinking. You should try it. It's great."

I made a sour face. "As if I haven't tried."

Aunt Clara's face lit when we finally drew near. She set her plate on a tall table near the buffet. "There you are! I'm so glad to see you." She wrapped me in a tight hug, then grappled for Grady, pulling him in too.

He patted her back, either in affection or like a pinned wrestler asking for release.

I wasn't sure which, but both made me smile.

"Already on dessert?" he asked, when she finally set us free.

"We start with dessert," Aunt Clara said.

"We have to," Aunt Fran added, moving in to give me a hug. "Everyone always overdoes it with fish at a fish fry, and there are never enough sweets to go around. You look beautiful tonight."

"You too," I said, stepping out of her hug.

"Grady," she said, sweeping her mischievous gaze to him. "How are you doing?"

I tried not to imagine the question as diagnostic. *Feeling weaker? As if you have one foot in the grave? Perhaps only three months to live?*

"Good," he said, setting a palm against his flat stomach and tipping his head toward the buffet. "Better now."

My aunts exchanged a look.

"Have you seen Susan Thames?" I asked, interrupting their silent exchange. "She has some paperwork for me, and I'd like to look it over with Grady while we eat."

Aunt Clara frowned. "Not in a while. She met with a mason before the party began. Trying to schedule repairs for the well, I believe. I'm sure she's in her office now."

"If she isn't already out here having a bite to eat," Aunt Fran suggested. "It's been nearly an hour."

"Daddy!" Denver's small voice rose above the din of the crowd, and we turned collectively to see him collide with Grady's legs and hips.

Grady bent to kiss his son's cheek, then tousle his hair. "Hey, buddy. How was baseball camp?"

"Great!" Denver said. "Coach says I'm a natural, and Denise promised I can stay up late tonight. She also said I can have four desserts! Hi, Everly!"

I crouched to hug and kiss him. "No wonder I like Denise so much," I said. "Do you think she'll let me have four desserts too?"

Denver's eyes sparkled, and he nodded.

Grady leveled Denver with a steady gaze. "Did Denise really say that?"

His son looked to my aunts for help. "She implied it," he said.

Aunt Clara nodded.

Grady narrowed his eyes. "How did she imply it?"

Denver wet his lips, looking everywhere but at his dad. "I asked if I could have five desserts and she said no."

Aunt Fran barked a laugh, already reaching for his hand. "Sounds like solid logic to me."

Aunt Clara followed behind them. "Come now. We have to hurry or there won't be four desserts left. That's the trick at a fish fry."

I smiled after them, warmed to my toes by the hope of a thousand similar memories to come.

Grady set his palm against my back. "I don't think I can adequately explain how much those two mean to me for what they've done for him."

"They know," I whispered. "My aunts see right through people, the good and the bad. It's nice until you want to keep a secret." I scanned the crowd for my dear friend and Denver's au pair. "Have you seen Denise?" It wasn't like her to be separated from Denver so long. At eight years old, he wasn't exactly a preschooler anymore, but she normally kept a closer eye.

"Waylaid," he said.

I followed his fresh frown face to Denise. She'd been waylaid by a group of men in khaki pants and polo shirts. I groaned, reminded of how difficult it was for anyone with the face and figure of a human Barbie doll to do anything without a fair amount of ogling and unwanted attention. She always handled it well, though she shouldn't have to handle it at all. Adults should simply know how to behave. Thankfully, I also knew that if any one of her admirers got out of line, Denise could and would flatten them.

Grady sighed. "I'm going to see if she needs a reason to leave that conversation."

"You're a good man," I said. "Can I meet you back here in a few minutes? I want to look for Susan and grab that file."

He nodded. "Sounds good. Be careful."

I smiled and shook my head. "Silly. Nothing nefarious happens at a fish fry."

CHAPTER

THREE

Northrop Manor was still and dimly lit as I made my way to Susan's office. Stanchions with velvet ropes guided fish fry guests to and from the restrooms. An easel at the center of the main hallway instructed readers to stay behind the ropes.

I ducked swiftly beneath the crimson dividers, then eased around the sign and hurried down the long, narrow hall.

The historic home creaked and moaned with age, slowing and startling me multiple times as I made my way to Susan's office. I stilled at the squeak of the back door opening and closing, followed by the sounds of low voices in the kitchen, presumably catering staff.

Susan's closed door was a welcome sight, far better than finding the office empty as I had before. A set of angry voices rising inside kept me from knocking.

I dropped my fisted hand to my side, unsure if I should wait my turn to speak with her or go away and give the quarrelers privacy. Their tones were harsh, words sharp and clipped, but nearly indistinguishable through the heavy oak between us.

As the argument cooled, Susan's even timbre became easier to distinguish. The other voice, however, remained low and deep.

I considered interrupting to free her from the spat or provide her a means of escape, like the one Grady had gone to offer Denise. But Susan's voice sounded nearer the door, and I tiptoe ran through the nearest archway and into the mammoth kitchen.

"Everly?" Amelia asked, appearing before me at the kitchen island. She held a chocolate-dipped strawberry halfway to her open mouth. Her red blouse, lips, and nails accented the fruit. Her straight, blond hair was twisted into a delicate knot at the nape of her neck, and she'd paired the red blouse with a black pencil skirt and matching Mary Jane heels. Backdropped by a gourmet French country kitchen, she could've been ripped from a magazine ad for better island living.

Ryan smirked at her side, his black dress pants and red tie coordinating perfectly with her ensemble. "What are you doing?" he asked, obviously amused.

"I—" I abandoned my goofy tiptoe sprint and strode more casually toward the marble island, listening surreptitiously for sounds of footfalls or voices in the hall behind me. "I thought I heard someone in here. I never expected it to be you. What are you guys up to?" I scanned them appreciatively once more. "You look fantastic. Tell me you didn't dress up for a fish fry."

Amelia lowered the strawberry with a frown. "No. Ryan took me out to dinner before we came here. Why were you running?"

"Just looking for a ladies' room," I fibbed, the words sounding more like a question than an answer. "Why are you two in the kitchen if you've already been out to eat? Wait." I did some mental backtracking. "Why go out to dinner if you were coming to the fish fry?"

The couple traded an odd look.

Ryan inhaled dramatically. "We were celebrating, then we came here for mingling and dessert."

"The desserts outside weren't enough?" I asked, helping myself to a piece of chocolate-covered fruit from the tray. "Now you sound like my aunts."

Amelia tapped her strawberry to mine in cheers. "The desserts outside are gone," she said. "The table was wiped clean when we arrived. We sneaked in here to see if the caterers had anything saved for later. This was all that's left."

I bit into the sweet, juicy treat with a flutter of my lashes and groan of delight.

Amelia soon followed suit.

Ryan shook his head at us, a smile tugging at his lips.

"Welcome back to Charm," I told him. "How was your flight?"

"I've had worse." He lifted his gaze over my shoulder, pointedly staring at the archway where I'd run in. "Don't you know where the restrooms are? Grady's mother-in-law lived here for almost a year, didn't she? Surely you visited then, and Amelia said Clara has an office here now."

Amelia wiped her fingers on a napkin and arched a brow. "He's right. What are you up to?"

I hung my head with a dramatic sigh, then darted back to the archway and peered into the hall. When I found the space empty, I returned to my friends and confessed. "I wasn't looking for a bathroom."

They listened to my story, grinning instead of being offended by my initial lie.

"I've truly missed you, Everly Swan," Ryan said fondly, drawing Amelia's back against his chest. "You never fail to entertain."

Amelia's smile widened, and she tipped her head back for a look at his thoughtful expression. "Ryan is thinking of moving here."

Ryan kissed her forehead sweetly, then lifted his eyes to mine. "I could travel to cover stories and work remotely as needed."

I finished my second strawberry without comment, thrilled to see my best friend smile.

"You should go back and knock on Susan's door," Amelia said. "We don't want to keep you, and I know how important getting that information is to you. Grab the file, then come find us. I want to know what's she's found."

Ryan nodded. "Agreed. Do share."

Uncertainty reared as I looked over my shoulder again. Had she known someone was listening outside her office door when she'd opened it? Had she seen me running away?

The sounds of furtive whispering pulled my eyes back to my friends.

Ryan was the first to look my way. "Make sure you come back when you finish," he said. "We have some news to share when you have time."

My gaze dropped to Amelia's left hand. Her ring finger was bare, and I couldn't imagine what else the news might be. "What is it?" I asked. "Something good or something bad?"

"Both," Amelia said. She took a deep breath and smiled, apparently unable to wait. "My publisher asked for a sequel to the children's book I wrote last year. *The Mystery of the Missing Mustang* has gone back to print eleven times. They've translated it into twelve languages. It's been a much bigger success than anyone expected, and all of a sudden, readers want more."

"That's fantastic!" I told her, rocking onto my toes with a burst of excitement. "Do you have an idea for book two?"

"I think so," she said. "I sent a couple of pitches to my agent this morning and she liked them so much, I might get to write them both."

My eyes caught on an oddly familiar figure outside the kitchen window. I watched as it moved swiftly across the darkened lawn, away from the party. A narrow shadow sailed unnaturally along the tree line in her wake.

"I received the call just after Ryan arrived and—" Amelia said.

I lifted a hand to interrupt her. "Sorry," I said, rushing to the window. "I think I just saw Susan headed away from the party, and someone might be following her."

My friends moved to my sides, squinting through the glass and into the night.

"I don't see anyone," Amelia said. "Are you sure?"

I trained my gaze on the place where the shadows had disappeared, and a strange sensation lifted the hairs at the back of my neck. "I think so."

Amelia set her hand on my shoulder. "I'll check her office, hang on."

"Wait up," Ryan called after her. He touched my arm, pulling my eyes to his. "We still need to talk tonight," he said.

I nodded, impossibly distracted by the feeling something sketchy was happening outside.

Ryan's footfalls softened as he followed Amelia.

I kept my eyes trained on the scene beyond the glass. The silhouettes of tall black trees swayed against an inky blue sky. The bevy of stars played hide-and-seek behind reaching limbs and racing clouds.

I stepped through the back door, listening to the night and asking myself if I should worry or be more patient.

Maybe Susan was meeting someone for a tryst or rendezvous.

Maybe it hadn't been her at all.

My heart hammered with the need to know what she knew about my family. Was it safe to marry the love of my life or not?

The door opened behind me, and I turned.

Amelia scowled. "I was gone for less than two minutes. You couldn't wait inside? Have you learned nothing these last few years?"

Ryan took her hand in his. "How about a stroll over the

grounds?" he suggested, nodding to indicate I should start moving in the direction the shadows had gone.

I led the way, waffling between feelings of fear and stupidity. "Maybe we should call her name," I said. "In case she and a second person came out here to be alone. I don't want to interrupt a secret rendezvous."

Ryan chuckled. "That would be awkward."

"Susan?" I called, projecting my voice into the night. When she didn't answer, I cupped my hands to my mouth and tried again. "Susan?"

Muffled voices carried to us on the wind, and I strained my eyes to see in the dark. "Do you hear that?" I whispered.

"Yeah," Amelia said, taking my hand in hers. "But if that's her talking, why isn't she answering? If we hear her, she must hear you."

A sharp scream of terror rent the night before I could answer.

We all froze, and Ryan cursed.

I knew instinctually the cry was Susan's.

"Grady!" I hollered, belting the word from my core as I launched in the direction of the solitary scream. "Grady!" I yelled again, louder and more desperately, bumbling blindly through the night.

My name rose on repeat behind me, projected from Amelia's frantic lips. "Everly!"

Ryan's low tenor relayed the gist of what had happened, in a one-sided conversation, presumably to someone by cell phone.

I pulled my phone from one pocket and activated the

flashlight app, vastly improving my ability to see in the darkness.

Amelia arrived at my side and clamped one hand over my forearm, fingernails biting into my skin. "Stop!"

We fell still together, panting as I swung the beam of my light across the ground, praying I wouldn't find Susan sprawled and lifeless, like so many others I'd discovered in these last few years.

"Everly!" Grady bellowed. His long, fit strides eviscerated the distance between us as I turned to watch his approach. Ryan followed on his tail.

Amelia released me a moment before Grady's arm was around my waist, turning me to him. His searching eyes were frantic, as they roamed my face, expression hard. "Are you okay?"

I nodded. "We heard a scream. I thought it was Susan, but no one's here."

Grady held me against his chest with one strong arm while he accessed the light on his phone. "Come on," he said, when the app was on. Then he slid his hand into mine. "We'll look together."

Something crunched unnaturally underfoot, and I stopped short, turning my light to the ground. The broken remnants of a small sea glass bead glittered in the grass.

I gasped softly, fear prickling over my skin. "Susan had a necklace on with beads like those when I saw her at lunchtime," I whispered.

A swipe of his light across the ground before us revealed more pieces of the necklace.

Grady tugged me forward, stepping carefully to give the beads a wide berth. "Watch out," he said, turning back to warn Ryan and Amelia. "Those could be evidence."

The other couple stopped moving, opting to wait it out where they stood.

The wishing well came into a view a moment later. One section of bricks was completely missing, the crumbling mortar having given up its hold. "Grady," I whispered, shining my light on the spot. "That damage is new."

He tucked me behind him as we approached the well. Grady raised his phone and adjusted the beam. A low cuss slipped from his mouth, and I poked my head around for a look at the cause.

Twenty feet below us, Susan floated, eyes open and unseeing in the shallow, murky water, her pale face covered in moss and duckweed.

CHAPTER
FOUR

An hour later, everything around me had changed. The peppy ambience of our town-wide celebration had been stripped away, along with most of the staff and guests. My great-aunts had helped pack the remaining food into small containers and were distributing them to guests on their way home. The process was slow, given the amount of food and fact no one could leave without first being interviewed and subsequently dismissed by local police personnel.

Thankfully, Denise had been permitted to slip away and take Denver home almost immediately. The same was true for a group of people Grady had been speaking with when he heard my screams.

Ryan and Amelia had gone home as well. I certainly didn't blame them.

I sat alone in the grass, knees pulled to my chest and heart pounding as Grady worked. A torrent of freshly unveiled trauma, from my presence at six similar scenes in half the number of years, twisted like a corkscrew through my heart. I concentrated on breathing and holding myself together, while everything inside wanted to break apart.

The coroner put his pen light away, finished poking and prodding Susan for now. He made notes on a clipboard at his side, and I wished I knew what he saw. Had someone pushed her? Or had she been making a wish, and the bricks gave way, causing her to fall? Where was the person we'd heard her speaking with before she'd screamed?

The ominous sound of the zipper on the coroner's bag sent chills up my spine, and I watched in fresh remorse as a pair of EMTs piloted her gurney back to the waiting van.

My mind flew through the details of the night as I watched them go. I replayed my conversation with Susan earlier and hated that I hadn't reached her sooner.

My presence might've saved her.

The memory of a man I'd seen earlier, at the entrance to Northrop Manor, returned to me. Susan hadn't wanted to meet with him. Had he returned all these hours later to finish something they'd started at lunch? Was he the man I heard her arguing with in her office? And who was he anyway?

A shadow stretched over me in the thin halo of light cast from crime scene spotlights set up around the well.

My friend and local EMT, Matt, crouched at my side. "Hey, Everly. You doing okay?" he asked, taking my hand gently in his.

I nodded, eyes full of tears at his kindness. It took longer than it should've for me to realize he wasn't holding my hand and gazing into my eyes so much as checking my pulse and pupils. Likely for signs of shock.

When he kissed my cheek and stood, then nodded to Grady, my suspicions were confirmed. "Okay," he said. "Call me if you need anything."

"I will. But I'm fine." I tried and failed to smile, then shot Grady an accusing glance, knowing he'd asked Matt to look me over.

He turned quickly away, as if he wasn't busted.

I often gave him a hard time, but in truth, I never minded that he looked out for me. It was actually one of my favorite things about him.

Several minutes passed before I got company again.

Amelia and Ryan folded themselves onto the grass at my sides, bookending me between them.

"You came back," I said.

They each curled an arm behind me.

"I will always come back for you," Amelia said. "Dad's on his way with Susan's husband. He and Mr. Thames are friends, so I had a feeling he would know where to find him. Apparently, he was on a fishing trip."

"Mr. Thames was fishing?" I asked, curiosity piquing. Was that unfortunate, or suspiciously convenient?

Maybe I was unnecessarily jaded and cynical.

Amelia leaned her head on my shoulder. "Cell reception was bad, so Dad radioed the boat, then met Mr. Thames at the dock and drove him here."

As if on cue, the ragged croaks of an emotional human broke through the white noise of a dozen first responders crawling the immediate area.

"Where is she?" A man with puffy eyes and a round

belly appeared several yards away. His hair was the color of rust, shocked through with flecks of white to match his beard. "Where is Susan? I want to see her!"

Grady stepped calmly into his path, lifting an arm to slow the guy's pace. "Mr. Thames?"

The man scanned the scene, eyes catching on me and my friends, briefly, before slipping away.

"I'm Detective Grady Hays," Grady said. "Charm P.D."

I watched in renewed horror as Grady explained the situation, and Susan's husband broke down in tears, collapsing into Grady's arms.

For a moment, I wondered, selfishly, if this was all a part of my curse at play. Had I somehow extended my bad luck to her, by asking her to dig into my family's lore? The eerie possibility clung to my skin like spiderwebs.

Ryan stood, then extended a hand to me. "Come on. Grady won't mind if we take you home. You can feed us and tell us we're pretty." He winked. "You know you want to."

Amelia followed his lead, standing and offering her hand as well. "Do you like my messy bun and comfy clothes?" she asked. "We changed while we were waiting for Dad to get a hold of Mr. Thames."

I scanned her revised appearance, realizing I hadn't really looked at her or Ryan since their return. Faded and frayed cutoff shorts replaced her black skirt. A Hufflepuff T-shirt replaced her blouse. "Your shirt is incredibly on the nose."

She smiled. "Thank you."

I dragged my gaze to Ryan, still waiting patiently, and said to Amelia, "Your boyfriend is a really nice guy."

"True." Amelia bent forward and took my hand, hauling me up. "He's almost as nice as my best friend."

"Hey," Ryan complained, moving in close as we turned to leave together. "I'm nicer than Everly."

Amelia shrugged. "She's a tough act to beat."

My aching heart warmed. I looked from my best friend to her boyfriend, thinking of the news she'd only half shared and his earlier insistence that we needed to make time to talk.

Grady passed us before I could ask Amelia what was going on. He was on his way back from the front of the manor where he'd escorted Mr. Thames. "Headed home?"

"Yeah," we answered in near unison.

Ryan shook Grady's hand. "We can stay with her until you're finished here."

Grady gave a stiff nod, then moved into my personal space, fixing me with concerned gray eyes. "I'll be there as soon as I can," he promised. "Let these guys take care of you until then."

I nodded, certain I'd cry if I tried to speak.

"Be safe," he whispered, stroking his thumb along my cheek.

My chest clenched, and Grady strode away before I could respond, answering the call of a uniformed officer in the distance.

Amelia tucked me back under her wing and towed me forward. "I hope you have lots of comfort foods and chocolate."

"Always."

Soon, Mr. Thames appeared again, seated alone under the bistro lights as we passed. His eyes were red and his gaze distant.

The coroner's van was gone, along with most of the party.

A smattering of staff and historical society members remained, speaking softly with officers nearby.

Susan's husband's pain rooted me in place, and my friends stopped with me.

"Everly?" Amelia asked, probably unsure why I'd frozen there or what I planned to say.

Truthfully, I didn't know either.

Mr. Thames raised puffy eyes to us. "She's gone," he said flatly. "And I wasn't here."

"I'm so sorry," I blurted, the despair I'd felt earlier, of being too late to save her, rushing back to overtake me. I couldn't imagine what it would be like to lose my spouse, and I never wanted to know.

"Why was she out there alone in the dark at this hour?" he asked. "How did she fall into a well?"

I bit my lip against the memory of a second shadow trailing her along the trees. A second voice whispering with her in the darkness. I'd told Grady everything I knew, and he'd nodded. But he hadn't told Mr. Thames. Why?

"We'll figure it out," I told Mr. Thames. "I promise."

His brow furrowed. "What do you mean? How?"

"I don't know. But Detective Hays and the local police are really good. I plan to help too, however I can. Susan meant a lot to me."

The man's mouth opened in question, but no words came out. Considering we'd never met, I supposed he might wonder who I was and how I'd known his wife.

Ryan angled himself between me and Mr. Thames, then he lowered his mouth to my ear. "All right, enough of that. Let's go before we find out his fishing trip was a ruse and you just announced to a killer that you're going to help him go to jail."

I felt my eyes widen as Ryan stepped away, and I fixed my eyes on the silent man before me. Was it possible the tears I'd seen were a façade? Tears of regret, not grief? Claiming to be on a boat at the night of Susan's death was a tidy alibi for a killer.

I made a mental note to talk to Amelia's dad about how he'd managed to reach Mr. Thames, and if the timing between his radioed call to the boat and the fisherman's arrival at the dock seemed right.

Ryan nudged me away and Amelia tugged my hand.

"I think he needs some time and privacy," she said softly. "You do too."

Ryan moved back to my side, leaning toward my ear once more. "Agreed. And you need to think before making any more promises like that."

I knew he was right, but my heart demanded I do something to help Susan. If I couldn't save her, I could at least help find her justice.

I cast a final look over my shoulder as we cut through the remaining cluster of people to the parking lot.

Mr. Thames stared as I drifted away.

ᕤ

I woke well before dawn, unable to sleep or even continue to try. The image of Susan, eyes wide and face covered in duckweed, had plagued me all night and eventually pushed me from my bed.

Maggie, the fluffy, ghost-white cat who'd come with the house, sat in my bedroom doorway. Her luminous green eyes flashed in a shaft of moonlight through my window.

I only started briefly, having grown accustomed to her random appearances and disappearances over the years. "Hello, sweet kitty," I said, bending to stroke her lovely fur. I had no idea how she got in or out of my home, but she never failed to return hungry. And I was always delighted to see her.

Maggie rose, arching into my touch, seeming to say she was glad to see me too.

She followed me to my open-concept, second-floor kitchen, a space I loved as dearly as my café downstairs. The appliances, cupboards, and countertops were sorely outdated, but the space had remarkable renovation potential. As soon as I found the time and money to tackle the work, the kitchen would become an inviting place to gather and a magical place to cook. Until then, I was content with the simplistic charm and history of the room. Like much of the rest of the home, being there made me feel as if I was visiting an era gone by.

The central space of my living quarters was used as a

living and entertaining area. A bank of windows and set of glass patio doors on the back wall provided an uninterrupted view of the sea. My master suite was on my left and a long hall led out of my living space to a number of additional bedrooms and stairs to the third floor on my right.

I'd painted the walls a soft gray-blue throughout and added a coat of winter white to the handcrafted baseboards and trim. A plush, cream-colored rug centered the living space, like a raft adrift on refinished hardwood floors. My couch, accent tables, and chairs were arranged neatly on top. I'd chosen airy colors for furniture and fabrics, enhancing the visual aesthetic of living in the clouds above the sea. The view outside my windows only added to the effect.

Maggie sat primly before her kitty dinette, cleaning her paws and face. I'd stenciled her name on a pair of white porcelain bowls I'd found while cleaning the third floor, then positioned them atop a white rubber mat with a delicate floral border. I liked to think she enjoyed the extra effort I made for her, which only encouraged me to do more.

I refreshed the water in her bowl first, adding a large ice cube for fun. Then, I unlidded a container from my pantry with the homemade tuna tarts and cheesy chicken chips she loved. "The crunchy ones are a new recipe," I told her. "The online instructions made them mushy, so I had to adjust. Let me know what you think."

She dug in, obviously eager to help with my research.

I stuck a pod in the single-cup coffee machine and pressed the button marked *Brew*.

Moonlight danced on the ocean outside my patio doors,

enticing me closer and giving me promises of peace. The sea never lied or disappointed, so I carried my freshly filled mug onto the deck. I left the door partially open for night air to rush in and to allow Maggie to slink out, if she chose.

I'd barely had my first tentative sip of coffee before a familiar flap of wings drew my attention to the sky.

Lou, my magnificent seagull and friend, landed lithely on the railing. He cocked his head as if to ask what I was doing up so early. He and I typically enjoyed the sunrise together, but that wouldn't come for another few hours.

"I know," I told him. "I couldn't sleep."

"Squawk!" he replied.

"You too, huh?" I asked, taking another small sip of my drink. "Did you hear about what happened to Susan?"

He performed a little two-step in my direction, moving to stand before me on the rail. He cocked his head again as I spoke, and his beady black eyes bored into mine. I was sure he understood me on some level. He wasn't wholly wild like other birds, and he sought my company often. Sure, I usually fed him when he came around, but I sensed there was something more there as well.

My great-aunts believed Lou and Maggie, were, respectively, the reincarnated souls of the wealthy businessman who commissioned my house for his mistress and my ancestral cousin, Magnolia Bane, the mistress. I'd chosen Maggie's name in honor of her, but I hadn't realized the man's name had been Lou until after I'd named the seagull. A strange coincidence, but a coincidence nonetheless.

Unfortunately for the original Lou, when his wife

learned about the affair, she walked into the sea. And when Magnolia realized her love of Lou had essentially caused the death of his wife, she threw herself off the widow's walk on my roof. Lou, having lost everything, died alone in my house years later, having slowly lost his mind.

I was thankful people were less dramatic these days and just got divorces.

Gossip resulting from the dramatic set of events had become fodder for campfire stories over the years. By the time I was born, everyone in town thought the house was haunted. Kids dared one another to get near the place when they passed by on the beach. I'd never accepted the challenge because that would've been trespassing, and if the place was haunted, I didn't want to be rude or disrespectful by entering uninvited. But I was never afraid.

To me, this home was the most beautiful in Charm, and I'd dreamed of seeing the inside one day. I'd assumed if that opportunity ever came, it would be because I knew the new owner, not because I was the owner. Now, the property was mine to maintain and love. And I truly did.

As for Lou and Maggie, if they were who my aunts believed, then I was honored to love and care for them as well. But I hoped my aunts were wrong.

Because if they were wrong about one legend, they could be wrong about another. I needed them to be wrong about our family curses.

CHAPTER

FIVE

I felt slightly more like myself by lunchtime, lost in the busyness of iced tea making and perfecting the presentation of my jerk shrimp kabobs on rice. The business side of my café counter was my happy place, and I hummed merrily to a Beach Boys tune as I squeezed a lemon over the meal.

Sun, Sand, and Tea occupied the better half of my first floor. The café was accessible through the foyer, by way of my front door. The previous owner had strategically removed a wall separating the kitchen and formal dining area to create a large space for entertaining. The result was a stunning seaside setup with breathtaking views of the ocean. I'd come back to Charm days before the home was listed on the market and with just enough credit and savings to seal the deal.

I'd immediately turned the kitchen and dining area into my café and scattered an array of tables and chairs across the wide-planked, whitewashed floor. Twenty seats in total, five at the counter and fifteen placed otherwise. My high-top bistro tables stood near the windows, while traditional four-seat sets formed a line down the room's center. Padded wicker furniture and a matching coffee table sat beside a set of bookshelves overflowing with any guest's next favorite beach read.

I'd chosen colors and fabrics for the café that would reflect the breathtaking views outside. Blues and greens for the sea, accents of tan and gray for the sand and driftwood. Punches of amber and scarlet to represent the magnificent daily sunrises over the Atlantic. The newly finished former ballroom was accessible via an archway on the north wall. I used the room for large parties and cooking classes, but nothing beat the views from my café.

Denise passed change to a customer at the register, then turned to me with a heavy exhale. "This place is hopping today. I hate to say it, but you might have to consider hiring more help."

I smiled, thankful she was right. Business was booming. "I asked Aunt Fran to talk to the Corkers about that," I said. "I hope to get someone hired and trained before the wedding."

"Good choice. Those Corkers are a hoot. You should ask Margie Marie," Denise suggested. "She's fantastic."

I made a mental note to do just that. "I will." I liked the idea of seeing my staff grow, and of the free time that would come with the change. Once Denver moved in, I hoped to be the one to pick him up from school sometimes, and I looked forward to spending fun afternoons together when I did.

The seashell wind chimes over my front door jingled, and a moment later, Grady walked into view. My heart hopped with excitement as he selected the stool across from me at the counter.

"Hey," I said, sliding a napkin before him. "How are ya?"

"A little better now." He nodded his hello to Denise before fixing a troubled smile on me.

I grabbed a clean mason jar from the drying rack and filled it with ice. "Is this about last night?" I asked, choosing my words carefully and lowering the decibel in case of listening ears.

His jaw tightened, and my insides followed suit.

I wanted details about Susan's death but knew he wouldn't volunteer them.

I positioned the jar of ice beneath Grady's favorite dispenser and pulled the tap. Old-fashioned sweet tea flooded the cubes, setting them afloat.

I regularly kept twenty flavors of iced tea available on the daily, repeating indisputable favorites, like Grandma's Old-Fashioned Sweet Tea, and swapping out others to test or showcase specialty and seasonal recipes. Strawberry basil, blackberry mint, and hibiscus were on the menu today, for example, but would be gone tomorrow.

I ferried the drink to Grady, then covertly placed a thick slice of my family's lemon cake onto a plate and delivered that too.

"Thanks." He smiled as he lifted his fork, and I waited for the cake to kick in.

The recipe went back at least two centuries and had been copied multiple times over the years for posterity. I'd happened upon various versions of the original while looking for new ideas to serve at my café. Surprisingly, the recipe hadn't changed too much over time. Some versions featured modernized processes or a revised ingredients list to save time and money, but the overarching results were the same.

I stuck as closely as possible to the original recipe, enjoying my connection to the past. I never minded the extra effort. One look at Grady's face when he took a bite made it all worthwhile. Knowing dozens of my ancestors had baked the same cake for their loved ones was mind-boggling, and I loved it. Men's names were doodled in the margins of each copy, and I adored the sweet subscript, *to bolster a hero's heart.* I'd added Grady's name to the newest copy of the recipe as well. It seemed like a tradition of sorts, and I loved including him in our family history. He definitely had a hero's heart, so it wasn't a surprise he enjoyed this cake most of all.

These days, I plied him, and him alone, regularly with my lemon cake, in an unspoken testament to my love and an admitted effort to settle him down. Grady was wound far too tightly for beach life.

The cake and I were working to change that.

Grady took another bite and moaned with delight.

Yep, definitely worth the work.

"Have you gotten any news since last night?" I asked, unable to wait any longer.

His chewing slowed and he caught me in his gaze. "Nothing substantial. Why? Have you?"

"No." I did my best to feign casual, even as my pulse began to rise. "Any chance you found out who Susan met with yesterday at lunch?" I asked. "Or who she argued with in her office last night?"

"I'm still working on that," he said. "I spoke with a mason this morning who visited the manor yesterday to provide a quote on repairing the well. He said the bricks were old and unstable, the mortar severely weakened by age. The side could've collapsed like it did at any time."

I wrinkled my nose. Was the mason suggesting Susan's death was an accident? Did Grady truly think that was a possibility? Or was he trying to keep me from looking into this more carefully? I cocked a hip and arched a brow. "Agreed," I said. "And Susan obviously knew that, hence the request for a repair quote, so how did she accidentally fall in?"

Grady's gaze shifted to Denise as she waved goodbye to another customer and pretended not to eavesdrop.

"She didn't fall," I whispered. "Someone else was with her, and she was pushed."

His eye lids dropped shut, and I knew I was right.

"You're trying to stop me from asking questions about this," I accused. "That's why you rushed off last night when you stopped by to check on me, and that's why you're being coy now."

Grady had popped in on his way home, told me things were fine, reminded me I was safe, then promptly ran away.

At the time, I'd assumed he was exhausted and preparing for a big day ahead. Now, I knew he was just getting out of my place before I asked too many questions.

"I was there," I reminded him. "I saw her in that well, and she was face up, which means she fell backwards." Only one thing could cause a person to back up with enough force to topple the bricks of a well, even old decrepit bricks. "Someone pushed her." I'd repeated my assertion with the fervor of someone who knew she was right.

Grady forked another bite of cake, his grouchy expression back in place. He hated when I nosed around his murder investigations, but I couldn't help myself. It was an affliction of mine we both had to live with.

"I never got the file from her office," I said, squaring my shoulders in preparation for a fight. "I was supposed to get it last night, which was why I went to find her and how I heard the argument." I should've knocked on her door and interrupted the fight, or at least stuck around to get a look at whoever had been in her office with her.

"I'm headed back to Northrop Manor this afternoon. I'll keep my eyes out for the file," he said. "Anything that has your name on it, or looks like research related to our query, will come directly to you."

I smiled sweetly at his unspoken declaration. *Therefore there is no need for you to return to that location.*

He'd clearly forgotten Aunt Clara kept an office at the manor now.

I had plenty of reasons to return.

"Thank you," I said, instead of correcting him. "Have

you heard anything about Amelia?" I asked. "She said she had something to tell me last night, but things went pear shaped, and I can't stop thinking about it."

He shrugged.

Denise shook her head too.

I checked my phone for signs of missed messages. There weren't any. "I left a message earlier this morning, and she responded with a text saying she had errands and would stop by as soon as possible."

Grady squeezed my hand. "Sounds to me like she wants to talk to you in person about something."

Worry twisted in my middle. Something was wrong. I could feel it, and I needed to know exactly what it was so I could panic properly.

Grady's encouraging smile and presence swung my mind to happier problems, and I searched under the counter for a set of sample wedding invitations I needed his opinion on. "Nicole at the stationery shop in Rodanthe dropped these off yesterday, and I completely forgot to tell you. We're supposed to pick one, then let her know which we like best." I set the samples on the counter between us. "What do you think?"

He wiped his hands and mouth with a napkin, then lifted the small stack of nearly identical ivory cardstock. "Do you have a favorite?" he asked.

"Not a favorite," I said, "but I like these two more than the others." I tugged two samples from his grip and set them beside his plate.

Grady discarded the rest of the pile and lifted the pair

I'd chosen. "In that case, how about this one?" He turned my favorite of the two to face me.

I ran a fingertip over the beautiful embossing and multiple textures, admiring the pretty loopy script. "Perfect. I'll give Nicole a call."

Grady offered me a high five. "That was easy."

"We make a great team."

"Indeed." His eyes flashed, and my cheeks heated.

"Next up is cake testing," I said.

Grady's eyes widened. "Nice. I've really talked that up to Denver."

I laughed. "Me too. I think he should have his own cake at the reception. When we talk to the baker about our main cake and the groom's cake, we should make sure Denver is represented as well. I don't care if he chooses ice cream cake or monkey bread. I want him to have whatever his heart desires, and I want to make it for him."

Grady rose and leaned over the counter to kiss me. "That would be very special, and he would love being included in that way," he said, shifting back as two-dozen onlookers stared. "What do I owe you for this delicious pick-me-up?"

I grinned, a little dizzy from the kiss. "How about your undying love and affection?"

"Done," he said. "Anything else?"

"Will I see you later?"

Grady's cheek ticked, and the lazy half smile I loved curled his lips. "That's the goal." He leaned in for another kiss.

Then, he was gone.

Denise shook her head as I came down from the clouds.

"What?" I asked, rearranging my features into what I hoped was a more normal expression.

"You get all doe-eyed and weak-kneed every time he touches you," she said. "I'd be completely embarrassed for you, if I wasn't so jealous."

I glanced around the room to find a mass of smiling faces, all who'd clearly seen the aforementioned doe eyes and weak knees. Unlike Denise, they were actively pretending they hadn't noticed. I should've been embarrassed, but my smile grew. What could I say? Grady made me happy.

The thought immediately ruined my mood.

I didn't want to lose him, and I wondered again if Susan's untimely death was somehow a side effect of my family's love curse? Had asking her to look into things been her kiss of death?

"Uh oh," Denise said, moving in close and lowering her voice. "I know that face. And whatever direction your thoughts are going, they are wrong. You need to stop."

I frowned. "I can't help it. I was right there. I should've been able to stop this. What if it's my fault because I asked her to help?"

Denise sighed and closed the remaining distance between us, engulfing me in a hug. "Honey, no. This is not your fault. There's no rational way to make it your fault, so stop trying. And before you start down your usual rabbit hole, trying to figure out what happened on your own, don't do that either. I can't take seeing you get hurt again, and Grady will fall apart if anything happens to you. He still blames himself for all the other messes you've wound up in while playing detective."

A couple carried their bill to the register and looked in our direction.

"I'll get that," Denise said, hustling away with a warm smile for the guests.

I opened my laptop. I couldn't help wanting to know what happened to Susan last night, even if all I did was complete a few online searches for details. Knowing anything was better than remaining in the dark.

I logged in and navigated to the *Town Charmer*, the anonymous local gossip blog everyone visited for the latest in community news and hearsay. Whoever ran the website and authored the posts was scarily accurate with their information, if a little biased in the reporting. Regardless, it was where I went for details, especially following a murder.

The blog's home page loaded, and I frowned at the headline.

SWAN'S SWEET TEA...AND SECRETS?

Images of me with Susan sat below the large, bold words. We'd been photographed having coffee at the café on Main Street. Then again, walking the boardwalk early in the morning and shaking hands outside Northrop Manor. The article speculated about our friendship and reasons for our meetings.

Based on Susan's reputation for digging up details, the

author guessed correctly that I'd asked her to look into something. The article ended with a prompt for reaction and response. What had I asked Susan to look into?

Countless community members hiding behind ridiculous usernames, like BeachyKeen41 and SandyCheeks75, had all sorts of nonsensical theories, everything from my search for a missing love child to a deep dive into Grady's past, uncovering hidden dirt before I finally committed to the brooding lawman.

I rolled my eyes. The speculation was bananas, but it was a welcome switch from the ongoing polls and reports about my wedding plans. Would I wear white? *Should* I wear white? Who would be the attendants? Who would be invited? And who would the town's favorite caterer ask to cater the most important event of her life?

"Okay," Denise said, hurrying back to me. "Is that the *Town Charmer*? What did I miss?"

I turned the laptop to face her, and she pressed her lips into a thin white line.

"At least the wedding isn't featured today," I said, in search of a silver lining. "That's something, right?"

Denise raised her eyes to mine and forced a patient smile. "The blog didn't stop covering your wedding. They gave you guys your own column."

I followed her gaze as she drove her forefinger over the laptop touchpad and clicked on a tab I hadn't noticed along the header. Wedding bells began to chime through the speakers, and an animated bride and groom, with mine and Grady's faces pasted on, raised and lowered their joined hands while a crowd of cartoon guests threw birdseed. A countdown clock ticked below our feet.

My shocked giggle turned sour as I took in the barrage of polls and questions included on the page.

How long after the wedding will we get a baby Hays out of this? Seashellie21 asked.

The answers ranged from ten years to two months, and I assumed it was my nemesis, Mary Grace Chatsworth-Vanders, who'd said the latter. Considering the wedding was three months away, and babies took nine months on average to bake, only she would suggest I looked pregnant already.

"The whole town is buzzing over this," Denise said. "Your wedding is a really big deal. Some are calling it a royal island wedding."

I sighed, unsurprised by the revelation. The town's obsession with my family's strange and lengthy history here was bound to draw significant interest. The alleged curses helped. No one had talked much about them before I'd accepted Grady's proposal. Now it was as if all my friends and loved ones were watching two cars about to crash, or Grady and me on a high wire without a net.

I refocused on the screen, and my attention stuck on the latest poll question: Is the Swan Love Curse real?

That was the question of the centuries.

I appreciated that the responses leaned in my favor, with No as a slightly more popular answer, but I groaned anyway.

Denise closed the lid on my laptop. "You are not cursed,"

she said. "I won't allow it. And I can't support you nosing into Grady's investigation right now. We need your head in the wedding game. Have you tried on any of your family gowns yet? Because as your bridesmaids, Amelia and I both want to be there to see you in every one."

"You really don't," I said. "Some of those dresses are older than my aunts. It's just a tradition that I try them on. I'll probably wind up with something from this century, which means I'll have to order from a bridal shop."

"Sounds like you've got some serious shopping ahead of you," she said. "Why not put all your energy and focus on that instead of trying to track down a killer?"

"I can do both," I assured her—and myself. "And no one needs to worry about my safety. I've been taking self-defense with Grady."

She laughed and performed a long stage wink. "I'll bet."

The seashell wind chimes rang again, and I perked up at the sound. "Welcome to Sun, Sand, and...oh." I rolled my eyes as Mary Grace strode to the counter. "I thought I detected the faint scent of sulfur," I muttered.

"What?" she said. "No grand welcome for me?"

Mary Grace's family had lived on the island until our middle school years. During that time, she'd spent her time convincing classmates I lived with my grandma and great-aunts because my mom had run off to join the circus to avoid raising me. The mean-spirited lie had caused me to rehash and reiterate the death of my mother dozens of times before I was thirteen.

I wasn't over it.

I grabbed the to-go order Denise had prepared in advance and set it on the counter. "One hundred dollars."

She handed me a twenty, and I made change.

The smirk on her face told me she had something smart to say, and I hoped she'd leave without sharing it.

"So," she said, causing me to bite my tongue so hard I winced. "Found another body, huh? Is that some kind of superpower? Or do you spend your time looking for a way to maintain the spotlight?"

I passed her the receipt and a few ones, thinking I could mash a cream puff in her hair if she wanted to share the spotlight with me. There were plenty of witnesses who'd probably been waiting twenty years for exactly that.

Instead, I sighed. "Have a lovely day."

She frowned, dissatisfied, cocking her head like a confused puppy. Then she looked pointedly at my middle. "I suppose you do provide plenty of room for speculation. How long before those nuptials?"

I narrowed my eyes and planted my hands on my hips, showcasing my rounded belly, earned honestly by the near-daily indulgence in absolutely incredible food shared with equally amazing friends. *Not* a growing baby. "I knew that was you on the blog," I said.

Mary Grace cackled. "I knew you would. And I don't care. I doubt you planned to invite me to your wedding anyway. Besides, the way you fall over bodies, there'll probably be two at the reception."

I glared as she laughed her way out the door.

She was obnoxious and rude, but she wasn't really wrong.

CHAPTER

SIX

I stewed the rest of the day. Mary Grace had gotten under my skin, but so had Susan's death and the realization my entire town was obsessed with my wedding. A wedding I wasn't sure should happen. One that would break my heart if it was canceled.

I closed the shop at seven sharp and grabbed the stack of books I'd borrowed from the family archive, prepared to return them and seek solace with my aunts. Somehow, being back in my childhood home always made my problems seem smaller and more manageable.

The café had been busy until closing, and several patrons had asked how I was doing, having heard I was the one to find Susan in the well. Most folks asked out of true concern. A few were clearly looking for an inside scoop. I did my best to be honest but coy, and I reassured all who asked that the truth would be found. Grady wouldn't let anyone go without justice, and I would help however I could.

Meanwhile, I had to clear my head.

I settled my satchel crossbody and nestled the borrowed books inside. Porch lights on and café lights off, I hurried through the front door and locked up quickly behind me.

I made it as far as Blue before I froze in my driveway.

The golf cart dripped with water, despite the clear blue sky overhead. Her seat and hood were dotted in hunks and mats of seaweed. Just as Susan's face and clothes had been.

A handful of coins were scattered over the seat and floorboards.

My heart clenched, and my fight or flight instinct kicked in. I was back in motion within seconds, running for the open doors of my carriage house.

I dove into Dharma, my 1969 VW Beetle, a gift from Aunt Fran, and slammed my hand against the lock as I powered up the car. A moment later, I jammed my foot on the gas and motored away.

Aunt Fran had passed Dharma on to me when Aunt Clara had purchased a Prius and given their mother's Bel Aire to Fran. Dharma had been a cherished part of Aunt Fran's youth, and like most things in my family, she was filled with memories and nostalgia. A baggie of dried flower petals and herbs hung from the rearview mirror by a thin leather rope for protection, placed there a lifetime ago by Aunt Fran's mother.

When I'd inherited the car, a Beach Boys eight-track had been stuck in the broken tape player, the volume cranked too high. Since then, the radio had been removed entirely and a modern apparatus installed in its place. The new stereo was a gift from Grady, complete with satellite radio and onboard GPS. I suspected the ability to track me if I ever went missing was Grady's gift to himself.

I pulled over three minutes later, after I'd reached the bustling streets of downtown, and texted Grady with shaky fingers.

The phone rang half a second after my message was delivered. Grady's face graced the screen.

I settled the phone in the holder on my dash and pressed the speaker button. "Hi."

"Where are you now?" he asked, foregoing any customary greetings.

"On Middletown Road. I was my way to the homestead," I said.

Middletown Road was a main crossroad through downtown, cutting across the narrow island's center like a belt between the ocean and the sound.

"I was on my way to visit my aunts when I saw Blue. I have books to return, and I didn't want to go back inside alone and wait. I just wanted to get out of there."

"Tell me you aren't walking."

"I took Dharma," I said. "I left Blue where she was, and I didn't hang around to see if there were any ominous messages or threats beyond the coins and seaweed."

"Wise," he said. "I'm on my way. I'll let you know what I find."

I swallowed the hard lump of terror and gratitude balling in my throat. "I'm sorry to bother you when I know you're already having a bad day."

"Always bother me," he said. "No matter what."

I smiled a little as relief eased my tight chest. "Okay."

"Okay," he echoed. "Now, who have you talked to about Susan Thames's death? I'm assuming the coins and seaweed are directly related, and you're personally involved, so I might as well get a list going."

I paused a beat to decide if I was offended. I wasn't. He knew me. "I talked to Amelia and Ryan last night. Also, my aunts. And I spoke to Mr. Thames on my way out. I talked with you when you came over before bed and again this morning. Denise and I talked a little at work today. Some café guests had questions, but I was tight-lipped on details. That's all." I mentally ran through the list, making sure I hadn't left anyone out. "It sounds like a lot, but I've barely spoken to anyone. You, Denise, Amelia, Ryan, and my aunts don't count."

Grady was quiet so long, I tapped the phone screen to see if the call had been dropped.

"Grady?"

He released a long breath into the phone. "Did you happen to declare your intent to find the killer to anyone at any point?" he asked. "To Mr. Thames or anyone inside your very busy café, where it might've been overheard by the killer? Where it might've been overheard by an innocent person who later, unwittingly, repeated it to the killer?"

I bit my lip and pulled away from the curb, angling into traffic, concentrating far too much to formulate an answer.

"I'll take that as a yes," he said, sounding irritated, and probably more than a little worried. "Call me when you're ready to leave your aunts' place. I'll swing by and follow you home, then walk you inside."

Forever my protector, I thought, the small smile returning. "I guess I'll see you later."

❧

My aunts lived in the home where I'd grown up. The same place they'd grown up, and where their moms and grandmas had grown up as well. The current structure was roomy, with multiple additions added over the years. Neat black trim lined the windows of the dark gray colonial salt-box, with matching black roof and door. Neatly cut grass ringed the exterior and an extensive garden and bee farm sat out back. In the front, an abundance of wildflowers pressed against the white scalloped fence running along a tidy cobblestone path to a red front door. The general interior style and décor was a collage of bygones past, but all aspects of technology, from appliances to smoke detectors and Wi-Fi, were fully modernized. Much more so than the actual residents.

I released a thankful breath as I shifted Dharma into park and made a run for the house. As usual, the door opened, and my aunts appeared before I reached their small porch. Much like I knew when Grady was near, they'd always simply known when I arrived. It was lovely to be greeted this way as an adult, but it had been incredibly difficult to get away with missing curfew as a teen.

"Hi," I panted, shaken from the coins and seaweed on Blue and slightly winded from the sprint up the walk.

"Hello, sweet girl," Aunt Clara said, greeting me with

a longer hug than usual, as if she also sensed my fear and anguish. Or perhaps it was written on my face.

Aunt Fran motioned me inside. "I was just preparing your favorite hot tea," she said. "Sassafras with ginger."

I followed my aunts into the kitchen and sank onto a three-legged stool at the massive center island. The room was warm and inviting, filled with nostalgia and the ghosts of our ancestors. I instantly breathed easier.

Colonial-blue cupboards with black hinges lined the walls above the appliances and below the island countertop. A deep farmhouse sink overlooked a window to the yard and gardens, showcasing the beauty of flora grown there. Above us, bouquets of herbs and flowers dangled from the rafters, handpicked by my aunts and hung to dry.

I unloaded the books I'd brought to swap, then the contents of my troubled heart and mind. Once I'd started, I couldn't seem to stop until every thought and feeling clouding my head was free and waiting for inspection. Twenty minutes and two cups of tea later, I deflated with relief, ready to be refilled with better things.

Aunt Fran refilled my cup and added a sugar cube as well. "That was a lot to carry on your own," she said. "I'm glad you trusted us with it."

They each rubbed a palm over my slumped back and shoulders, infusing me with their love.

I inhaled the eternal hope, feeling lighter by the moment, then dropped a second cube of sugar into my tea. "I'd be lost without you," I said. "I probably don't tell you that enough."

"You don't need to," Aunt Clara said. "We know."

I leaned my head on her shoulder briefly, watching the flames dance inside the oversized fireplace on one wall. The stone hearth and chimney had originally served as an oven, but for as long as I could remember, a simple black kettle hung from a chain above the flames, simmering water with fresh orange peels, cinnamon sticks, and rosemary to sweeten the air.

"I'm glad you're here," Aunt Clara said. "It always feels more like home when you're here."

Aunt Fran hummed her agreement.

"Thank you," I said. "I feel guilty dropping things on you like this," I admitted. "I know you never mind, but I like to see you unburdened and happy."

"We're happy when you let us help," Aunt Clara said. "Even if all we can offer are listening ears and sage advice."

"Advice she never takes," Aunt Fran said.

"True," Clara agreed.

I puffed my cheeks and blew out a breath, knowing they were mostly right. "I try to do what you suggest," I said. "But it's as if there's a mischievous, rebellious nut living in here." I pointed to my head. "And she just can't leave things alone. I can't rest until I have answers. I go nearly batty anytime I try."

My aunts exchanged a look, probably forecasting my upcoming rant.

"Who would douse poor Blue in water, coins, and seaweed?" I asked, knowing the answer from similar past experiences. Obviously, Susan's murderer.

"Well," Fran began, "someone clearly wants to send a message."

"It's a warning," Aunt Clara said. "Whoever it was must know you saw Susan in the well and that you're looking into that. It suggests that if you don't stop prodding, you'll be the one covered in seaweed next."

Aunt Fran gave her a comically blank expression. "What?" Aunt Clara said.

I smiled at Aunt Clara's genuine confusion. I had asked. She was simply providing an answer. "I agree with your assessment," I said.

"All right," Fran said. "I suppose the next logical question is who could know those things about you? Who knows you saw Susan pulled from the well and that you're looking into her death? Also, please don't look into her death. You always get hurt when you do this."

"I won't get hurt," I said. "All I've done so far is read the *Town Charmer* and ponder the big picture."

Aunt Clara furrowed her pale brows. "Why meddle again at all?"

"I'm not meddling. I haven't done anything yet. Also, I can't help myself."

Aunt Fran clicked her tongue.

"What do you guys know about Susan?" I asked, suddenly eager for information. My aunts knew everyone in some capacity. Maybe they had a clue I could use. "Who could have possibly wanted to hurt her? I thought everyone loved her."

Both aunts shrugged, either not having any answers or not wanting to share it.

"Give me something," I said. "Please?"

Aunt Fran sipped her tea, eyes locked on mine. "I suppose," she said, setting the cup down carefully. "Susan might've dug up something someone didn't want known. She was our best local researcher, after all."

I nodded, feeling the weight of real possibility in her suggestion. "Any idea how I might find out who else she was helping?"

Aunt Fran tapped a finger against the edge of the counter. "I believe she works with a lawyer on Lighthouse Road. I don't know much about the office, but I'm sure you can find all that online."

"Or," Aunt Clara said, clapping her hands before popping off her stool. "You can let Grady handle this while you focus on the wedding."

"Have you been talking to Amelia, or was it Denise?" I asked. Then another thought came to mind. "Have either of you heard any news about Amelia lately? She told me there's something I need to know but hasn't told me what."

Aunt Clara beamed. "Is she marrying Ryan?"

"Probably," I said. "Eventually, but I didn't get the feeling that was on her mind right now. She tried to talk to me at the fish fry, but I got distracted, and now I can't reach her. I think she's avoiding me, but she texted to say she would stop by as soon as she could."

Aunt Fran frowned. "Sounds like she wants to talk to you in person."

I sighed. "That's what Grady said."

"Must be serious," Aunt Fran said. "I hope everything's okay."

"Me too," I whispered, as much to myself as to my aunts.

Aunt Clara offered a sweet smile. "Why don't you exchange your books in the archives while Fran and I gather a few of the ancestral wedding gowns for you to try? You can fill us in on Amelia's news when you know more."

Knowing I was stuck, and making mental notes to find the law office on Lighthouse Road first thing tomorrow, I agreed.

"Until then," Aunt Clara concluded, clapping her hands together, "we can finally get this tradition started."

Aunt Fran nodded in agreement, and the energy in the room began to vibrate.

෨

By the time I'd made the short trip through the home to the family archives, and back with a fresh set of books, my aunts were waiting in the parlor.

Six white garment bags lay over the back of an antique settee. Each had a note attached with the names of brides who'd worn the gown before and the dates of their weddings.

I padded onto the floral mauve carpeting and lifted the nearest option with a resigned smile. "Here we go," I said, surprised by the apparent glee in my voice.

My aunts rushed from the room, pulling the pocket doors closed behind them.

"Holler if you need help with the buttons," Aunt Clara called. "We'll be right out here when you're ready."

I pulled the zipper and eyeballed the item inside the bag. I didn't have to remove it from the hanger to conclude with certainty I couldn't get a single inch of my modern-day, size 14—okay, maybe size 16—body into the early nineteenth century gown. The same was true for my second option.

Based on the number of names on each tag, quite a few Swan brides, and our cousins, had been petite in the extreme. I wasn't one of them. I hadn't been born with a small frame or appetite, and my metabolism had all but walked off the job by my twenty-sixth birthday. Regardless, dress one and two looked a lot like high-collared night gowns, and not at all like anything I'd consider appropriate for a wedding. I zipped both back into their respective bags and moved on.

Next was a Civil War era number, crammed into a bag thrice as large as the first two combined. It took several seconds to free the entirety of material from its holder, and many more seconds for me to wash the images of Scarlett O'Hara from my mind.

I stepped into the layers of fabric, determined to be a good sport, and raised the zipper as far as possible before calling Aunt Clara and Aunt Fran.

The pocket doors swept open dramatically, and my aunts appeared, wheeling an oval mirror on a stand. They placed the mirror before me, then came to my sides.

They oohed and aahed while I stared, stupefied.

A fitted bodice formed a V at my hipbones, where the

first of three distinct layers of material circled my legs in tiers to the floor. A mini version of the skirt hung delicately around my shoulders, and an accessory bag attached to the larger garment bag contained a lace fan, gloves, and massive hat.

"I believe this one requires a hoop," Aunt Clara said.

Eventually, my eyes dried out from staring, and I began to blink.

"What do you think?" Aunt Fran asked with impossible sincerity. As if she wasn't seeing the same thing I was. "It won't take long to let it out or hem it a bit. Whatever you need."

Aunt Clara turned to examine the names on the tag. "Oh, Franny," she said. "Our grandmother wore this one."

"You're not smiling," Aunt Fran said, ignoring her sister's statement. She'd fixed her eyes on mine in the mirror. "This isn't the one. Take it off."

Aunt Clara nodded. "She's right. Just leave it with the bag when you change. Fran and I will see to everything before bed. Try the next one."

They exited, pulling the doors closed once more, and I moved on.

Bag four was from the same time period, roughly 1851 to 1872.

I spent a couple of minutes figuring out what was what, then wedged myself into the long muslin gown. Small, embroidered flowers adorned the material in a polka-dot pattern. The sheer sleeves ended in lace cuffs and bows at the wrists. The high collar rolled all the way under my chin and itched a little. A series of small, domed buttons walked down my sternum from clavicle to waist. Behind me was an enormous, intricately fastened bump: a bustle that appeared sturdy enough to stack plates on, or perhaps knock people out of my way at the buffet line.

"Are you ready?" Aunt Clara called.

"Yep."

We repeated the previous dress reveal.

Aunt Fran calculated the necessary alterations. Aunt Clara read the names of previous Swan brides who'd chosen this fine specimen. And my face gave away my lack of enthusiasm, so we moved on.

I skipped the next dress, after hefting it off the settee and nearly crumpling under its weight. "Too tight," I fibbed through the door.

"It's okay," Aunt Fran called. "The last one should fit. It was our mother's."

I paused before opening it, understanding they'd set it at the far end for a reason. Saving the best for last and all that. It would mean a lot to my aunts to see me try it on.

"Everly?" Aunt Clara called. "Have you spoken to Grady about the man with all the questions at my shop?"

"I mentioned it last night," I told her, sliding into the soft material. "We're both keeping our eyes out, and I plan to ask Pearl for more details when I see her next. Meanwhile, I think you should get some pepper spray."

"I'd hate to hurt him," she said.

"Don't." I pulled the zipper, then opened the pocket doors. "If you ever feel threatened, use the spray. No permanent damage will be done, and you can always apologize later, if needed. Your safety is more important than manners."

I went back to the mirror and smoothed my hands over the expensive material that slid like cool butter against my skin. "What do you think of this one?"

The lovely Edwardian gown was ivory in color and made of a variety of lace, over a built-in silk sheath. The effect was remarkably dreamlike, and I imagined running through craggy moors. I appreciated the simple design, modest neckline, and short sleeves. I even liked the wide length of satin that wrapped around my middle and tied into a bow at the back, its tails hanging dramatically to my ankles.

"You're smiling," Aunt Fran said. "Is this the one?"

I hadn't realized I was smiling, but the reflection before me proved her right. Unfortunately, I hadn't been thinking about the dress.

I was imagining Aunt Clara, the sweetest, most harmless human I knew taking out a stranger with pepper spray because he asked one too many questions. The image was hysterically funny, and my smile widened.

"This is it?" Aunt Clara asked, stepping between me and the mirror.

"It's very nice," I said, careful not to turn down their mother's gown.

Aunt Fran marched to her sister's side, brows raised. "Are you sure? I was certain you'd have to try them all at least twice."

"I like it," I said.

Aunt Fran sighed. "But does it make you feel beautiful, powerful, and as if you never want to take it off?"

"No," I admitted, "but it's definitely my favorite so far."

"There are dozens more," she said. "You've barely gotten started. This probably isn't the one."

"Actually," I backpedaled at the thought of dozens more, "I love it."

My aunts frowned.

"Why don't I take it with me and try it on at home with Grandma's pearls and proper undergarments," I said.

Aunt Clara crossed her arms. Never one to argue, she said, "Well, don't let Grady see it, just in case. If you decide to wear this one, you won't want to bring on any bad luck."

I nearly swallowed my tongue at the thought. I most certainly did not need any bad luck. I still wasn't convinced marrying him wouldn't be his death sentence. "I'll hide it the minute I get home," I promised.

The women nodded, and I texted Grady to say I was ready to go.

His response was instant: I'll be there in ten. This seaweed business put me on edge.

Then: Self-defense tonight. Are you in?

I suppressed a squeal. Normally, I wasn't a fan of the self-defense classes Grady insisted upon, but tonight, any time spent in close physical contact with my beloved sounded like exactly what I needed.

I'm in.

Suddenly, my recent threat seemed like much less of a bummer.

CHAPTER
SEVEN

An hour later, Grady and I sat on my living room floor, red-faced and breathing heavily. Our self-defense lesson had gone the way these lessons always did. He grabbed, and I escaped. Repeatedly. Until we'd run through every hold he could think of a dozen times, and I was out of breath. Then we did them all again. The plan was clearly to turn me into a female Houdini.

"See," I panted, resting back on my elbows against the carpet. "I can escape anything. I will never be in danger again."

"Getting free is the end goal," Grady said. "But it might not always be as simple as breaking an attacker's hold and running. If your assailant has a weapon, you could be badly injured in their attempt to stop you." He pierced me with sincere, fretful eyes, and an onslaught of terrifying memories replayed in my mind.

Grady and I had both been shot at in the past few years, and when the aim was right, no one could outrun a bullet or an arrow. Once the damage was inflicted, the odds of running at all were nil.

"You should be able to fight back if necessary," he said. "I hope it never comes to that, but if you're ever in a situation where you need to defend yourself again, I want you to know with confidence that you can. So please humor me and try."

I stretched onto my feet and adjusted my rumpled T-shirt and cotton shorts. "I don't like violence," I said. "When I think about fighting, I get panicky. I don't want to be the kind of person who needs to prepare herself for fist fights."

"You don't want to," he said, rising with me. "But you might have to. Did any of your past abductors care about your comfort zone while attempting to toss you off a cliff or your roof, or drown you in the ocean?"

I set my hands on my hips. "If I start punching people, how am I any better than the people who've attacked me?" The reasoning might not make sense to Grady, but I felt a deep need to be better than my previous abductors.

"So don't go around hitting people," he said. "Fighting back isn't the same as being an assailant. Fighting back means being a survivor, and Everly..." He inched closer and dropped his voice to a whisper. "If I can't keep you out of harm's way, I need to at least know you are equipped to survive it."

I relaxed against him for a moment, winding my arms around his back and listening to his heart beat strong and steady beneath my cheek. His skin was warm through the soft cotton T-shirt and sweatpants he'd worn for the occasion. When I backed away, he patted the space where my ear had just been.

"Hit me," he said. "We'll run through a couple of the attack exercises we worked on before."

I rolled my eyes and turned for the kitchen. "How about a snack instead?"

Grady snaked one arm out and caught my wrist gently in his grip. "Not yet," he said, towing me back to him. "I have to tell you about something that happened."

My limbs felt like stone as I imagined what he might say next. Nothing particularly good came to mind. "What?"

"A gargoyle fell off the town hall today as I was leaving. It cracked the sidewalk about eight inches in front of me."

"What?" I squeaked, twisting against his grip and easily breaking free. "How?"

"They're reroofing," he said. "I guess all the activity loosened the sculpture at its base."

I stared. This wasn't Grady's first near-death experience since our engagement. "How many times have you nearly died since your proposal?"

He frowned. "Don't start that again. You aren't cursed. I'm not going to die, and a falling gargoyle isn't proof of anything. Besides, I was dealing with weird stuff like that long before I proposed," he said. "I only tell you these things now because I plan to spend the rest of my very long life with you, and if I don't tell you, you'll be mad."

He wasn't wrong about that last part.

"What happened to you before our engagement?" I asked, focusing on this new revelation.

Grady laced his fingers with mine. "Let's see. I fell off a fishing boat last year. I've been thrown from multiple horses, and an elderly driver mistook Reverse for Drive and nearly ran me over in a parking lot."

I stared. "When did you first recognize this pattern?" I asked, mentally retracing my timeline since the night our paths first crossed.

"It's not a pattern," he said. "It's life. I'm a cop and an outdoorsman. Stuff happ—" He stopped speaking mid-word and his eyes widened, obviously recalling something important. "The first time was during a hike in the maritime forest." He rubbed a heavy palm across his forehead, down his cheek, and over his lips. "A tree fell right in front of me. It was huge. I didn't even hear it give way. Suddenly, it was just there, slamming against the path in front of me. It shook the ground. If I'd have been moving a little faster, or started my hike a few seconds sooner, I would've been pounded into the ground like a nail."

"Jeez." I grimaced at the awful visual. "Why didn't you tell me that? That's horrible!"

"Yeah," he said, looking slightly paler than I was accustomed. "That was the year we had all the snow. I was out enjoying the first warmish day after Christmas."

"After you kissed me under the mistletoe," I said, feeling the wind rush from my lungs.

How long had I been falling in love with Grady Hays?

"That's the year," he agreed. "Now, let's practice a couple attack moves before we call it a night."

"I've already mastered one of those," I said. "One is plenty."

Grady looked into my eyes. "It's really not."

I turned to walk away, and he grabbed me. I clutched his arms in my hands, then bent suddenly forward, lowering my center of gravity and disrupting his. I tucked into a ball and used the momentum to throw him over my head before I jumped back onto my feet.

Air whooshed from Grady's mouth as his back collided with the floor, long limbs splayed.

The sight of his stunned expression sent a rush of panic through me, and I flung myself onto the rug at his side. "Oh my goodness. I'm so sorry!" I said. "But it's a good move, right? Are you okay?"

Grady laughed and pulled me closer as he caught his breath. "You're fast."

I smiled, and he rolled.

In the next heartbeat, our tides had turned, and I was pinned beneath him.

"I'm faster," he said, melting my bones with his hooded and adoring eyes.

My heart danced in response. "I like your move better," I whispered.

"Oh, yeah?" he asked, huskily, slowly lowering his mouth to mine. "I've got a few more."

৯৯

I woke in an all-around terrific mood the next day, if a little sore from my romp with Grady. The morning continued to improve when Amelia stopped by unexpectedly for breakfast.

I let her in with a hug, and I left the door unlocked because Denise would be in soon to start her shift, and apparently Ryan was on his way as well.

"So, what's up?" I asked, arranging fruit and yogurt parfaits on the counter. One for each of us, and two more for Denise and Ryan when they arrived. "I've been on pins and needles waiting for your news."

"Sorry. I wanted to talk to you in person," she said. "I was interrupted the other night, and the news is pretty important."

I thought back to the last time I'd seen Amelia and recalled she'd been attempting to tell me the details of her new book deal when I saw Susan running off into the darkness. "Ugh," I said. "I am so sorry. You had wonderful news, and I ruined it. Please, tell me everything. You have my undivided attention." I popped a grape into my mouth and took the seat beside her at the counter.

Amelia smiled. "Okay. It's kind of a big deal," she said. "People are finding out, and I wanted you to hear it from me."

I lowered my spoon into the parfait, and a sense of unease rolled over my skin. "What is it?"

"Webflix purchased the film and television rights to my book, and they plan to adapt the story into a series of thirty-minute shows for children. It's the main reason they're sending me on a major book tour."

My heart and brain jolted with excitement, but Amelia appeared as if she was bracing to drop a bomb.

I pressed my lips together and waited for her to go on.

"The book tour has almost a hundred stops across the country, which means I'll be gone for the better part of a year. I'll get short breaks between regions, and I can fly home whenever I want, but things are going to be really different for a while. I won't be here, and I'm going to miss so many things."

My bottom lip wiggled.

Amelia's eyes misted. "You don't need to worry about me, because I won't be alone. Ryan is coming along. He hated the thought of me traveling by myself for such a long amount of time, so he's writing a series of articles that coincide with my travel route. Dad will manage things at Charming Reads, and everything will be great." Her cracking voice and reddening cheeks were at odds with the upbeat words. "I'm going to miss you."

I wrapped her in a hug, mind boggled by the enormity of her news, and hating to see her cry, even if they were happy tears.

She sniffled and pulled away, wiping her eyes. "I know it's a lot to take in, but it's all really good news, and it's the perfect time for me to do something big like this. I'm not married. I don't have children. The only thing tying me here is the shop, and Dad agreed to take over so I can go. I'm going to ask Clara to make sure he eats and does things outside of work so he doesn't starve or get lonely in my absence. He and I have always been a pair, since Mom left. I'm not sure what he'll do without me around."

I took a steadying breath and let it all settle in. "When do you leave?"

"Two weeks."

"Holy crab cakes!"

"I know." Amelia sighed. "It was a shock for me too, but Webflix and the publisher want to start building buzz right away."

I bobbed my head, nodding as I searched for the right words. "Well, you can count on me to check in with your dad too, and Aunt Clara basically thinks he hung the moon, so he's going to be well cared for. No. Actually, he's going to be pampered and spoiled by all the doting and attention. You're going to hate us when you get back."

"Really?" she asked, a small smile breaking through her tears.

"Yes. And you," I said, creating a long, dramatic pause, "are getting a Webflix series!"

The room was silent a moment before we broke into screams and bear hugs, giving in to the joy.

"I'm so happy for you," I said, meaning it in my bones. "This might be the best news I've ever heard. You deserve every perfect thing life has to offer, and I want it all for you."

She wiped frantically at her wet cheeks. "Thank you. I want the same for you, and I promise I won't miss your wedding. I've already made arrangements to fly home for the entire week, so I can be the best maid of honor who's ever had the honor. And I want to start by helping you find the perfect dress."

"Oh!" I bounced onto my toes. "I have a dress. Hang on."

I ran to the utility closet where I kept my broom, vacuum, and household cleansers, then returned with the garment bag from my aunts' house.

Amelia wrinkled her nose. "You keep your wedding gown with the grout and toilet cleaner?"

"I didn't want Grady to see it," I said, hanging the bag on the hook where I kept my apron. I unsheathed the heirloom dress and opened my arms near it like a game show hostess. "Ta da!"

Amelia shifted her attention from me to the dress, then back. "That's the one you picked? From a couple centuries of options?"

I lowered my arms. "I only saw six," I admitted. "I tried on three. This was the best of those. I don't have time to try on dozens of dresses. This one is really pretty. Isn't it?"

She nodded. "It's a very nice antique wedding gown. Well deserving of prime placement at any fashion museum."

My seashell wind chimes jingled, and Denise appeared, followed by Ryan.

"Hey!" she said, hugging Amelia, then smiling at me. "Look what I found loitering on the boardwalk out front."

Ryan offered a sheepish grin. "I was trying to give the two of you as much time as you needed. I filled Denise in about the book tour and the other thing on our way to the door."

I frowned, unsure what he meant by *the other thing*.

Denise grabbed the parfaits on the counter and passed one to Ryan. "I am so excited about all of this. You have no idea. I love to travel, so I'm insanely jealous. And I can't wait until Denver sees your story on Webflix. He will flip his little lid. I'm totally going to take a picture of his face the first time he sees the show."

Amelia smiled, but it didn't quite reach her eyes, which were still focused on me. "I promise I won't miss the wedding," she repeated.

"I believe you," I said. "Really. And I'm truly happy about all of this. It's wonderful."

Ryan stepped past me, eyes fixed on something over my shoulder. "Whoa." He sauntered, wide-eyed, to the garment bag and gown hanging against the wall. "What on the ever-loving green earth is this?"

"My wedding dress," I said. "What do you think?"

He shook his head slowly. "No."

Denise pushed a spoonful of parfait into her mouth and averted her gaze.

Amelia motioned Ryan back to her. "The dress is Everly's choice, and she likes this one."

Ryan balked, then pointed at the dress, as if my gown spoke his point for him.

Amelia flipped her attention to me. "There's something else I want to talk to you about."

"Is this the other thing?" I asked.

She nodded. "It's about what happened to Susan."

I raised a hand to stop her because there was so much more I wanted to know about her book tour. "It's fine," I told her. "We can talk about that later." My investigation into Susan's death was barely off the ground and could definitely wait until we'd properly celebrated Amelia's news.

"I know you too well to think you'll let her death go," Amelia said. "And I worry. I don't want you getting wrapped up in this investigation like the ones before. Going after a killer on your own could get you hurt again, or worse."

Ryan and Denise moved into position, flanking her sides.

I raised my chin, prepared to defend *my* position on asking a few small questions at the law office where Susan worked, as soon as I figured out which one that was.

"So," Amelia said. "We want to help."

"What?"

Ryan smiled. "What do you know so far? And what can we look into for you? With the three of us on your team, we'll find the truth in a quarter of the time it would take you on your own. Consider us your research assistants. Gophers and PAs."

I pressed my hands to my hips and narrowed my eyes. "I don't need gophers or PAs. I just need friends, and you two already have plenty to do."

"At least keep us in the loop," Amelia said. "We want to know what's going on, and what you're up to."

Denise nodded. "Then you can't fall off the grid for long without one of us knowing where you were and when you vanished."

I shivered, hating the reminders of other times I'd gone temporarily missing during an investigation. The causes and related experiences weren't good.

"Besides," Ryan said. "We're in a hurry. Amelia won't relax until this is over, and it will be hard for her to leave town if you're still muddling along. So I'm working on reconnaissance to speed the whole thing up. It'll help if you share what you know so far."

When none of the people in front of me burst into laughter or called out *just kidding*, I decided not to look a gift horse in the mouth and recapped the little information I had. Then I waited for my team's input.

Ryan sighed heavily. "Sorry. I just can't concentrate." He waved a hand toward my dress. "Can we see you in it? Because I'm not understanding how this is what you want to be married in." He turned a baffled look on Amelia and Denise. "And I'm not sure why you two aren't more concerned."

The ladies exchanged looks.

"She likes it," Denise said. "That's all that matters."

Amelia nodded. "And I'm sure it looks better on."

They all looked my way.

"Fine," I growled, slipping the dress from the hanger and carrying it into the ballroom. "I'll change. You brainstorm. I hear Susan worked at a law office on Lighthouse Road, so I planned to start there."

"Good." Ryan projected his voice so I could hear. "I asked around about that crying man at the crime scene," he said.

"Her husband," I called back.

"Only technically," Ryan said. "He and Susan were in the middle of a divorce. He lives on their boat. She stays at the house. It's supposedly amicable, but it does make me wonder."

I huffed a humorless laugh. "How many divorces are

really amicable?" I asked, hurrying to button the dress over my cutoff shorts and T-shirt.

"Exactly," Ryan said. "That guy was shedding a lot of tears for a man in the middle of a divorce."

"He was pretty upset," Amelia agreed.

"Are you thinking crocodile tears?" I asked.

"Maybe," Denise said. "The spouse is always a good place to start in cases like these. I'm sure Grady did."

"Oh!" Amelia called. "If Mr. Thames is living on the boat, maybe he wasn't even on a fishing trip like he said. Dad didn't mention anything about a pending divorce."

"The boat makes a nice alibi," I said, tying the wide satin bow as neatly as I could with hurried fingers. "Ryan? How did you manage to hear about the couple's split before Mr. Butters? You've barely been in town a day."

"I heard some ladies gossiping about her death over coffee at a café, so I introduced myself and they spilled their beans," he said.

I imagined Ryan flashing his unfairly charming smile, and I was certain the gossiping women had been powerless against it.

Finally ready, I lifted the material of my skirt so it didn't drag on the floor, then hurried back to my friends.

The trio turned to face me.

"What do you think?" I asked, running my palms over the soft material.

Ryan performed a slow blink.

Denise tipped her head. "It looks better on you than it did on the hanger."

"Thanks, I think. Amelia?" I raised my brows at her, hoping she would see a diamond in the rough. "What do you think?"

"I think Susan Thames was an institution on this island for historical accuracy and research," she said, returning to her parfait. "Aside from being a kind and generous person, she's a real resource lost and definitely deserves justice."

"Come on," I said. "I meant the dress, and you obviously hate it."

"I don't," she lied, busily spooning fruit and yogurt into her mouth.

"Take another look," I begged. "Try to imagine me with a veil and bouquet. Grandma's pearls and some lipstick."

Amelia gave me a long appraisal. "You're going to be the most beautiful bride this island has ever seen. It won't matter what you wear."

"Thank you," I said, appreciating the effort. "The gown is a little bland right now, but it'll be great with the right accessories and when my hair is done."

Denise set her empty parfait cup in the sink, nodding in support. "I'm sure this dress will be perfect. And, now that I'm thinking about it, Susan's last name sounds really familiar. She might've helped Senator Denver with the sale of Northrop Manor to the historical society."

I tensed. "Susan worked for an attorney's office on Lighthouse Road."

"Krebs and Chesterfield?"

A bolt of excitement shot through me as the seashell wind chimes jingled once more. "I don't know, but I'm going to find out."

Denise lifted a finger to indicate I should hold my thought. Then, she hurried toward the foyer to redirect whoever had arrived. We didn't officially open until eleven. The sign on my porch said so, but some folks still tried their luck anyway.

I looked to Amelia and Ryan. "I'm going to talk to someone at the law office before the café gets busy. Do me a favor and don't mention this to Grady," I said. "I don't want to worry him."

My spidey-senses tingled, and I raised my eyes to find Grady, standing with Denise in the archway to my café.

"Oh, hello," I said, chuckling nervously. "What brings you around this morning?"

His eyes narrowed, and I folded my hands innocently at my waist. "Apparently, I'm here to stop a coup."

Ryan took Amelia's hand. "We were just on our way out. It was nice to see you, Everly. Call if you need anything."

Amelia waved her goodbye, then hurried along beside him, mouthing the word *sorry* over her shoulder. She practically ran past Grady on her way out.

Denise was nowhere to be seen.

Cowards.

Grady's expression suddenly softened, and his eyes roamed slowly over my limbs and torso.

I followed his gaze to the wedding gown I was still wearing, and a tiny cuss jumped from my tongue.

He'd chased away my first investigative team, and now I had to get a new dress.

CHAPTER
EIGHT

After a brief but heartfelt chat with Grady, we came to the usual agreement. I would do what I wanted, and he wouldn't like it. At least this time, if my curious nature got me into trouble with a killer, I knew some self-defense. Not that I planned to meet the killer on my first official outing. Generally, that kind of run-in took significantly more effort and a few additional threats.

I kissed Grady goodbye and coaxed Denise back into the café to prepare for opening. Then, I climbed into Dharma, feeling confident about my odds of staying safe at the law office.

"Ready?" I asked the vehicle, running my palms lovingly over the steering wheel before gunning her engine to life.

Traffic was light, but I kept an eye on my rearview mirror anyway, checking for tails as I cruised through town. Thankfully, the route I took involved a long, two-lane stretch of road lined in sand dunes for a mile. If I was being followed, it would've been obvious.

I slowed to take the turn onto Lighthouse Road and quickly spotted a brightly colored patch of retail shops and offices on my right. I parked in the small lot outside a clapboard house painted in the coral shades of sunset and only a few dozen yards from the beach. A Krebs and Chesterfield sign on the door confirmed I was at the right place.

I hurried to the double glass doors and smiled at a life-size cardboard stand-up of two gray-haired men in suits, standing back to back, arms crossed. Attorneys Krebs and Chesterfield, I assumed.

Inside, a cluttered desk, presumably belonging to some kind of administrative assistant, faced the entryway. A pair of closed office doors graced the wall behind the desk. One attorney's name was stenciled on each. I scanned the room for signs of the missing gatekeeper and wondered if that person had been Susan Thames.

"Hello?" I called, rapping my knuckles against the desktop and shifting my eyes from one closed door to another.

Were the attorneys in there now?

"One minute," a woman's voice called, drawing my attention to an open doorway I hadn't noticed on the side wall.

"No problem," I said, craning my neck for a look into the small room.

Only a smattering of papers on a conference table were visible from my vantage.

I sidestepped a few inches, while I was still unchaperoned, and scanned the open files on the desk before me.

Each manila folder was tagged with a name and an

address. The contents appeared to be title work for the sales and purchases of homes and businesses. A few of the files were discolored, presumably from age, their edges soft and tattered. I nudged the stack of folders a bit, attempting to get a better look at the addresses typed across the labels on their tabs.

Three of the four files were for Northrop Manor. The other was too faded to be legible.

"Hello! So sorry!" the woman's voice called again, from a significantly closer position.

I jumped and spun, squelching a yelp of guilt for peeking at the files.

A stout, busty woman in a purple shirtdress and chunky black heels smiled at me. Large, round-framed glasses sat high on her naturally upturned nose. Her long brunette hair had been carefully arranged in a retro moptop style circa Beatlemania.

I was sure she'd love my car.

"Hi!" I said, moving quickly away from the desk, one hand outstretched in greeting. "I'm Everly Swan."

She seemed to pale as I approached, and her gaze slid briefly to the desk where I'd been poking around. "Oh, dear."

"Do you work here?" I asked, suddenly wishing I'd brought something from the café to break the ice. "I own Sun, Sand, and Tea, the iced tea shop in the big Victorian home on the beach."

The woman nodded slowly. "Of course. I'm Faye," she said, seeming to shake off the mini-stupor. "I know who you are. I should've recognized you straight off, but my head's all over the place today. You understand."

"I do. You worked with Susan Thames."

Faye nodded again. "It was terrible, what happened to her."

"Yes," I agreed. "Would you mind if I asked you a few questions?"

Faye seemed to consider this a moment before motioning me to follow her. "This way."

We entered the room she'd just vacated.

The space was well lit with a large oval table at the center. Serious-looking tomes filled sturdy wooden bookcases against one wall. Metal filing cabinets lined the other. I suspected the space pulled double duty as a conference area and legal library.

"Please," Faye said. "Sit. Can I get you something to drink?"

I lowered into the nearest chair. "No, I'm fine, thank you. I'll only take a few minutes of your time."

She selected the seat across from me and folded her hands on the table. "I don't mean to stare," she said. "It's just that you're practically a local celebrity. I feel as if I should ask for your autograph. The only way this would be more exciting is if Detective Hays was with you. Then I could ask you both to sign a photo or something." She smiled at her joke.

At least, I hoped it was a joke.

She waved a hand between us, as if to erase the strange comments. "I ramble when I'm nervous. I know the circumstances are terrible," she said, "but my friends are going to be so jealous. We eat at your café sometimes, hoping to catch a Graverly sighting. Now, here you are. Asking to talk to me."

I raised a finger to halt her. "I'm sorry," I said. "I'm confused. Can we just…" I circled my finger in a rewind motion. "A what sighting?"

Her cheeks reddened. "Graverly," she repeated.

I pushed my chin forward, brows high. "What?"

"It's your celebrity couple name with Detective Hays," she clarified. "Grady and Everly. Graverly. We considered Sways, but this had a better ring."

My lips parted, but words eluded me. So I stared.

"We follow all your cases," she continued. "I didn't know you knew Susan until I read this morning's post on the *Charmer*. Were the two of you working on something together?"

I squinted, trying to see a path through all the cuckoo. Unable to find one, I decided to keep asking questions. "When you said, 'we follow all of your cases,'" I began, "Who do you mean by 'we'?"

Faye frowned, somehow managing to look as confused and befuddled as I felt. "The Sippers," she said.

I shook my head. "I don't understand."

"Your followers." She paused, as if waiting for me to say, "Oh, those Sippers." As if her words made any sense. "We're the ones ready to help if you need us. The name's a little silly, I guess. It's because you make literal tea, and we sip up the figuratively spilled sort. The Corkers chose the name. We all just went along with it."

"The Corkers named my followers Sippers."

"Exactly." She laughed. "I suppose we shouldn't be surprised our name's a little quirky. They called themselves Corkers. Maybe someone else should've named the Sippers."

I rested my elbow on the table and set my chin in my palm to keep my jaw from hanging open. I wasn't sure I wanted a group of followers, or how I felt about them being called sippers.

"If Susan was working on something for you," Faye said, eyes brightening, "I could take over. I'm pretty good at research, and I've got plenty of time. Is that why you're here?"

"No," I said, struggling to get my thoughts back on track. "I hoped you could tell me what Susan was working on the last few days or so, aside from my project."

"Oh." Faye's shoulders slumped. "I'm not sure what she was up to. She was tight-lipped about her projects outside the office."

I nodded, making a mental note that Susan was possibly working on something for someone outside the office. "When was the last time you spoke with her?" I asked. "Did she seem like herself? Were the two of you friends? Did she mention anything was bothering her?"

"That's an odd set of questions," Faye said, a small frown forming on her lips. "It sounds as if you're looking into her for some reason. Was she in trouble? She didn't seem the type to do anything illegal or unsavory." A long, quiet beat later, she gasped. "She just died. You think it wasn't an accident."

"Maybe," I said, recalling belatedly that Charm P.D. hadn't yet declared the death as a murder.

Faye covered her mouth with both hands. "Someone killed her."

"I just want to know what she was working on."

She pressed her lips together and tapped a glossy purple fingernail on the desk. Her fat gold and diamond rings were impressive too. "You're welcome to take a look at her desk, maybe work some of your Swan magic," she said. "If you're interested. I'd love to watch a master in action."

I stood, eager to poke around and purposely ignoring her adoring tone.

We returned to the main room, and Faye led me to the desk I'd been snooping at earlier.

"There you are," she said, leaning against the wall, presumably giving me space to work.

"This was Susan's desk?"

She nodded. "I work in the filing room."

I crept around to the business side of the papers, no longer worrying about being caught. "Are either of the attorneys in?" I asked, eyes darting to the closed office doors. "Maybe one of them has an idea what she was working on." Or a few minutes to talk before I leave.

"They're typically not in until after ten," Faye said.

"Right." I smiled.

Charmers were on island time. Mornings and evenings were for being outdoors, enjoying good food and company, not toiling in a stuffy office. As a result, most businesses, outside medical practices and the service industry, kept truncated late morning to late afternoon hours.

"Has anyone from the police department been around?" I asked, opening and closing drawers in search of a hand-written letter or flashing lights with the killer's name attached to it.

"Not that I know of," she said. "Why would the police have come around?"

I bit my lip, forgetting again that news of foul play hadn't yet been announced. Even the Charmer hadn't said a word. "What about Mr. Thames?" I asked, intentionally ignoring her question. I glanced over my shoulder when she didn't answer immediately.

Faye scratched behind her ear. "It's not something folks talked about, but she and Burt were separated."

"I see," I said.

Ryan's intel was right. I kind of wished I'd beaten him to it.

"I hate that this happened," I whispered, a fresh wave of sadness sweeping through me. "She helped so many people."

Faye offered a sad smile. "She had a true gift for dig-ging up details. The things she found didn't always make everyone happy, but she was the best at finding the truth."

"How do you mean?" I asked, giving up my quest for a smoking gun or confessional in the creaky metal desk.

"In divorce cases, for example. Some couples can get sneaky and underhanded when it's time to call it quits. Both sides want to leave the relationship with as much as they can while making sure their former partner leaves with as little as possible. Some try to hide money or assets. Susan always found the things they hid. Business partners do the same when it's time to dissolve the union. She looked into all of that."

I took a moment to let that sink in. "I had no idea." I'd imagined Susan as a historian. The idea she worked at a law firm was odd, but mentally manageable. Picturing her up to her elbows in messy divorce cases was almost too pedestrian to be real.

"You see a person's true colors when they have something to lose," Faye said. "I've even seen Realtors falsely inflating property values just to dupe an out-of-towner or an uneducated buyer. The Realtor gets a bigger commission on the larger sale, and the buyer is never able to sell for what they paid." Faye shook her head. "Things can get dirty where money is involved."

I knew it was true, but it still seemed awful. I rubbed my temple as my mind circled back to the bigger question at hand. "How about Susan's separation? Was her divorce amicable? Or was it getting messy?"

Faye scanned the world outside the glass door, then took a few steps nearer. "I think the divorce is nearly final, if it isn't already. I can't be sure, because Susan was so private, but it's been a long while since the initial split. I remember Burt wanted to give things another chance. He was heartbroken when she asked him to move out last year. They never had any children. If the case isn't final yet, I suppose all the marital assets go to him."

That sounded like a solid motive to me. I needed to pay Mr. Thames a visit, maybe take him a casserole for condolences and see about that divorce status.

The main office door opened, and Faye sprang away from me, knocking a file from Susan's desk in the process.

I picked the papers up and returned them to their place, noting the familiar realty logo on a number of pages inside. Beach Royalty Realty. Mary Grace Chatsworth-Vanders's company.

I *really* didn't want to need information from her.

Two men in gray suits paused briefly to stare at us.

My heart hammered at the sight of the younger man. I'd seen him waiting for Susan outside Northrop Manor the day she'd died, and she hadn't looked forward to meeting with him.

"Mr. Krebs!" I guessed, taking a fifty-fifty chance. I cringed at the shrillness in my voice, then shoved my hand out in greeting toward the older gentleman. "I'm Everly Swan. I run Sun, Sand, and Tea, the iced tea shop at the beach. I was a friend of Susan Thames."

I'd apparently guessed right. Krebs shook my hand, eyes sliding from me to Faye, then back. "I'm aware of who you are, Miss Swan. I'm sorry for your loss."

"Thank you. I'm sorry for your loss as well," I said. "I understand Susan worked here. She was very good at what she did. She must've been an incredible asset."

Krebs's frown deepened. "She will be difficult to replace."

The younger, dark-haired man narrowed his eyes, probably sensing I was up to something, or noticing the flashing neon sign in my still-startled expression that said as much. "I'll wait for you in your office," he told Krebs. "I have another appointment in an hour."

Faye, Krebs, and I watched as he strode through the door behind the desk and rounded the corner, out of sight.

Krebs's heated gaze traveled over me, then across the desk and the mass of open files at my side. "Faye," he said, voice low and jaw locked. "You weren't going through those files with Miss Swan, were you? Or discussing any details of our cases with her. Because that would be both highly unethical and illegal."

Faye kneaded her hands and turned nervous eyes on me.

"No. No!" I laughed. "Nothing like that. I was only here to use the phone. Faye let me call for a ride because my car battery died," I said, formulating the world's worst excuse for my presence.

Faye tented her brows. "I'm glad to help anytime."

I set my hands on the door and looked at my car, clearly visible through the glass, and I groaned internally. I couldn't very well get in and drive away now. I also couldn't conjure someone to pick me up.

"Someone is on the way to pick you up?" the attorney asked.

"No. No one was home," I said, continuing the dumb lie. "I'm just going to walk."

I scurried onto the sidewalk before he could ask any more questions or I could say anything to make matters worse. I didn't want to get Faye fired or myself arrested.

Grady would kill me. If I was lucky, Krebs would go into his office quickly and close the door, eliminating his view of Dharma.

Until then, I turned on my toes and started walking.

CHAPTER NINE

I headed for the beach, drawn to the water as always when my head was full and my heart was heavy. I considered taking a seat in the sun once I'd arrived but couldn't convince my feet to stop moving.

Instead, I marched onward, heading back toward town as my mind reeled with an overload of information, from the fact Susan sometimes dug up information that ticked people off to the appearance of Mary Grace's company logo on the file from Susan's desk.

I couldn't even begin to process the fact people secretly called Grady and me Graverly. Or that some of those same people called themselves Sippers.

I blinked my eyes, concentrating on my senses instead of my muddled thoughts.

The scent of sunblock rose on the wind, woven with the sand and sea. Sounds of gulls and children's laughter filled the air. My heated skin and the familiar slip of my steps in soft, dry sand slowly lowered my heart rate.

Eyes open, I delighted in the fling of sandpipers racing the waves and brightly colored kites soaring proudly overhead.

Before I'd realized how far I'd gone, a whiff of grilled burgers and greasy fries pulled my attention toward the boardwalk, where Charm's main shopping area had come partially into view. Pops of color on awnings and signs peeked through the dense foliage of the marsh along Ocean Drive, and I marveled at the speed in which time had passed.

The trip back to town was significantly faster without the hindrance of traffic and roadways. I felt a little like Lou, who always took the direct route place to place. For earth-bound humans, like myself, the beach or boardwalk was a similar option. No need to navigate around neighborhoods, national forests, and landmarks. No waiting at stop signs and crosswalks for pedestrians, cyclists, or geese to cross the street.

I turned to look back in the direction I'd come, unsure if I should turn around or keep going. Undecided about when to pick up my car, but certain I was ready for some shade, I headed for the town hall. If Aunt Fran had driven to work, she could take me back to my car.

I picked up speed as images of a falling gargoyle moved to the forefront of my mind.

Grady's life had been endangered so many times since our first kiss, it was impossible not to list that fact in the Cursed column of my mental spreadsheet. What would happen at the end of our wedding vows, when he was told to kiss the bride? A tidal wave? Falling satellite from space? If he survived that, what about the honeymoon?

I stopped a few minutes later, peering up at the rooftop of the town hall, shielding my eyes with one curved hand. Just as Grady had said, one of the winged statues was missing. My heart skittered as I examined the sidewalk and found a deep divot where the figure had landed.

"Everly?" Aunt Fran stepped through the building's front doors wearing oversized sunglasses and a giant black hat. "What are you doing here?"

I waved. "Walking. Are you leaving?"

"I have a council meeting in thirty minutes, but I need some fresh air before it begins," she said, popping up an old-fashioned parasol. Also black. Her pale gray silk blouse fluttered in the wind. Her long black skirt billowed. "The Corkers are pushing for more activities to spice up their lives, while Charm traditionalists are pushing back on the number of things I already have scheduled. All of these people are taxpayers, but the Corkers are also volunteers, activists, and donators. I can't make everyone happy, and I don't want to be persuaded to cater to the Corkers, much as I agree with them, for fear it will look as if I sided with the money. I want everyone in Charm to have a truly charmed experience."

Sheer exhaustion was evident in her eyes, tone, and posture. I couldn't ask her to drive me anywhere right now, and I wouldn't risk making her late to her meeting.

"Hey," I said, joining her in a small patch of shade thrown by a nearby tree. "You're doing an amazing job. Don't let anyone tell you otherwise, and don't try peddling that nonsense to yourself. You're the first mayor this town has had in my whole life who truly cares about what the population wants. I think it's honorable that you're trying so hard to make everyone happy. But it's an impossible goal. And you shouldn't make yourself miserable trying to reach it."

She heaved a sigh. "I know you're right. You're very wise, and infinitely kind."

"I get those qualities from you," I said. "You, Aunt Clara, and Grandma did a bang-up job raising me."

Fran gave a small smile. "We certainly tried. Thank you for saying so." She squeezed my hand, then took a few deep breaths. "Where are you headed?"

"Nowhere," I said. "I was on the beach and decided to get out of the sun."

She tilted her head. "Anything I can help you with?"

I lifted one shoulder, then let it drop. "Any chance you know what Susan Thames might've been working on the other night? Aside from researching our family? Or who she met with during the fish fry?"

Aunt Fran's eyes shifted in thought. "Anyone accessing historical property records has to sign in at the desk. We keep the file room locked, and Susan spent a good portion of time there."

I beamed, following the tilt of her head to the town hall doors. "Excellent. Mind if I take a look now?"

"Knock yourself out," Aunt Fran said. "I'm going to walk around until I find my zen, or the council meeting begins, whichever comes first."

I had a feeling I knew which that would be, but I kept it to myself.

I kissed her cheek, then hurried inside.

Elaine, the town hall receptionist, smiled at the sight of me. "Everly! How are you?"

"Wonderful. Thank you."

We exchanged brief pleasantries, then I asked her about Susan and the file room.

She performed a stage wink, and I frowned. "Of course." She riffled under the counter a moment, then raised a spiral notebook into view. "Everyone signs in here."

I accepted the book and dragged my fingertip over the page, scanning the various signatures, in search of one in particular. I tapped the line with Susan's name. "She was here earlier this week. Do you know what she was looking into?"

Elaine shook her head. "No, but it was something from 1970 or earlier. We're working to scan all the records and upload them to the website so folks don't have to come in, but we've only made it back to 1970. Anything before that is still boxed and filed in the back."

I turned the pages of the book, noting the appearance of Susan's name on repeat. "Wow." Aunt Fran hadn't been kidding. "She came here a lot."

"Quite."

"Do you mind if I take a look in the back?" I asked.

"Not at all." Elaine passed me a pen and pointed to the notebook.

I scratched my name on the next available line, then added the date and time.

Elaine smiled and handed me a key. "Turn the light on when you go in. Turn it off when you leave. And Everly?"

"Yeah?"

"I'm here if you need anything." Elaine repeated the awkward, drawn out wink from my arrival, and I hurried to the door behind her desk.

"Thank you!" I let myself into the unexpectedly large room and paused to let my eyes adjust. Light filtered in through blinds on two tall, narrow windows, showcasing dust particles in the air but not doing much to illuminate the overall space.

I ran my hand along the wall, flipping the light switch. Rows and stacks of boxes filled numerous massive shelving units that nearly reached the ceiling. "Holy cannoli," I whispered. How would I ever figure out what Susan was doing in here?

Narrow planks of dark wooden flooring stretched out before me, leading to a single folding table and chair.

I walked the central aisle, pivoting my head left and right to take it all in. Periodically, small white labels on the shelving units caught my eye, identifying the years and first letters of files contained therein. I made a loop around the space, acclimating myself and admiring the extreme organization. I decided to start with what I knew.

Susan had been researching my family, and she'd been working to repair the historic well Northrop Manor. Several files I'd seen at the law office had contained the manor's address.

I pulled the boxes and files on Northrop Manor and my

family homestead. Then, I started taking photos. Knowing my time was limited, I snapped pictures of anything and everything that might be worth a closer look when I got home.

When it was time to go, I repacked the materials as neatly as possible, then returned them to the shelves. I beetled through the door, turning out the lights and locking up on my way to the receptionist's desk. I paused only long enough to leave the key and wave goodbye as I passed. Elaine was on the phone, and I didn't want to bother her. Also, Denise needed to leave Sun, Sand, and Tea soon to pick up Denver from school, so I needed to be back before that happened.

The relentless southern sun was out in full force as I hustled back down Middletown Road to the beach, then through the sand toward the law offices.

I mentally planned my route, plotting short cuts and imagining where vehicles might bottleneck, slowing my return home by car. My little bracelet thrilled as my heart rate climbed, celebrating the impromptu workout.

My resulting smile fell as Krebs and Chesterfield came into view.

Dharma sat exactly where I left her, in the small lot outside.

And she was coated in heavy, dried clumps of seaweed, a handful of coins scattered on her seat.

CHAPTER
TEN

Grady arrived ten minutes later, looking unimpressed and incredibly tired. He greeted me with a scowl and a kiss on my forehead. "You okay?"

"Better now," I said, crossing my arms as I followed him around the car.

"Witnesses?" he asked, raising his eyes to the law office and handful of nearby shops.

I shook my head. "Krebs and Chesterfield was closed when I got back. I haven't gone into any of the stores to ask if anyone saw what happened."

Grady raised his cell phone to the car and snapped photos from various angles while I told him everything I'd learned from Faye. And about the way Krebs had glared.

"Faye said the police hadn't been around to talk to the office staff yet, so maybe that's a good place to go next," I suggested. "See what everyone else here has to say."

He shot me a droll look. "Good idea."

"I'm not trying to tell you how to do your job," I said. "I'm just thinking out loud."

"Do you think any other way?"

I returned his bland look. He was lucky I kept as much as I did to myself. "I texted Denise while you were on your way. She closed the shop so she wouldn't be late picking up Denver," I said, changing the subject. "She explained the situation, then handed out to-go boxes for unfinished meals and free desserts in apology. She said everyone understood."

Grady snorted softly. "You live in a town of enablers."

I smiled. "You live here too. Did you know we have a fan club?"

Grady cast me a questioning look. "Who does? Your family?"

"No. We do," I said, motioning between us. "They call us Graverly."

His curious expression pinched. "Graverly? That's... morbid."

"It's our names," I said. "They mashed them together. Like a celebrity couple."

Grady stopped taking pictures and straightened, setting big hands against his hips. "This is my punishment for falling in love with a nut," he said. "This and the fact all our personal business is covered daily on a public website. The Corkers are right. Folks around here need more to do with their time."

I grinned. "The Corkers gave us our name."

"Figures."

"That's what I said. And they call the fan club members Sippers."

"Zippers?" He shot me an incredulous face.

"Sippers," I repeated, smile growing impossibly wide. "And if you'd just tell me who runs the *Town Charmer*, I could ask them to back off a little on the Graverly features."

He lifted a finger. "Don't call us that. We're the Hayses."

I frowned. "Not yet we aren't, and I can't take your last name. You know that."

"Why not?"

"It's tradition." Surely we'd talked about this.

He turned a glare in my direction, pausing once more to stare. "Explain, please."

"Swans just don't do that. Swans are Swans. Men take our last name."

He barked a laugh. "Maybe when it behooved the couple. When women couldn't own businesses or property. Or as a way to keep your inheritance. Not now, in the twenty-first century."

I moved my hands to my hips, mirroring his stance and not appreciating his tone. "Exactly. It's the twenty-first century, and women don't have to take their husband's names. We don't have to do anything."

"I'm not changing my last name," he said. "That would mean changing Denver's last name or having a different name than my son. I won't do it. Amy's tombstone says Hays. Denver is a Hays. You will be a Hays."

I set my jaw, as determined not to settle as he was, and

with equally important reasons. "I won't break a centuries-old tradition."

"Then hyphenate," he said, voice edging closer to growly than I preferred.

"I will consider it if you do," I countered. "There's no reason both you and Denver can't hyphenate. It won't cause him to lose the link to his mother. It will only add a link to his present and future."

Grady pinched the bridge of his nose.

"You can think about it," I said. "We don't need to make any hard decisions for three months."

"You say that a lot," he said, dropping his hand away from his face and fixing me with his standard cop face. "Three months isn't that long, and every decision that matters is already made."

I bit my tongue against the urge to confess I couldn't marry him if I wasn't certain he'd be safe.

"Everly," he said slowly. "You aren't cursed, and we will prove that. Either by finding documentation that shows this whole concept was blown out of proportion over time, or by the passage of time itself. I have big plans to say I told you so on our golden anniversary."

I considered pointing out that letting time set the record straight wouldn't be romantic or grand if he was struck by lightning at the altar, but I kept that thought to myself too. Instead, I did what I always did and changed the subject again. "Why won't you tell me who the gossip blogger is?"

He'd discovered the truth about the responsible party after something posted during our last murder investigation had put me *and* Grady's case in danger. He'd promised the blogger he wouldn't reveal their identity to anyone, and so far he'd kept his word—despite countless hours of begging and endless failed manipulation attempts on my part.

"It's not my secret to tell," he said, just like always. "But I have mentioned that a reveal like that, for someone as curious as you, would make a magnificent wedding present."

I pursed my lips. He wasn't wrong.

"I had a chance to talk to Mr. Thames," Grady said, stealing my move with the subject change. "He and Susan are divorced."

"They're getting divorced," I said, correcting him with the gossip Ryan had acquired and shared.

Grady eyeballed me. "It's been finalized. I saw the paperwork myself."

"Huh," I said, a little surprised and wondering what that might mean on a larger scale. "If they're not married anymore, I wonder why he was so upset that night."

"They were married twenty years," Grady said. "You spend that much time with someone, you probably don't want them pushed down a well."

"Depends," I said.

He slid his eyes my way. "Should I be worried?"

I smiled. "Not if you toe the line," I teased. "Still, I can't help wondering if a few of Mr. Thames's tears were formed by the guilt of having knocked her over the edge."

Grady cringed. "That's dark. Why don't you let me take the investigation from here?"

"Because I still have questions," I said. "Like who was

the man Susan met at Northrop Manor after lunch that day? Because he was just here this morning, with Krebs."

Grady scratched his eyebrow. "So you came to Susan's place of employment, asked a bunch of questions about her death, were seen by multiple people, including a guy you know the victim had a problem with, and your car was vandalized afterward. Is that accurate?"

"It's a fair summary of my morning," I said. "But I also walked to the town hall, talked to Aunt Fran and Elaine, then signed into the records room to see what Susan had been looking into before her death. A couple of hours passed between my visit to Krebs and Chesterfield and my return to find Dharma covered in yuck."

Grady pulled me to him in a loose embrace and pressed a kiss to the top of my head. "You're killing me, Swan. Now, come on." He turned me by the shoulders and steered me to his truck. "I'm going to have someone finish processing your car and the immediate area. I'll ask them to have the car washed and returned to you later today. Meanwhile, let's just get out of here."

"Okay," I agreed, shuffling along ahead of him, "but who was the guy I saw with Krebs today?"

"Leave this alone, Everly," he said. "I'm saying it with love, but make no mistake. I do mean it."

I climbed into the truck and buckled my seat belt, not appreciating his refusal to answer. "You know I can call the law office tomorrow and ask who the guy was."

"You can call," he said, closing my door. He rounded the hood and climbed behind the steering wheel. "But attorney-client privilege will stop anyone who works here from telling you anything." He shifted into drive and pulled away from the little office building.

I couldn't help wondering if that privacy law would stop Faye or another Sipper from sharing the man's identity.

Grady covered my hand with his, then raised it to his mouth and kissed the backs of my knuckles. "I'm sorry your car was vandalized, but I'm glad you're okay."

I rolled my head against the seat back to stare at him. "Thank you for coming to my rescue."

"Always," he vowed.

I smiled and squeezed his hand.

Color rose high on Grady's cheeks a moment later, and he stole a look in my direction. "I'm sorry I saw you in your wedding dress today. You've been on edge about bad luck already, and my timing was awful. For what it's worth, I think the dress is nice, and the rule is for the groom not to see the bride before the wedding. It has nothing to do with seeing the dress."

I sighed. "It's all right, but I'm not taking any chances. I'll pick out another dress. There are plenty more at the homestead, and I'll need more research books from the archives in a few days anyway."

Grady's pinched expression didn't ease. "I have a few books at my place too. I'll get back into research mode as soon as I wrap this case."

He parked outside my home several minutes later and turned to me with a storm of emotion behind his eyes. "You looked beautiful in that dress. I don't say it enough, but you are the most beautiful woman, the kindest human and gentlest soul I've ever known. I would marry you in bare feet and cutoffs, covered in sand, floating in the sea, riding on horseback. Anytime. Anywhere. As long as you'll have me."

I unbuckled my seat belt and threw myself at him, wrapping him in a hug. "It's hard to think of myself as cursed when you keep saying things like that," I muttered against his neck.

"You are not cursed," he promised, for roughly the billionth time.

And I hoped more than anything he was right.

❦

I woke the next morning with plans to visit Mr. Thames. After hours of scrolling through the social media feeds of both Susan and her ex the night before, it seemed reasonable to speak to him about my concerns. Regardless of how long they'd been separated, they'd been married long enough for him to know her better than anyone else. Assuming he wasn't her killer, he could be my greatest resource.

It had only taken a few clicks to discover Burt Thames not only lived on his boat, he used it for his business as well. He was a fisherman who regularly chartered the boat for group excursions, and he took plenty of pictures for his personal and business social media pages. Many of those images included a deeply tanned woman with platinum hair and a plethora of string bikinis. The website listed her as his office assistant, and I'd noted her as a point of interest in my case.

I'd talked things over with Lou at sunrise, and he'd gotten all worked up about the details. He'd squawked and flapped his wings as I explained about the blond, clearly in agreement. Based on the volume of photos and apparent level of comfort between her and her photographer, presumably Burt, she was likely a love interest.

Now, I just had to wait for Thames Boating and Fishing to open so I could set up a time to chat. Hopefully, while I was on the premises, I'd get a firsthand look at the dynamic between him and his office assistant and know if I was right about the romantic element.

The only other lead I'd gained online was found in Susan's social media feed. She had a surprising number of posts on the rumored hauntings at Northrop Manor. She'd never struck me as a believer in ghosts or the supernatural, but she'd been especially interested in one particular accident that had claimed the lives of four men about eight years before I was born.

According to the follow-up articles I'd read, a crew of construction workers had been crushed to death during a major reconstruction of the manor's foyer, when several beams, and the roof they were supporting, collapsed. I vaguely recalled my grandma and great-aunts talking about the accident over midnight pancakes when I was small. They'd known the workers and the families left behind.

I checked my watch, anticipating Denise's arrival and making a mental reminder to hire another helper soon.

When it was finally nine o'clock, and Mr. Thames's business officially opened, I pulled up the website and gave the phone number a call.

"Thames Boating and Fishing," a husky woman's voice answered.

"Hello," I said. "Can you tell me if Mr. Thames will be in this morning? I'd like to swing by and speak with him for a few minutes, if possible."

"Let me check the schedule, hon," she said, snapping her gum into the phone's receiver. "Be right back." She put me on hold, then returned to the line a moment later. "Looks like he took a group out at dawn today, and it's nonstop for him through the night. If you want, I can pencil you in for later this week."

I groaned and shut the laptop, bummed by the change of plans. "I'll call back tomorrow," I said as pleasantly as possible, then disconnected.

Today, I'd have to pursue the only lead I'd been trying to forget about.

Today, I'd have to ask Mary Grace for her help.

CHAPTER
∽
ELEVEN

I walked so slowly to the realty office, my rubber fitness bully buzzed twice, demanding I BE MORE ACTIVE! If it wasn't for the GPS chip, the thing probably wouldn't have believed I was moving at all.

I couldn't believe I was moving, intentionally, in the direction of Mary Grace's new business. I swung my arm around to appease the bracelet, making it believe I'd gone wild at its command. If only I could soothe my internal despair as easily. Mary Grace and her husband, Councilman Vanders, were shiny, sneering blights on my overall life experience in Charm. Thankfully, they were usually easy to avoid.

Vanders annoyed me for multiple reasons, from relatively petty behaviors to wildly offensive comments. For example, he lived on an island but preferred spray tan to sunshine, and his painfully whitened teeth were at blinding odds with the fabricated tan. *Petty.* His womanizing comments and misogynistic jokes, however, were nauseating and unequivocally offensive.

Mary Grace's outlandish self-importance, and a lifetime of unpleasant run-ins, worked double duty to kindle the fire she'd lit in middle school by badmouthing my mama.

My complete inability to rise above it all made needing Mary Grace's help all the worse.

I cursed my insatiable curiosity and prayed for a distraction as I dragged my way to her office. The silent request was answered almost immediately.

A buff, blue-eyed cowboy caught my eye up ahead as I crept along the sidewalk on Main Street. My ex-boyfriend and current friend, Wyatt, spoke with a group of youngsters in matching red T-shirts and jeans. Their shirts had cartoon horses sandwiched between the words Cowboy Club, and they all wore dusty boots and hats like Wyatt's. He'd dressed in his usual white T-shirt and blue jeans and inviting smile.

A woman with a notepad and pen took the group's orders outside my favorite ice cream parlor. She wrote blindly on the paper while her hungry eyes gobbled up the six-foot snack before her.

Wyatt whooped when he noticed me and extended a hand in my direction. "Well, if it isn't Everly Swan," he boomed, tugging me in for a hug when I drew near. "It's always good to see you, E. I believe you know my little cowpokes. Pokes, say howdy to Miss Everly."

"Howdy, Miss Everly," they returned.

Wyatt worked for the island's nature center, monitoring and studying the wild pony population. He also ran a summer cowboy camp for young folks. He taught the students what it meant to be a cowboy. Not just roping and riding, but respect for nature, wildlife, and people. Kids loved it, and their mamas lined up for any excuse to talk to our resident retired rodeo star. Wyatt paid no attention to the lusting mamas, much like he ignored the ogling waitress. In recent months, he'd only had eyes for Denise. He claimed otherwise, but one look at him in her presence told the real story. They'd been a couple, briefly, and I suspected the split had come when one of them, or both, had gotten spooked by the potential loss of their friend, should the romance fail. I couldn't imagine that happening. They were great together, so I hoped they'd figure things out soon.

I smiled brightly back at the swarm of tiny cherub faces. Wyatt brought them to Sun, Sand, and Tea for drinks and treats at least once a week, so I was getting to know them better all the time. "You must've been very good to get ice cream for breakfast," I said. "How's your morning so far?"

"We saw a snake!" Tommy, a boy in glasses, declared.

"Oh, my!" I widened my eyes and pressed my palms against my cheeks like the kid from *Home Alone*. "Are you okay?"

"Yeah," Tommy assured. "I fought him off with my bare hands!" He pulled the sleeve on his T-shirt back with one hand and made a muscle.

A little girl in braids, who I recognized as Olivia, crossed her arms. "He's a dummy," she said. "He wasn't even supposed to be near the marsh. He could've been bitten, and he didn't fight that snake. He ran away. Mr. Wyatt said he was lucky he didn't see an alligator."

"All right," Wyatt said, clapping his big hands together

with a chuckle. "Let's get our hands washed before we eat."
He motioned to the public restrooms at the side of the
building, then moved to stand between the sets of doors.
"Ladies on the right. Men on the left."

I followed along as the kids divided in waves, entering
their respective restrooms. Wyatt was amazing with the
kids, and I smiled at the swell of pride in my chest. He'd
grown into a centered, respectable man. Not at all like the
reckless bull rider I'd once fallen in love with. And I was
glad for him. Though, it still floored me to hear him say
things like "Let's get our hands washed before we eat." I'd
seen Wyatt eat untold numbers of meals while covered in
blood, sweat, and grime during long days of training on
the rodeo circuit.

"They aren't getting ice cream," he clarified. "They're
getting Belgian waffles with strawberries, whipped cream,
and cinnamon syrup."

I offered a crooked grin. "The ice cream might've had
less sugar."

He fixed broad hands on narrow hips and locked his
bright eyes on mine. "What are you up to this morning?"

I made a disgruntled sound, instantly bummed by the
reminder. "Research."

"Looking into what happened during the fish fry?" he
asked.

I tapped a finger to my nose.

He grinned. "Anything I can do to help?"

"No. But I might need bail money soon," I only half
joked. "I'm on my way to talk to Mary Grace, because her

company logo was on some files I saw at the law office where Susan worked. No one's been able to tell me what Susan was working on when she died, aside from researching my family, so I figured a chat with Mary Grace was in order."

Wyatt rubbed the scruff along his jaw, concern lining his brow. "You know researching your family didn't have anything to do with what happened to Susan, right?"

I shrugged.

He turned to face me directly, then stepped into my personal space, creating a private cocoon for just the two of us to speak freely. "Researching your family didn't have anything to do with what happened to Susan," he repeated. "It absolutely did not, and I'm here to tell you that as often as you need to hear it. So if you start thinking otherwise, give me a call."

A riot of cowpokes emerged from the men's bathroom, eliminating my chance to respond. The children were soaked in water and nearly collapsing in hysterics.

Olivia appeared next, striding from the women's restroom and stopping behind Wyatt. She kept him between her and the chaos while she stared in annoyance and disapproval. "Boys are ridiculous."

I smiled. "Yeah, but they're a lot of fun if you can get past the noise."

"Good grief!" Wyatt hollered, trying to catch and separate the group. "Did y'all wash your hands or just climb right into the sink and turn on the water?"

The group exchanged mischievous grins, then attacked him with sopping hugs.

I jumped back, shooting a look of camaraderie to Olivia. "Good luck! Gotta go!" I called. "Y'all come round my place next time. I'll make brownies!" I waved to the pint-sized mob as I hustled away on an outburst of laughter.

A balding fortyish man standing outside my aunts' shop looked up at the sound of my cackling, then turned slightly away. He spoke into a cell phone, relaying details about products sold at Blessed Bee, and gave a favorable description of my aunts before noticing I'd stopped beside him. "I have to go," he told whoever was on the other end of his call, then tucked the phone into his pocket and addressed me with a worried expression. "Can I help you?"

"Maybe," I said, wondering if this was the man Aunt Clara thought was stalking her. I worked up my sweetest southern drawl and most welcoming smile just in case. "I'm Everly Swan. I own Sun, Sand, and Tea. That's the iced tea shop in the big Victorian on the beach. My great-aunts, Clara and Fran, own this place." I hooked a thumb over my shoulder, indicating the bright yellow store behind me. "I overheard what you said about their products. It sure was nice. Are you thinking of making a purchase? Maybe I can help with your questions?"

He blinked, clearly caught off guard. "Alexander Lehman," he said. "I'm a big fan of the American Honeybee. The shop is pure genius. I'm deeply impressed by your aunts' work."

"Thank you. Me too. Have you had a chance to speak with them? I know they'd love to meet a fellow bee enthusiast." I held my smile as I eyeballed him. He appeared harmless, but so had plenty of bombers and serial killers. "Where are you from, Mr. Lehman?" Not from North Carolina with his clipped, hurried speech. It was possible he was a new transplant, but even folks who were new to island life didn't wear dress shoes, slacks, and button-up shirts in July, unless the shirts had big tropical flowers. The trousers and shiny shoes were always a no, outside a professional office space.

"Chicago," he said, making things infinitely clearer. "Your family is from here?"

I nearly laughed. "For a few hundred years now," I said.

I turned for a peek through the shop window, where Aunt Clara had painted fat yellow honeybees flying loopy paths over puffy white clouds. I hadn't noticed her Prius at the curb, so I couldn't be sure if she was working at the shop today without giving her a call or going inside.

The man's phone rang, and he turned away to answer. "Lehman." He laughed at whatever the caller said, then lifted his hand in goodbye to me and strode away without another word.

"Chicago," I muttered, staring after him. Folks didn't say goodbye up north?

I made a mental note to see what I could find online about Alexander Lehman from Chicago as soon as I got home. Meanwhile, at least he was moving away from Blessed Bee.

And sadly, so was I.

A few blocks later, I arrived at Beach Royalty Realty, opting to tell my aunts about Mr. Lehman later and just get the worst of my day over now.

Like ripping off a bandage.

The office was a U-shaped new construction covered in white shake. Well-tended flowers grew in window boxes and planters near the door, adding to the abundant curb appeal. A blue door and yellow shutters gave the structure a quaint cottage feel, but the courtyard and fountain at the center of the U created the allure of something much grander.

A rectangular sign on a set of exterior steps encouraged folks to *Climb up and Enjoy the views*.

I did as directed, still slightly procrastinating my time with Mary Grace.

A flat roof lined in waist-high reinforced plexiglass walls awaited me. Colorful Adirondack and rocking chairs invited folks to sit a spell. Coordinating pillows with nautical prints added to the charm.

I inhaled humid ocean air and turned to take in the distant sights of the sound and sea. Signs posted sporadically on the plexiglass explained the island's size, in geography and population, as well as all the beauty residents could find within. From national parks and historic lighthouses to maritime forests, wild ponies, and endless access to the Atlantic.

The attractive displays of local facts were obviously meant to enchant and engage potential new residents, but the words were all one hundred percent true. I couldn't imagine living anywhere else or why anyone would want to. Watching the sunrise from my deck each morning was addictive, and I looked forward to the experience every single day.

When I was with Grady, on his side of the island, in the evenings, we rarely missed a sunset over the sound. I doubted any place on earth could compare to Charm's offerings.

Selling homes in our community should be easier than selling water to thirsty people. The flora and fauna, history, community, and beauty alone were priceless, and things I appreciated more every day. I couldn't help wondering if Mary Grace felt the same way or if the informative posters were just a means to an end. Nothing more than hollow words she hoped would turn into cash. In some ways, it was easier for me to imagine the latter. Otherwise, she and I had something in common. And if that was the case, I suspected the temperature was falling in Hades.

On the roof, however, it was blazing hot, and I needed to get on with my day.

I trudged back down the wooden steps and forced myself to enter the building's front door.

The office's interior was an open concept floor plan, with views of the courtyard through floor-to-ceiling windows and a set of French doors on the opposite wall from where I stood. Between the front and back doors were two desks and several small seating areas to entice and schmooze clients. The overall aesthetic was beach house chic, and much to my dismay, I loved it.

Mary Grace smiled sinisterly from her seat behind a large, whitewashed desk against the far wall.

"I knew you'd make your way over here eventually," she said, rising onto her feet and moving smugly in my direction. "Took you longer than I expected, but I suppose the *Town Charmer* and your little fan club has built you up unnecessarily." She crossed thin arms and tapped long red nails against her unnaturally tanned skin.

"Hello," I said, as pleasantly as possible. "This is a beautiful office space."

"I know that," she said. "Now, go on. Tell me why you're here." Her self-satisfied expression, along with her welcome statement, suggested she already knew.

I took a steadying breath and considered my word choice carefully. I couldn't afford to upset her when I wanted something she had. *Information.*

Her smile grew as I silently struggled, glaring at her perfect face, hair, and bleach white capris. The low-cut red blouse and cinched belt showcased her slender figure, despite a gaggle of offspring. "Flustered?" she asked.

"No."

"Hmm. Let me read your mind," she said, pressing a finger to her temple. "You're here because you know I handled the sale of Northrop Manor to the historical society when the senator left town, and you want details about the transaction."

I forced a tight smile, thankful I hadn't needed to explain. "That is correct."

"So, you need my help," she said, dropping her hand to her hip.

I squirmed, and her eyes twinkled with delight.

I bit the insides of my cheeks, hating to need anything from a woman who went out of her way to irritate me, purely for her entertainment. I longed to turn and walk away, but I needed justice for Susan more than my comfort. "Is there anything you can tell me about your experiences and interaction with Susan Thames? Maybe something she did or said that stuck out to you? Rubbed you the wrong way? An odd question or comment in regard to Northrop Manor?"

Mary Grace dragged her gaze over me slowly. Judgmentally. "First, I want an invitation to your wedding."

"What?"

"Your wedding," she said. "I know you don't plan to invite me, and I hate being left out. So I want to make a deal."

"You want to come to my wedding," I parroted, confused. "Because you don't want to be left out."

She shifted her weight and tipped her head. "That is correct," she said, echoing my earlier words.

I weighed my options and glanced at the exit behind me. On one hand, Mary Grace was the type of woman who might show up at the ceremony in a white gown and do her best to steal the show. Spread a mean rumor or do any number of things to frustrate, upset, or otherwise ruin my wedding day. On the other hand, there was an unprecedented hint of vulnerability in her expression that made me wonder if she was somehow hurt by the fact I'd had no intention of inviting her. The entire town would be welcome at the reception, but the ceremony was meant for close friends and family.

"Do you know something?" I asked.

She nodded.

"Fine," I said. "I'll add you to the ceremony guest list, but it's going to be a very small event. Only about twenty guests."

"Twenty-two," she said, lifting her fingers in a peace sign. "I'm bringing Vanders as my plus-one."

"Right." I imagined addressing my husband by his last name and failed, then I remembered Mary Grace and her husband were aliens, or robots, so it was good I couldn't relate.

She extended a hand, and we shook on the deal. "Well, I'm not sure what you'll make of it," she said casually, getting right down to business, "but when I was working with Susan on the Northrop sale, she asked me to pull all the paperwork I could get my hands on regarding any previous sales of the manor. She didn't say why, but she was quite interested."

I thought of the posts on Susan's social media, about the roof collapse and the lost construction crew. "Did she mention an accident from the last century involving four local workers?" I asked. "It happened at the manor."

"No, but I was able to get files on nearly eighty years of sales, and she was happy with that."

"Any chance I can get copies of whatever you gave her?" I asked.

She shrugged. "If it will help."

I struggled to keep my jaw from swinging open. "Really?"

"Why not? I don't need them anymore. So don't mention

it. Literally," she said. "No one needs to know I'm working with you on your nonsense. Just make sure I get that wedding invitation. Otherwise," she warned. "I will crash your big day and you'll regret it."

I had no doubt.

She handed over the papers with an expectant look.

"You're a real peach," I said. "Invites go out in a few weeks. Yours will be in the mail." I turned to leave, then thought of one more thing and turned back. "Any chance Susan asked about the Swan homestead?"

Mary Grace cocked her head, interest clearly piqued. "No, why?"

"Just curious." I turned away again, relieved and glad to be heading out.

"Everly?" she called.

I dared a look over one shoulder, prepared for one of her usual quips or jeers. "Yeah?"

She pursed her lips and rolled her eyes. "If there's anything else I can do to help with your snooping, let me know. You might not like me, but I liked Susan. Your snooping suggests her death wasn't an accident, which is what folks have been whispering about since the fish fry. If they're right, I want to be on the right side of this. Her killer should be punished."

I nodded, then walked out with a strange sense of peace. The exchange with Mary Grace had been uncharacteristically civil and possibly one of the nicest we'd had in twenty years. I couldn't help wondering if it might've been the first step in a long road to healing between us.

I strangely hoped it was.

Blessed summer sun warmed my cheeks as I moved onto the sidewalk and lifted my chin skyward, absorbing the moment before heading back to work.

Cold water smacked hard against my upturned face, stinging my eyes and temporarily stealing my breath.

A plastic bucket bounced against the sidewalk nearby, followed by a smattering of loose change, both apparently dropped from the realty office's deck.

I pulled hunks of stringy seaweed from my hair, face, and shoulders.

And I screamed.

CHAPTER

TWELVE

Thirty minutes later, I sat beside Grady in his pickup truck. There hadn't been any witnesses to my attack, including me, and the crime scene was small, mostly just my face and a child's sand pail at my feet. So it wasn't long before all the clues had been processed, and we were on our way back to my place.

I'd taken notice of a white midsize SUV with a sticker of a volleyball in the window as it drove away from a nearby parking lot minutes after my attack. I didn't see the driver, or have any real reason to give the vehicle a second thought, but the timing struck me as hugely coincidental, so I'd made a mental note.

Then again, the paranoia might've been the seaweed talking.

Grady parked in my driveway and plucked a string of dried seaweed from my hair with a grimace. "This makes three mornings in a row. Your daily threat rate is picking up."

I puffed my cheeks and blew out a long exhale of frustration. "It's hard to believe Mary Grace was only a few yards away and she's not the culprit."

Grady cracked a smile. "Do I even want to know what you were doing at her office?"

"No," I said. "Probably not, but now I have to invite her and Vanders to our wedding, so that's on me."

He raised his brows, expression caught somewhere between disbelief and amusement. "There has to be one heck of a story there."

"Don't ask," I said. "Are you hungry? I can make us something to eat before Denise heads out."

"Nah, I'll grab a bite later. For now, I want to walk you safely inside and get back to work. I've got a murder to solve."

I huffed a dramatic sigh. "Yeah, yeah."

Grady pulled a beaded metal necklace from beneath his shirt and rested the attached badge against his chest. "Detective," he said, pointing to the credentials like a caveman.

I groaned, having seen this routine before.

"Tea maker." He turned the pointing finger toward me and booped my nose.

"Stop it."

He grinned.

I shook my head. "You know it's not that complicated to get a private detective's license. I read up on it a few months back. If I was a PI, we could work these cases together."

Grady's tanned face slowly paled.

I worried for a moment he might pass out. "Kidding," I said, though I'd been deadly serious. A few silent moments later, the color began to return to his cheeks.

I stared through the windshield at my house and the family curse barged back to mind. "Any chance you've had time to dig up something useful about my family?" I asked.

"Very little," he said with an apologetic shake of his head. "I pulled coroner reports from the system going back several decades, but nothing is digital before the 1970s. I'll have to get my hands on paper files from the years before then."

"Building permits and deed titles are the same way," I said.

He nodded, as if he already had that information. "I'd hoped to get through the material I have before now, but the new murder case has caused me to temporarily press pause."

Unfortunate, but understandable. "Have you heard anything about a construction accident that killed a crew at Northrop Manor about forty or so years back?"

"No, why?"

"I don't know," I said. "Susan mentioned the tragedy a few times on her social media feed, and she was involved with the property's most recent sale." Not to mention she'd been killed there as well. "I thought the facts might be connected."

Grady nodded. "Good point. I'll keep that in mind. Anything else?"

"Not on the investigation," I said. "But I ran into a

balding, fortyish man outside Blessed Bee today who was on his phone telling someone about my aunts' products. He might be the one she thinks is stalking her. I tried to find out, but he walked away. Didn't even say goodbye." I shot Grady a sideways glance and shook my head, then opened the passenger door. "All I managed to learn is that his name is Alexander Lehman and he's from Chicago."

Grady sucked his teeth, probably fighting the urge to tell me not to talk to strangers. "I'll check that out too."

"Don't worry about it." I waved him off and climbed down from the truck. "I can plug his name in online, check out his social media profiles and any business affiliations. It's no problem. I just wanted to keep you in the loop."

Grady met me at his bumper and walked me to the house. "How about I see if he has a criminal record before you talk to him again?"

"Fine." I lifted and dropped a hand.

Grady caught me around the waist when we reached the top porch step.

"Hey! What are you doing?" I gasped. "I smell like seaweed and I'm all wet."

He pressed a kiss to my forehead, my cheek, and my nose before planting a toe curler on my lips. Clearly, he was unconcerned by my sogginess.

Heat rushed through my chest and went straight to my brain, burning away all coherent thought. "Wow," I whispered, struggling for balance when he released me.

"Back at ya," he said. "I've got to go, but I need you to promise you'll stay here and be safe until I get back."

"You're coming back?" I asked, a flare of hope rocking me onto my toes.

He fought a smile as he ran the pad of his thumb across his bottom lip, hot eyes still locked on my mouth. "As soon as I possibly can."

Hallelujah! I held the porch post to stop myself from lunging for him when he headed back to his truck.

"Do me a favor until then," he said, opening the driver's side door. "Stop looking into Susan's death. Let me handle this."

I grinned and waved. "Be safe out there, Detective Hays."

"You didn't answer me," he said.

"Because you don't like it when I fib."

Grady rolled his eyes and climbed behind the wheel with an exasperated laugh. "Touché."

ॐ

Forty minutes later, I'd rushed through my shower and was on my way to work.

I bounced down the interior staircase, tucking my Sun, Sand, and Tea T-shirt into a pair of khaki shorts. I brought a pile of books from my family archives with me, inspired by Grady's goodbye kiss and promise of return. I really wanted to marry that man.

Denise smiled at the sight of me. "You look happy."

"I am," I said, stacking the books on the counter and taking a quick inventory of café guests.

Mercifully there were only a few. I needed the business, but I also needed time to talk to my friend without dozens of listening ears.

I smiled at Denise and patted the books. "Care to help me look for proof my family curse is just an old threat designed to keep ne'er-do-well men from setting their sights on innocent female Swans?"

"Absolutely." Denise selected a book from the top of the pile and opened it. "I think you jest, but it seems like a real possibility," she said. "No man would pursue a woman they didn't truly love if he believed the union would likely kill him. Only the head-over-heels, our-love-conquers-all types would take that kind of chance."

"Agreed," I said. "And since I'm getting nowhere on the murder case, I figured I would redirect my energy to solving the mystery of why all the men in my family have dropped dead prematurely for the last couple of centuries."

"And I shall help." Denise turned the page of her tome reverently, apparently awed by the aged yellow paper and delicate, faded script. "I love the mix of journaling and to-do lists, recipes and poetry."

I followed her lead.

"We can call Amelia and Ryan, if you want," she said. "Cover more books faster. They really want to get involved and help with anything you need."

I sighed. "I know, but I want Amelia to be happy, not stressed out, and she's got a million things to do in preparation for the trip she's about to take. She should concentrate on that, and spending time with her dad. If we come up with any small projects, I'll reach out to Ryan and he can split the job with her."

Denise smiled. "Sounds like a plan."

Around us, the handful of patrons chatted and ate while hidden speakers played an array of popular oldies and beach songs. Business was steady for a long while, without being busy, and we easily pulled double duty as researchers and tea servers.

A few dozen pages into my book, I noticed a pattern in the main text. "I think this one is some kind of summary of several other books," I said. "Like a massive table of contents for a set of encyclopedias. Almost as if an ancestor decided it would be nice to have an overview of main points from other books, and they attempted to create that here."

Denise moved closer, scooting her book along the counter with her. "Nice."

"Yeah," I agreed. The possibility sent a thrill through my chest. If the book was what I thought it was, I'd be able to skim the pages until I found something of interest, then I could jump to the book with more detailed information on that subject. I wouldn't have to read every page of every book, searching for a needle in a haystack. The concept was genius, and I wished I could thank whoever had begun the summary process.

Denise peered over my shoulder. "I love that so many of these recipes were written with prayers and well-wishes for those who'd eat the finished products."

I smiled. "Me too. Grady's lemon cake was created to bolster a warrior's heart," I said softly. "I love that."

She patted my back.

A pair of guests headed for the register, and Denise peeled away to handle their payment.

I trailed my finger over the faded pages, scanning through content summaries of other archived books. A few pages later, I came to what looked like an iced tea recipe from long before folks in Charm had the luxury of ice. The year scribbled beside the title was 1831.

"I'm back," Denise said, hustling to my side. "What did you find? I can tell by your face it's something good."

I flattened the open book on the counter and pointed to the page. "It's a recipe called restorative punch, but I think it's an iced tea. Look. One pint of double strength tea," I read. "Boil, strain, and pour over one-and-a-half sugar loaves. Mix with sweet cream and claret."

Denise pulled back. "What's a sugar loaf?"

"Compacted white sugar. Like giant versions of the cubes served with traditional tea service."

"Okay," she said slowly. "And claret is wine?"

"Yeah." I smiled. "Now, there's an iced tea flavor I haven't tried."

Denise snorted. "It's the Swan answer to Long Island Iced Tea. You can call it Charm Island Iced Tea and serve it at your bridal shower."

I formed a little O with my mouth. "I am absolutely making this as soon as possible," I said.

"Perfect," she agreed. "Who doesn't need to be restored by a little alcoholic tea punch once in a while?"

I turned my eyes back to the page, giggling, and struck

suddenly by an overwhelming need to know the original purpose of every Swan family recipe.

"When are you looking at more wedding dresses?" Denise asked. "I'd like to come this time."

"Hopefully soon," I said. Because I wanted to get a closer look at all the family cookbooks. ASAP.

CHAPTER
THIRTEEN

M y aunts arrived early the next morning with a stack of books from their archives and six more dresses. Five in garment bags. One in an archival chest.

I welcomed them with coffee and freshly made waffles.

"Dig in!" I told them, carrying the gowns into the ballroom. "I ate on the deck with Lou this morning so I'd be ready when you got here."

Aunt Fran nodded approvingly. "That was smart planning ahead."

"Thanks!" I laid the garment bags side by side across a table I typically used for cooking classes, then examined the tags. Aunt Clara and Aunt Fran had chosen dresses from the mid to late 1900s this time, so I had big hopes.

Aunt Clara poked her head through the archway from the café, a broad smile on her face. "These Belgian waffles are heaven. Is it a new recipe?"

"No. Just a new twist on an old favorite," I said. "Wyatt and his little cowpokes inspired me. I'm glad you like them.

I added cinnamon to the batter. There are more fresh berries and whipped cream in the fridge. Syrup is on the counter."

"We're already on that," she said. "Any luck identifying my stalker?"

"Kind of," I said, frowning through a pang of guilt. I'd been so caught up in reading the books from the archives, I'd completely forgotten to search for Alexander Lehman online last night. "I saw someone outside your shop that might've been him," I explained. "I got the guy's name, but nothing else, and I haven't had a chance to do any digging. But I shared the name with Grady, and he's checking for a criminal record."

"Thank you," she called over the familiar sound of whipped topping sprayed from a can.

I unzipped the first bag and resolved to slip in and out of the dresses as quickly as possible. I'd be married in the first gown that didn't make me look like a parade float. "This dress was made for Clarissa Bane," I said. "Was Clarissa a relative of Magnolia's?"

"She was," Aunt Clara said. "That's why I brought it. You have a great synergy with Magnolia's spirit here in this house. You've made Charm's most famous haunted house a home."

"And added a thriving business," Aunt Fran said. "We thought you might want to try a few gowns from Magnolia's family."

I bobbed my head, accepting the wild thought process that had landed these specific gowns on the day's agenda.

"A few of our cousins borrowed dresses from Swans

over the years and vice versa," Aunt Fran explained. "A few were returned and saved. Magnolia didn't have any direct descendants, of course, but her sisters, aunts, and their children all married at some point."

I freed the first gown from the bag and gave it a careful once- over. "It's pink."

"Yes," Aunt Clara said. "The 1940s were an interesting time. Things were less formal after the war. Silk and satin were harder to afford, so brides leaned on lace and taffeta." She poked her head through the archway and pointed a finger at the dress in my hands. "It's casual. I thought you might give it a try."

Casual, I liked. Pink, on the other hand, I wasn't as sure about.

Aunt Clara returned to the café, and I pulled the dress on over my shorts and T-shirt.

I tugged the zipper up my back and concentrated on breathing in the tight, unforgiving fabric. Then, I turned to the mirror I'd carried down from my living quarters and assessed my reflection.

The pained expression on my face seemed right, but it was unclear if the ruddy color of my cheeks was simply the glow of rosy material against my skin or if my unnatural pallor was due to lack of oxygen.

Regardless, I wasn't getting married in pink or taffeta.

I strained to reach and lower the zipper by a few inches, then I shuffled into the café to show my aunts.

"What do you think?" I asked.

Aunt Fran stopped chewing and set her fork onto the

plate before her. "How is it that this gown is at least forty years newer than some of the ones you tried on at our place, but it looks infinitely more out of style?"

Aunt Clara shot her a cross look. "Careful," she whispered. "This might be her favorite."

"It's not my favorite," I assured. "It was probably quite lovely on Clarissa, but I don't think it's the one for me."

Aunt Fran waved me away. "No worries. Try another."

I headed dutifully back to the ballroom, glad to be peeling the current dress off. "Amelia sent an email last night confirming some wedding day details," I said. "So far, she's booked the minister, a company for chair, table, and linen rentals, a string quartet for the ceremony, and a DJ for the reception. She says a florist is going to be in touch with you about centerpieces and bouquets later this week. I thought it would be nice to use flowers from the family gardens."

"Excellent," Aunt Clara said. "I love that idea. And Amelia. She's so sweet and organized. I'm going to miss her while she's away."

"Me too," I said, chest tightening at the reminder. I willfully pushed thoughts of Amelia's year-long absence from my mind as often as possible. I'd been gone eight years, chasing Wyatt across the Midwest on a rodeo circuit and attending culinary school in Kentucky, but I hated the idea of Amelia being away. Even for a year. It was inexcusably selfish, but true nonetheless. She'd been a constant in my life, before and after my time away. Life simply wouldn't be the same without her.

Aunt Fran appeared in the ballroom and helped me

with the zipper. "How's the investigation into Susan's death going?" she asked, liberating me from the pink taffeta fiasco.

I nearly laughed. "I'm spinning my wheels, getting nowhere fast, and someone has doused two of my vehicles and my head in saltwater and seaweed." I stepped out of the dress and passed it to Aunt Fran.

She offered an encouraging smile as she wrestled the fabric back onto the hanger. "You must be making some kind of progress, or you wouldn't be receiving any threats."

I sighed and moved to the next bag.

Aunt Clara strolled in to join us, one hand on her presumably full stomach and satisfaction on her brow. "If it helps, I don't think local police are having much luck either. I'm sorry to hear about the seaweed."

"Thanks," I said. "I wish I knew who was doing it." It had to be Susan's killer, trying to scare me off the case, but per my usual, I had no idea who that might be. I paused before the next garment bag and looked to Aunt Clara. "How do you know the police are struggling with this case?"

She pursed her lips, gathering her thoughts a moment before explaining. "Several officers have been on site at Northrop every day since the fish fry. They walk the grounds and the manor, looking all around as if there's something they know they're missing. The whole place was closed for a few days, but it's reopening for office workers this morning. I'd think we'd be back to business as usual if they'd found whatever it is they're looking for."

"Maybe," I said, curiosity freshly piqued. What were

the officers looking for? And why hadn't Grady shared this little tidbit? "They'll figure this out soon," I said. "It's a small island, and information travels fast. Even Mary Grace shared some details I needed." I frowned at the memory. "Eventually, all the pieces will come together."

My aunts' expressions turned to shock at my mention of Mary Grace, then to something more like concern.

Aunt Fran was the first to rearrange her features and pretend my statement wasn't wholly bananas. "Mary Grace helped you?"

"No one is more surprised than me," I said. "She had a caveat, of course."

"Of course," Aunt Fran echoed. "What does she want?"

"An invitation to my wedding," I said, still not quite believing it myself. "For her and Vanders."

Aunt Clara patted my arm gently. "It would be nice for the two of you to make amends. She's certainly difficult, but not everyone can be as innately lovable as you are."

I laughed, imagining the lineup of folks who'd readily deny that claim.

"I mean it," she said. "Some folks struggle with relatability, and kindness doesn't come naturally. Selfishness and a whole host of other behaviors that are designed to protect us from harm come naturally. Kindness is learned. Maybe Mary Grace learned to sharpen and lean on a different set of skills when she was young, and it stuck."

I thought of all the times my grandma had told me not to judge other people's choices, because I didn't know their options, and I hated the fact so many kids grew up without that kind of love and guidance. "You're right," I said. I didn't know the first thing about Mary Grace, outside of our interactions.

Maybe my wedding day would be a turning point for more than one of my relationships.

"What's next?" Aunt Clara asked, looking at the row of garment bags.

I unzipped and stared. Option number two was a white tea length number in matte satin from the early 1950s. It screamed Audrey Hepburn, and I thought the style was getting closer to something befitting my generous hourglass shape and plucky personality. "Cute."

Aunt Clara read the tag while Aunt Fran helped me step into the puddle of material. "Our cousin Fairchild wore this one," she said, shooting a bland, unimpressed expression to Fran. "She was always such a pill. And absolutely rotten to us anytime she came to visit. Another Bane," she told me.

"You didn't like her?" I asked, stunned by Aunt Clara's tone and word choice. Calling her cousin a pill was just about the worst thing I'd ever heard her say.

Aunt Clara lowered her gaze in apparent guilt for speaking ill of another human being. "She was quite a bit older than us. It's possible she just didn't like children. Our mama sewed this gown for her from pieces of other gowns. She did a remarkable job."

"She did," I agreed.

Aunt Fran raised the zipper at my back, then turned me toward the mirror. "The Bane women were cursed with unparalleled beauty. It brought them suitors from far and wide. Unfortunately, they didn't all get a proportional amount of brains to go with their looks. And they often chose the most gregarious man instead of the right one."

I considered being cursed with beauty and didn't hate the idea. It seemed to me the real problem was all that unwanted attention from gregarious men. I instantly thought of Grady and smiled. He was sincere and often stoic. A thinker. And a protector. I'd prefer his quiet, abiding affection over excessive or contrived congeniality any day. I just hoped my love for Grady wouldn't bring him any harm.

I frowned and fluffed the skirt of my gown, examining my reflection.

Aunt Fran ran her fingertips along my side, evaluating the fit of the bodice. "What do you think of this one?"

"It's nice," I said, looking away from the mirror, ready to focus on something other than my impending vows. I turned my back to Aunt Fran and lifted the bulk of my wild brown locks onto my shoulder so she could lower the zipper. "Do either of you remember a construction accident at Northrop Manor that killed several workers a long time back?" I asked.

"Of course," Aunt Clara said. "It was terrible. Four good men lost their lives. Women and children were widowed and left without fathers. It was the worst, most senseless tragedy we've had in Charm, outside the boats and sailors lost to the sea."

"Agreed," Aunt Fran said, as I shimmied out of the dress and passed it her way.

"Any idea why Susan would've been looking into that accident recently?" I asked. "She mentioned it a couple of times on her social media, and she asked Mary Grace to pull sales records for the manor going as far back as possible."

My aunts exchanged baffled looks, then shrugged.

"None," Aunt Fran said.

Aunt Clara unzipped the next bag. "I suppose there could be information in her office to help you understand what she was up to. Northrop is open to workers today, and I'm sure Oscar would let you in to see me if you find the time to stop by."

"I'll bring lunch," I said, suddenly filled with energy. "Susan had a file for me too." I'd nearly forgotten about it. "I was supposed to pick it up the night of the fish fry and didn't. Grady said he'd bring it to me if he found it. Maybe it's time I go find it myself."

My seashell wind chimes danced in the next room, and my aunts and I stilled for a collective moment.

"It's just me," Denise hollered, her footfalls echoing across the café floor.

"Oh!" Aunt Clara exclaimed. "Lovely! You're just in time. Everly's trying on dresses in the ballroom."

Denise appeared a moment later, mouth open and eyes narrowed. "You didn't even call me? Does Amelia know what you're doing?"

I lifted a palm to stop her protest. "There are dozens of gowns at the homestead. These are just a few. It's going to be a long process. Trust me, you've missed nothing so far."

"I'm still calling Amelia," she said, pulling her phone out.

I shook my head and turned to the next bag. "I have three more, then I want to run to Northrop Manor with Aunt Clara and see about a file in Susan's office. She had information for me that I still need." And maybe if what she'd found disproved the family curse, I could have more fun trying on the next round of wedding gowns.

Aunt Clara pulled the physical definition of gauche from the bag and frowned. "I thought I left this one at home."

I hiked a brow. "Are those feathers?"

"Glory," Aunt Fran said. "It's like a peacock and a swan had a baby. Put that away. I completely forgot about the feathers. Abilene was obsessed with Vegas showgirls."

I didn't bother asking for details on the statement or the bride. Instead, I checked my watch and turned to the archival box while Aunt Clara wrestled the plume-covered monstrosity back onto its hanger. The tag on this one was dated 1824, more than a century older than the other gowns my aunts had brought today and significantly outside the age span they'd mentioned. Below the year was a single name. Evangeline Everly Swan. I'd always known Everly was a family name, but I'd never heard of anyone with the name aside from me. I could only imagine what I would find inside the layers of acid-free paper, if only one woman had ever chosen this dress.

The seashell wind chimes jingled again, and Denise leaned through the archway. "Amelia's here."

"Hello!" Amelia called.

Clara and Fran perked up and left me, heading quickly into the café. Denise followed.

"I heard your wonderful news," Aunt Clara called. "Congratulations!"

"Thank you!" Amelia answered.

And I was alone with the gowns.

I tugged the antique-white material free from the container and marveled at the strange connection I felt with it. I smiled at the lively conversation in the next room as I freed a seemingly endless length of train and splayed it over the ballroom floor. Despite the gown's age, it was in perfect condition.

Aunt Clara gushed about how much she was going to miss Amelia, and her voice trilled as she discussed ideas for spending time with Mr. Butters.

Aunt Fran peppered my friend with questions related to the tour stops, unabashedly elated by the thought of traveling the country.

Denise rattled around behind the counter, clinking and filling empty tea jars with ice and taking drink orders for the little group. I'd made a pot of coffee to help us all wake up, but Southern ladies required sweet tea for a proper chat.

I turned my attention back to the deeply feminine, off-the-shoulder straps of the gown in my hands. I admired the impossibly soft fabric and tiny white appliques flowing down from the shoulders to the waist, then a few inches further. The neckline plunged moderately and the design pinched slightly at the waist before exploding in gratuitous layers of gauzy fabric that billowed to my toes. I imagined myself in the gown, barefoot, and walking peacefully across warm sand, the train of airy material blowing behind me.

My heart rate began to rise with the image, and my hands shook in anticipation as I dove headfirst into the gown, scooping my way beneath the skirt and working my arms through the elegant straps. I hoped it would fit, or that it could be altered if needed, and I breathed easier as the dress fell flawlessly over my figure, as if it had been made just for me.

A small sound broke on my lips as I turned to the mirror and saw my reflection. Unexpected and senseless tears welled in my eyes. I couldn't explain the torrent of emotions piling and churning inside me, because I'd never experienced anything like them before. All I knew was that the woman standing before me in the mirror was a goddess. She was peace and love and joy.

And somehow, she was me.

"Oh, my." Denise breathed the words, pulling my attention to the foursome of friends and family gathered behind me.

My aunts covered their mouths with their hands. Their eyes glistened with tears like mine.

Amelia took photos, moving slowly to capture me from every angle.

And Denise just shook her head. Awestruck. "You look enchanted," she whispered, inching slowly closer. "I've never seen you look more beautiful, and Everly, on your worst day, you are hands down the most gorgeous woman I know. This…" She motioned to me and the dress. "Is something else entirely. I don't even have words."

Tears spilled over my cheeks, and I turned to hug her in

thanks, all the while wondering if there was any way I could wear this gown every day. Forever.

My aunts and Amelia joined the hug, enveloping me in their loving embraces.

And though it didn't need saying, I couldn't help stating the overwhelmingly obvious aloud. "This is the one."

CHAPTER

FOURTEEN

I rode my bicycle to Northrop Manor at 10:45, having packed sandwiches and fruit for Aunt Clara and Oscar at 10:30, then timed my departure so I'd have just enough time to pedal over and arrive at the earliest acceptable minute for lunch. The thrill of finding the perfect dress still flowed through me, and I was both giddy and stupefied over the strength of the emotions tied to it. No one had ever mistaken me for a girlie girl or a human who cared two twigs about fashion, yet here I was, in love with a big, dramatic, breathtaking gown.

I laughed with disbelief and joy as the radiant summer sun heated my skin. Today felt like a day of positive and miraculous things. Maybe the answers I needed were in the file Susan made for me, and maybe the news was good.

Maybe my life was about to change.

White bakery bags bounced merrily in the basket over my pale blue fender as I cruised the weathered, sun-bleached planks of the boardwalk. I couldn't wait to deliver the meals to Oscar and Aunt Clara. I could almost feel the file on my family's history in my hands.

Whatever I learned about my possible curse, I'd find a way to get through it. Either I would uncover definitive proof that the Swan love curse was a lie, or I would find a way to overcome it. And not some flimsy problem-patch that worked on television shows and in the movies. I knew loving one another enough wasn't the answer. My mother had died following the untimely loss of my father, because she'd loved him too much to live without him, even for the sake of their only child. So I had no delusions that our love was somehow better or stronger than theirs.

If I needed to work around the curse, then I'd have to find something clever and significant to do the trick. Because I was marrying Grady Hays. I'd felt it in my bones when I stared at my reflection in the gown. The sensation of déjà vu had been so powerful, I was sure I'd lived the moment before. It was as if my heart and head had already been down this path, and my body merely had to wait three months and perform the motions. The deal had already been sealed by fate.

There was a profound peace with that knowledge because I wouldn't marry Grady if it would hurt him. Which meant there was a way. And I would find it.

I parked my bike near the front entrance of Northrop Manor and scanned the lot for Aunt Clara's Prius. She'd claimed her usual spot beneath a mossy-limbed oak.

A white SUV sat along the edge of a grassy access road in the distance. I told myself it wasn't the same vehicle I'd seen after my attack outside the realty office, then I gathered the bags from my basket and hurried through the door to greet Oscar.

"Miss Everly," he said, hooking his thumbs behind his belt. A large walkie-talkie hung from one side, weighing the leather strap down at an angle. "I heard you were coming today."

I set the bags on the table before him. "I thought you might enjoy sharing lunch with Aunt Clara again."

"You thought right," he said, lifting the phone receiver from his desk. "I'll let her know you're here."

"Just tell her the food was delivered," I said, winking conspiratorially. "I'll catch up to her in a few minutes."

"Everly?" Grady's voice turned me around before I could sneak away. He narrowed his eyes. "The manor's closed to the public today."

"I'm just delivering lunches," I said, waving goodbye to Oscar and heading in my fiancé's direction. "If I'd known you were here, I'd have brought you something too."

Grady frowned. "What are you up to?"

I grinned. "What do you mean?"

He looked me over, head to toe, then scrutinized my face. "You're…chipper."

"I'm always chipper," I said, closing the distance with a little hop in my step.

"No," he said, lowering his voice. "You're always pleasant and polite, but you've been burdened since I put that ring on your finger. You rarely look like that," he said, flicking his attention to the broad smile on my lips. "At least not in public," he amended, a grin tugging his lips.

I laughed. "I've been worried. That's all," I said. "You know about that."

"And you're not worried now?" he asked. "Has something changed?"

I hooked my arm with his and beamed up at him. "It's a girl thing," I said. "And it's a secret for now."

"Ah." He pulled me in close and kissed my cheek. "You found a dress."

"How do you know that?" I asked, considering the possibility he was secretly psychic. It would explain how he was such an insightful boyfriend and detective.

"You told me your aunts were bringing dresses this morning," he reminded me.

"Right." I smiled. I'd given myself away. "What are you doing here?" I asked, recalling Aunt Clara's assertion that officers had been lurking around the manor and grounds every day in search of something.

He scrubbed a finger against one eyebrow. "There was a squabble earlier over who gets the contents of the well," he said. "Some attorney showed up claiming their client owned mineral rights to the property and that included anything found underground here. The historical society says the well and its contents are theirs. I broke up the bickering and told them to handle it in court. I stuck around to take another look at the crime scene."

"Susan said the well has been used as a wishing well for decades," I told him. "Apparently, there are some pretty old coins down there. At least a few could have significant value."

Grady dropped his hand from his face to his side. "I really don't care what's down there or who has the legal rights to it. I just can't allow them to go around arguing and disturbing the peace."

"Fair," I said, wondering if the debate was directly related to Susan's death or if her fall down the well had simply brought light to the possibility of valuable coins on the property. Coming up empty, I recalled my reason for being at Northrop Manor in the first place. "Have you come across the file Susan had for me in her office? I'd like to pick it up while I'm here."

"I saw it briefly when I stopped in to check my team's progress on processing her office," he said. "I was called away, and I left it on a cabinet near the door. I'd planned to grab it the next time I was here but haven't been back."

"No problem," I said. "You've had your hands full. I'm here now, so I might as well get it today."

We moved to Susan's office door and paused. A notice from the Charm Police Department was posted on the historic wood, ordering everyone without approved purpose to stay out. Grady used a key to let us inside.

The space looked entirely different than the last time I'd been there. Everything had been inventoried and itemized, with yellow and white tags marking the contents of her shelves, desk, and filing cabinets.

"Wow," I said. "You guys left nothing untouched."

"We gave it all a brief perusal," Grady said. "She did a lot of work for a lot of people, so it's hard to say what will be helpful in catching her killer. A thorough overview was a good start." He collected a thick manila folder from the top of a nearby cabinet and passed it my way. "This was clearly marked for you, and since I knew what it was about, I didn't flip through it. I'd planned to look at it with you that night."

"No time like the present," I said, immediately opening the cover.

Inside, papers had been stacked in groups, paper-clipped together along the tops in tiny piles. Birth records. Death records. Marriage certificates. Various deeds and leasing agreements for businesses and properties. A handful of articles from local papers.

Grady grunted softly beside me. "I have most of this. It's all public record, available to anyone with enough time to pull it. Your family already keeps a detailed list of births, deaths, and marriages as part of the family tree, so I didn't bother printing most of that. Death records will show you the causes and age of men who married into the family and died."

"Perfect," I said, still thumbing through the documents. "Look at this." The last stack of papers wasn't about my family. It was labeled Northrop Manor. I pulled it free for a closer look.

"What's that?" Grady asked.

I turned the pages in his direction. "Why would she have put this in a folder with my stuff? Swans have never owned any part of this place."

Grady reached for the papers with a frown. "Nothing in this office was out of place. I've never inventoried anything so methodically archived."

In other words, I realized, hearing what he hadn't said, *Grady didn't think it was an accident*. "You think she wanted me to see these papers?" I asked, confusion wrinkling my brow.

"Or she was hiding them from someone," he said.

"She had an appointment on the morning she died with the guy I saw at Krebs and Chesterfield. And I heard her arguing in here with someone that night. Faye told me Susan sometimes dug things up that not everyone wanted brought to light, like inflated property values, hidden real estate, or other assets in business ventures and divorces."

"Faye?" Grady asked.

"The administrative assistant I spoke with," I said.

He bobbed his head, eyes scanning the paperwork. "Right."

"Have you been out there to interview the staff yet?"

"We're working on it," he said.

I closed the manila folder and hugged it to my chest. "Between this and the stack of books my aunts brought over this morning, I have plenty of material to keep me busy for a while."

"Want some help later?" he asked, ushering me back out of the office.

"Always." I smiled, while he locked up. "Come by after work? I'll provide the sweet tea and lemon cake."

"It's a date."

Grady walked me to my bike and kissed me chastely goodbye. He kept the stack of papers from the file with Northrop's address and went back inside.

I watched him walk away, mentally stuck on the fact Susan had tucked a set of papers into my file that weren't meant for me. It didn't make any sense. Susan was much too organized to make a mistake like that. I stored the folder under one crooked arm and walked around the building, thinking of the other odd thing I'd learned today. According to Grady, someone was trying to claim the rights to the contents of the well Susan was having repaired. The same well she'd died in.

Poorly timed coincidence or something more?

A figure came into view as I crossed the lush green lawn, and I tensed when I recognized the man's face. Unsure if I should continue forward or turn back, I slowed my pace and went with plan C.

I brought Grady's number up on my phone screen and hovered a thumb over the call button as I approached.

The man Susan had wanted to avoid the day she died turned in my direction, hands in pockets, shoulders slumped. It was the same man I'd just mentioned to Grady a few minutes prior. Did Grady know this guy was here?

Why *was* he here?

"Miss Swan," the man said, lifting his chin in greeting. He was tall, with black hair and icy blue eyes. He wasn't much older than me, somewhere in his thirties, maybe. He wore khaki pants and a three-button polo shirt in nautical blue. Dressed for work, I supposed, but I wasn't sure what that job might be. An attorney, perhaps?

I performed a small hip-high wave, careful to keep my phone screen hidden and Grady's number at the ready.

"I'm Casey Winters," he said. "I heard you were the one who found Susan."

"I was. How do you know my name?"

His lips quirked on one side. "Doesn't everyone know your name?" he asked. "I saw you the other day at Krebs's office when I dropped by to discuss a dispute with him."

"About the well's contents?" I guessed.

His brows rose and his gaze sharpened. "I guess the rumors are true. You do know all the local scoop. How'd you hear about the well already?"

"It's a small island," I said. "Why the sudden interest in what's down the well? Hasn't it been there for a hundred years?"

He raised and dropped one shoulder in a halfhearted shrug. "Susan's death brought attention to the fact the well exists. My clients likely hadn't given this property any thought in years; the mention of a wishing well got them wondering if anything of value was down there."

"And you thought you'd try to help them get ahold of it if possible?"

"That's my job," he said, a slight, self-deprecating smile on his lips. "Clients want legal paperwork drawn up or idle threats thrown around, and I get it done."

I examined the hard lines and sharp angles of his cheekbones, nose, and jaw. He had a youthful air about him, a carefree posture, and a tan line on his ring finger. I would've thought him handsome, if I liked preppy former athletes, which I was certain he was. And if I didn't suspect he might be capable of murder. "How did you know Susan?" I asked him, presuming they'd met through their work, since I'd seen him at the law office where she'd worked, but unwilling to jump to conclusions.

His smile fell. "Krebs represented my ex-wife in our divorce."

"Oh." I pressed my lips together and glanced at my phone screen, afraid I'd just kicked a beehive. "Did she dig up something you wanted to stay hidden?"

His brows dove together and his easy-breezy demeanor disappeared. "Actually," he said after a long, tension-laced beat, "Yeah. Susan helped my ex ferret out all the details of my overseas holdings, and it cost me an unbelievable amount of money. I'd been saving since I turned eighteen. I've worked since I was fourteen. I put myself through law school. My mom's a waitress in town, and my dad's a fisherman. College was a luxury we couldn't afford, but I wanted something more," he bit out. "So I did the right things and I saved all I could. I'd planned to help my folks retire in a few years. I wanted to pay off their house and take care of them when they were old. Because you might not realize it, but waiting tables and fishing doesn't come with superior healthcare or any kind of retirement package."

I took a baby step back, feeling the surge of anger and loathing in his words, despite their cool delivery.

"I waited until I was thirty-three to marry," he continued. "I thought I'd taken my time and chosen well. But my ex is from money on the mainland. Her father is in politics, and she has a massive trust fund. She resented me for moving her to the island, where she couldn't shop for couture or get five-star spa experiences and eat in Michelin star restaurants, so she divorced me after a single year. She said I chose this place over her happiness, and she made it her mission to hurt me however she could. She knew about the money I had saved for my folks, and she told Krebs to go after it." His hands balled into fists, and he slowly flexed and straightened his fingers, clearly fighting the barely tamped anger. "I hid that money after I realized the kind of person she really was. Maybe I shouldn't have hidden it, but Susan dragged it to the surface and now it's gone, along with my plans and my folks' chance to grow old without punching a timeclock until they die. My ex probably spent my entire life savings in a single trip to Europe. It meant nothing to her, but she took it out of spite and jealousy, and Susan helped. So, yeah, Susan Thames wasn't exactly my favorite person."

The phone rang in my hand, and Grady's number appeared onscreen. Not because I'd put it there, but because he was calling.

"It's Detective Hays," I said, stumbling back several feet, before turning into a quick rhythm of strides toward my bike. "Hello?"

"Everly?" Grady asked. "Is that you crossing the lawn from the well? I thought you went home?"

I broke into a jog, eager to put as much distance as possible between Casey Winters and me. "I'm leaving now," I said. "See you tonight."

I disconnected and jumped onto my bicycle, pedaling quickly away. I didn't look back or try to find Grady's location.

Instead, I breathed deeply, wondering if Casey had been angry enough to kill Susan for what she'd taken from him and his folks.

And I savored the satisfaction of interviewing my first solid suspect.

CHAPTER

∽

FIFTEEN

My phone rang on the way home, and I slowed my pace to take a closer look at the local, but unfamiliar, number. I coasted to a stop and planted my feet, thankful for the moment to catch my breath. "Hello?" I answered.

"Hello, this is June from Thames Boating and Fishing," a woman said. "I believe I spoke with you about talking to Burt?"

"Yes," I said. "That's right." I'd completely forgotten my plan to visit the marina. After the complicated exchange with Mary Grace, being attacked with seaweed, and discovering my dream dress, questioning Mr. Thames had totally fallen from my mind.

"He took a small group out earlier, but they're heading back now. Burt will be here in about twenty minutes. If you're still interested in speaking with him, you should be able to catch him before he heads home for a late lunch. He's got another excursion scheduled this afternoon."

I checked my watch and deliberated. It was after twelve,

and Denise typically stayed at Sun, Sand, and Tea until three. The marina was a long walk from my current position on the boardwalk, but I had my bike. The whole thing would take some hustle, but I wanted information and Burt Thames had it. "Okay," I said. "I'm on my way."

"All right, hon," she said. "I'll put a note on his desk. What's your name? I didn't catch it last time."

"Everly," I said. "See you soon."

I disconnected and scanned the world around me, letting my gaze drift over happy couples, frolicking children, and other smiling faces on the beach. No signs of killers armed with coins and seaweed. In fact, no one seemed to notice me at all. A good sign I wasn't being followed. And a blessing that would allow me to pedal a little more slowly on the trip back the way I'd come.

Thames Boating and Fishing came into view seven minutes later. The building was small, a single-story structure on wooden stilts near the sound. The siding was blue, the roof was metal, and a giant cartoon marlin was painted on one exterior wall. One of those big, red, inflatable tube men marked the turn for an adjacent gravel lot.

I parked my bike near the short flight of steps to the open front doors, then hurried inside.

Half the interior was set up like a typical gift shop, with every kind of trinket and T-shirt I could think of, all emblazoned with the business logo. A double set of patio doors opened to a rear deck and clear view of a private pier reaching into the sound.

A group of teens loitered on the dock, talking, laughing,

and soaking up the sun. Their perfectly tanned skin and complete ease suggested they were locals passing an afternoon with their friends. The presence of our local high school's mascot on one guy's skateboard and another's kid's baseball hat cemented the theory. Their rumbling laughter raised my lips into a smile. It felt like yesterday that Amelia and I had spent our days much the same, without a care in the world, and not a single clue life would ever be any different than it was at that moment.

Nostalgia lightened me impossibly further.

"Can I help you?" a female voice asked.

I turned to follow the sound, and my smile wobbled a bit when the woman came into view.

The blond from the photos online greeted me with a broad, cheerful smile. She was peppy-looking in the extreme and decidedly youthful for her age, which I guessed to be near fifty. She wore one of the shop's T-shirts with cutoff shorts and flip-flops.

I immediately appreciated her fashion sense, but her incredible figure suggested she either ran ten miles a day or never ate Nutella from a jar with her finger. Maybe both. And that made her significantly less relatable.

"Hi," I said brightly. "I'm Everly. We spoke on the phone."

"Oh, of course," she drawled. "I'm June. Burt's in his office. You can follow me back."

I trailed her down a short hallway, reminding myself not to jump to conclusions. It could be a coincidence that a murder victim's recent ex-husband had a staff member who was gorgeous. It didn't mean the two were romantically involved or that the relationship had been the reason for the divorce. Furthermore, being a possible adulterer didn't make him a killer.

We stopped at an open office door, and my jump-to-conclusions mind kicked into high gear. Maybe June killed Susan to have Burt to herself. Or maybe she killed Susan because Burt still loved her. Or Burt killed Susan to stop her from bringing something unsavory to light in their divorce, like the situation with Casey Winters and his ex-wife.

"Knock knock," June sang, rapping her knuckles on the doorframe.

"Come on in," a gravelly voice answered.

June stepped aside, and I peeked in.

The room was small, barely large enough for the battered metal desk with a single chair on each side. Burt was a large, barrel-chested man who likely had to inhale deeply and slide against the wall to reach his side of the desk.

"This is Everly," June said. "I believe she's looking to book a group excursion."

His gaze was hard as it fixed on me.

"No." I raised a palm in apology for the apparent confusion. "I don't want to go fishing. I just wanted to talk to you for a minute." I looked from him to her, then back. "I'm sorry if fishing was implied. It wasn't intentional."

June frowned.

Burt cleared his throat. "June? Can you give us a minute?"

"Sure," she said. "Take as long as you need, and just

holler if there's anything I can do." Her tone was soothing and kind as she spoke to him. The glare I received on her way out was neither.

In fact, if looks could kill, I wouldn't have lived to finish my thought.

Had I earned the cold look because Burt asked to be alone with me? Or was it something more?

"I recognize you," he said, tapping both thumbs against the desk's edge. "I saw you at Northrop Manor the night Susan died. Some folks said you found her."

"That's true," I said. "It's the reason I'm here." I examined his features and posture before continuing. "You were very upset when I saw you before. Understandably," I added. "So I was surprised when I learned you and Susan were divorced."

He sat back, dragging his hands onto his lap. "Is there a question in there somewhere?"

There were dozens of questions. I just wasn't sure how to ask any of them directly.

I flailed internally while he stared.

"Look," he said flatly, irritation sharpening the word. "I see what you're doing. And your boyfriend has already questioned me at length. So I'm going to save us both a lot of time and tell you to go talk to him. I've said all I have to say about Susan, our divorce, and her death. Asking me to continually rehash the loss of my first love is cruel, and I'm not doing it again. This isn't about you, so stop being selfish and let me heal."

I opened and shut my mouth like a fish out of water,

stunned for multiple reasons. He knew Grady was my boy-friend? Sure, it was a popular topic in the community, but I'd never heard of Burt before his wife died. So how did he know me? He didn't seem the sort to care about gossip or frequent the *Town Charmer*. Also, he'd called Susan his first love. Did that imply there was another love after her? Was it June? And lastly, he'd called me selfish, and I took extreme offense.

"Susan was my friend," I said, bristling. "I want justice for her. I thought you would too. You don't have to talk to me, but I'm going to do whatever I can to find the person who hurt her. I'd hoped you'd want to help."

His gaze hardened.

"Mr. Thames," I pushed on. "Do you have any idea who might've lashed out at Susan? Anyone who might've had a problem with her? An ongoing conflict or a recent butting of heads?"

The floorboard outside the office creaked, and I turned to spot June half-hiding in the hallway.

Burt growled. "What are you doing there?"

She bit her bottom lip and gave a sheepish frown. "I couldn't help overhearing what y'all were saying," she said. "And I just wondered if maybe Susan's death is linked to whatever's had her so tied up lately."

I shifted my attention to Burt, then back to the woman standing hesitantly outside the door. "What does that mean?" I asked. "How was Susan tied up?"

Burt scrubbed a big hand over his face and down his beard. He pushed his fingers through his hair and slid his eyes to meet mine once more. "Susan had been hard to reach for a few weeks. Extra busy with something she wouldn't talk about. I don't know what, so don't ask." He pressed onto his feet and baby-stepped sideways around his desk. "I need some air. I've got less than an hour to grab lunch before my next charter."

I opened my mouth to ask a follow-up question, but it fled my mind when Burt stopped in the doorway and wrapped June in an embrace. Then kissed her. I averted my gaze and considered covering my eyes when the couple before me deepened the kiss.

"I'll see myself out," I murmured, sliding carefully around them a moment later. "Thank you for your time."

I was back on my bike in a flash and counting the minutes until I'd see Grady again. He wouldn't like hearing I'd met with Burt Thames, but the kiss I'd witnessed seemed like something local law enforcement needed to know about. ASAP.

ைை

My afternoon flew by at the café. I enjoyed each customer's company and made notes on my suspect list between cooking and waiting tables. I also skimmed a few of the books my aunts had delivered from the archives, using napkins to mark pages I wanted to revisit when I had more time.

After work, I changed into a pair of cotton shorts and a tank top that only clung to the parts of me I didn't mind accentuating. I ran a brush through my hair before pulling it back into a ponytail. The night air was calling me, and I didn't want to spend my night peeling hair from my face and eyes.

I moved the book with summaries of other books, and the file I'd picked up at Susan's office, to my kitchen counter. Then I topped a tray with two chilled glasses and a pitcher of iced Old Fashioned Sweet Tea. I added plates, forks, and a fresh lemon cake as well. Next, I opened the sliding glass doors to my deck and let the balmy night air swirl in.

"Squawk!" Lou screamed, the moment I pulled the door wide.

"Hello, handsome," I said. "How's it going?"

"Squawk!" he repeated, agitated and two-stepping along the handrail, wings outstretched.

"What's wrong?" I asked, picking up on his unmistakable tension. A sliver of fear coiled in my chest, as I realized he might be trying to warn me about something.

I gave the deserted beach a careful look before returning my eyes to him.

My phone buzzed and fear spiked in my chest.

"Goodness!" I slapped one hand against my pounding heart and pulled the device from my pocket. The words EMERGENCY UPDATE appeared on the screen in red block letters, and I shivered.

"The *Town Charmer* sent out an alert," I told Lou.

I'd turned the blog notifications off weeks ago because I was tired of seeing my wedding plans scrutinized and evaluated. I'd turned the feature back on when I woke this morning, not wanting to accidentally miss any scoop on Susan's murder.

I tapped the link and waited to be directed to the post.

Lou bounced and complained more fervently, and a sense of foreboding coursed through me. He craned his neck, as if he might be able to read the post over my shoulder when it loaded.

Finally, the site appeared, and I read aloud to Lou. "It is with a heavy heart that I post the following message from an unknown source, who demands their words be made available on my feed immediately. I don't condone this behavior or support this message in any way, but it was made clear to me that not posting these words would result in swift and immediate action against Everly Swan."

My head went light and my noodle legs bent unexpectedly, dropping me into the rocking chair on my deck.

"Squawk!"

I swallowed hard and continued. "I hate bullies and threats, but I cannot in good conscience take a stand that will result in injury to another human being, so here is the message. And to whoever wrote this, I'm not alone when I say you will be found, and you will be sorry."

I released a shaky breath and wet my suddenly parched lips before continuing.

Everly—
You refuse to take a hint, so how about
I spell things out for you in poem?
I'm done playing games.

I'm now seeing red.
Keep asking questions
You'll be the next dead

My airways constricted and light danced in my periphery.

The killer stepped up from silent seaweed warnings to making a public threat against my safety. The resulting shock and fear was a knife to my chest. I'd barely made any progress in my quest for truth, yet someone was ready to kill me over it. And they apparently didn't care if the whole town knew.

I tapped the phone's screen with trembling fingers, accessing my texting app through tear-blurred eyes.

I wanted to live!

My phone rang and Grady's face appeared onscreen before I could tap out a message.

Apparently he'd gotten the blog notification too.

CHAPTER

⚬

SIXTEEN

An hour later, the initial wave of terror caused by the threat post had subsided, and the icy chill of fear had finally left my bones. Grady had arrived within minutes and made everything better. He'd plied me with the sweet tea and lemon cake I'd set out to share, and covered me in reassuring words and hugs. The effort had worked wonders.

More importantly, and most impressively, he'd made a single call to have the threat removed, and within minutes, it was gone. Then in true, direct, and unapologetic Grady fashion, he replaced the threat with a message of his own.

To the one who threatened Everly Swan,
I'm coming for you.
Grady Hays

Grady had crossed his arms when the new message appeared, hot resolve coloring his stare. He hadn't signed the promise with his official Charm P.D. title because the words didn't come from a detective. They came from my fiancé, personal protector, and friend. I felt a little bad for whoever had just picked a fight with a tea maker and wound up in the ring with her cowboy.

"Water?" he asked, carrying a tall glass onto the deck with him. He'd cleared our tea and empty plates while I sat in a heap of comforted exhaustion on my deck chair.

"Thanks," I said, accepting the offered drink. "For everything. For putting up with me and for sticking up for me." I sipped the cool water before setting it on the table at my side and reaching for Grady's hand.

He took the seat beside me with a frown. "I don't put up with you, Everly. People put up with squeaky shoes and hangnails. I love you. And I will always stand up for you. Defend you. Listen and comfort you. I'm here to be what you need me to be. The same way you are all those things for me. You don't have to thank me for loving you."

I batted my stinging eyes. "I'm not sure you're real sometimes."

He shook his head and pressed a soft kiss against my temple, as if I'd said the most ridiculous thing in the world. "Maybe you could prove your devotion by leaving this investigation alone," he suggested, lips quirking into a barely-there grin.

"Or," I countered. "Maybe you can come with me while I kick tires and shake trees. When the killer inevitably comes for me, you'll be there to slap some cuffs on whoever it is and call it a day."

Grady chuckled, eyes alight with humor. "I can be your sidekick?"

"Sure," I agreed. "I'd allow it."

He barked a laugh and began to rock, clearly happy in the moment, despite the way the night had begun. He smiled at Lou, silently watching from the rail. "What are we going to do with her?"

Lou stood taller and fluffed his feathers, morphing into a gray-and-white, beaked puffball. He stretched his wings when he smoothed himself, in an impressive show of grandeur.

I presumed this was the equivalent of a human's exaggerated shrug. At least he'd stopped squawking when Grady had arrived.

"Just be careful out there doing your detective thing," I said, squeezing Grady's fingers and feeling the itch of fear return.

His expression softened as he peered back at me in the moonlight. "I'm good at what I do," he said gently. "I'm well trained and far more experienced catching killers than this person is at being a killer. You don't have to worry about me. And before you say it, your love is not cursed."

I sniffed, fighting a sudden tidal wave of emotion, and thankful for a fiancé willing to repeat those words as many times as I needed to hear them. I suspected I could never hear them enough. Not when random forest trees and cement gargoyles were trying to squish him while he hiked a trail or walked down the street.

"Everly." He turned in his seat, reaching for my face. He

cupped my cheeks and ran his thumbs along my chilled skin, leaving paths of heat in their wake. "Your love is not a curse."

"You're betting your life on it," I warned.

"Yes, I am." He looked into my eyes and a small smile returned to his face. "Since you're making nice with Mary Grace Chatsworth-Vanders now, I got a call from her husband."

I blanched. "What? When?"

Grady returned his hands to the arms of his rocker. "Earlier. He invited us to dinner with them. A double date. Just us two couples."

I stared blankly. "Did you ask if he had the wrong number?"

"No." Grady laughed.

"Did you tell him he had the wrong number?"

Grady shook his head.

I grimaced. "Dinner with the Chatsworth-Vanders? I hope I'm not sick that day."

He snorted, and I relaxed against my chair. "Here's better news," he added. "The bank approved Denise's paperwork. I'm sure you'll hear about it from her tomorrow, but she's officially buying my house and property. Which means our horses can stay where they are, and Denver can keep his old room for nights he spends with her."

"When will he stay with her?" I asked, feeling oddly greedy for any lost moments with him.

"Anytime Denise makes special plans with him, or he misses the old place," Grady said. "Whenever we want to do married people things."

I wagged my eyebrows, and he laughed.

"I meant short trips and weekend getaways, but I like where your mind's at, Swan." His smile widened comically, and his blessed dimple sank in.

Thinking of marital things brought another question to mind. One I'd been wondering but hated to bring up in case I didn't immediately like the answer. "Do you want more children?"

Grady stilled and his smile fell. He searched my face before speaking. "Do you?"

"Yes, but I understand if you don't. Denver's getting older, a younger sibling wouldn't have the same impact on him now as it would've if they were closer in age. And you're older too, maybe beyond the point when changing diapers and not sleeping for a year or two sounds like a good time."

He curled his hand over mine on the arm of my rocker, an expression of awe and sincerity on his handsome brow. "I would love nothing more than to have a baby with you. Late nights, dirty diapers, and all. I wasn't sure if that was something you'd want, so I've never asked."

I raised his hand in mine and pressed it to my cheek, then looked out at the darkened sea. Silver streaks of moonlight rippled over the water's surface, countless stars dancing above. *This is happiness*, I thought. These moments. These talks. With this man at my side.

The word husband circled in my brain, and Burt Thames's face appeared, wrecking my moment of good vibes. "Did you have time to check on Susan's ex-husband's alibi?" I asked. "He was really upset the night she died, but when I visited him, he kissed his employee right in front of me," I said, widening my eyes for emphasis. "Kiss-kissed," I clarified. "Like PG-13 kissing."

Grady frowned. "First of all, please stop questioning my suspects," he said flatly. "I mean that, and secondly, Burt and June were on the boat together at the time of Susan's death."

I mirrored his unpleasant expression.

"Does that help you cross them off your list?" he asked, not seeming genuine about the question at all. "You should probably also know Burt was the one to file for divorce last year. He left Susan for June. They've been trying to agree on the details of the split since then. Nothing hostile, just a lot of property and assets to sort after a marriage that lasted so long."

I rocked my chair slightly, recalling Burt's comment about Susan being his first love. "If you think that's enough to eliminate him as a suspect, I'll agree," I said, willing to accept Grady's opinion as accurate. I ignored his bland expression. I'd agreed, hadn't I?

So that left Casey Winters on my suspect list.

"Any more on Aunt Clara's possible stalker?" I asked, changing the subject before I stressed Grady out with too much talk of the investigation.

He visibly relaxed a bit. "I've got a unit following her, but my guy hasn't noticed anything suspicious, and I don't think Clara needs to worry. I looked up the name you gave me, and Alexander Lehman appears to be a respected businessman. He owns some franchises and invests in start-up companies. Maybe he's interested in one of their products for his stores."

My brows rose. "That's interesting." I loved the idea of my aunts' brand in other stores.

"Which reminds me," Grady said, tapping his phone screen before I could ask any follow-up questions on the subject. "I need to head home, but I have some Swan family news to share."

I waited impatiently while he accessed a file on his phone, then referenced the screen as he explained his findings.

"You know I believe the concept of all Swan husbands dying untimely deaths is subjective," he said. "And that people all across the world die too soon every day, which isn't proof of a curse, only the fragility of life."

"I do."

He paused to smile. "And the word curse is inarguably subjective."

"Yes," I said, having heard this all from him before. My muscles tensed in anticipation of whatever he was building up to.

"Human life expectancy has increased greatly over the decades. A farmer from the last century, for example, performing hard daily labor, possibly without quality water and substantial food to sustain him, would've considered fifty a long life. So we have to remember we're looking at this potential curse and its alleged proof through a twenty-first century perspective."

I waited.

"Do you know how Fran and Clara's grandfather died? Their mother's father," he clarified.

"He was kicked in the head by a horse," I said. "The freak accident had left their young grandmother a widow with three little girls to raise alone. His loss was a horrific burden on them financially, and they'd often gone hungry as a result."

Grady nodded. "It was an unfortunate, but not uncommon scenario for farmers then," he said. "He was forty-six years old."

I lifted my shoulders in an exaggerated shrug. "Are you suggesting forty-six was a full life a hundred years ago?"

"Not at all, but take a look at their marriage certificate." He passed me his phone.

The photograph of a faded yellow document centered the screen.

"Fran and Clara's grandparents married when she was nineteen and he was twenty-five. They had three daughters and were married twenty-one years. That hardly feels like a curse."

Grady swiped the screen, bringing another image up for my examination. "This woman was a baker and a holistic healer of some kind. I found her in the archive books I borrowed from your aunts. People thought she was a witch for making the same kinds of products your aunts sell at their shop today, plus teas and other home remedies that have since been proven to help with everything from upset stomach to insomnia."

"I hate that people did that," I said. "Making up lies and tossing accusations about people and things they didn't understand is awful and cruel," I said.

Grady smiled and a flicker of humor passed in his eyes. "This lady relished the rumors," he said. "Her writing is fun and snarky. You would've liked her, but apparently she was born and died in the 1800s. She was a beekeeper and lemon farmer. I still have the book at my place. I'll bring it with me next time."

I focused on the digital image of a page in a book. A sketch of hands leaving flowers on a gravestone. The text was long and wordy, a mournful lament. The author had apparently lost her beloved too soon and hated facing life without him. My heart broke and I turned to Grady. "This is sad, and it supports the curse."

Grady used his thumb and first finger to enlarge the image, bringing only the tombstone into view. The man's name was Silas Swan, and based on the years indicating his birth and death, he'd lived to be eighty-one. "Unless she married him in his golden years, this suggests not all Swan husbands die young or soon after marriage. Based on her poem, I think it's clear she loved him. I'm still looking for their marriage certificate to confirm the year, but that's more likely to be somewhere in your family archives than on file in town. And these are just two examples of couples in your family who enjoyed a lifetime together. I suspect the more we dig, the more of these we'll find."

I nodded woodenly, hope rising in my heart as I moved the image around onscreen, reading the poem beneath the sketch.

A gust of wind swept over my deck, causing Lou to bob and shift or be blown away. And a shiver rocked down my spine as the poet's name came into view at the bottom of the page.

Evangeline Everly Swan.

CHAPTER

SEVENTEEN

I spent the next morning making party plans for Amelia's luncheon send-off. I'd been so wrapped up in my own drama that I hadn't given her amazing news the amount of enthusiasm it deserved. Probably because I didn't want her to go. It was easier to pretend she wasn't leaving than to face the fact I'd spend a year without her right across town. Selfishness aside, a proper party was in order, and I would make it a good one.

Denise wiped the counter beside me, peering sideways as I made notes and lists. Her long blond ponytail hung over one shoulder as she worked, a tiny corkscrew curl at the bottom.

"I'm fine," I told her for the dozenth time. "Grady handled the blog threat, so I'm focusing on a party to celebrate my best friend's book tour."

She dropped the rag into my prep sink and set her hands on her hips. "Don't play cool with me," she warned. "A cold-blooded killer bullied the *Town Charmer* into posting a public threat against you. This is huge and very scary," she said. "Whoever did that was downright brazen."

"Yes, and that is why I'm trying not to think about it."

She huffed. "Clearly. Based on the number of piña colada pies in this refrigerator you were up all night not thinking about it."

I glanced at her, dragging my attention from my notes. She knew me well. Baking always calmed my nerves and helped me process my thoughts. "Have you tried the pie?"

She gave me a be-serious face. "Yes, and if I try any more of the pie I'm going to need a bigger pair of pants to go home in. It's addictive."

I smiled. "Thanks." According to my grandma, piña colada pie had been a favorite of my mother's. I rarely made it because thinking of my mother had set me on edge until recently. I'd been mad that she'd left me and sad that my new life hadn't been enough to make her stay. But lately, I was learning to accept things I couldn't understand. It had taken me thirty years, but I'd finally stopped trying to put myself in other people's shoes so I could make sense of their behaviors. For starters, I had no idea what their footwear looked or felt like, and even if I put the shoes on, it was still *me* wearing *their* shoes.

So I'd resolved to love and accept people as they were, without inserting my opinions on their behaviors. The concept of individuality was complicated at times, but it'd been on my mind more than ever as I'd pored through the family archives. Examining a hundred lives across multiple centuries was a profound reminder that everyone was doing the best they could with what they had, from material things to health and circumstance.

"Maybe I should serve the piña colada pie at Amelia's luncheon," I said. "What do you think?" I pushed my party notes in Denise's direction.

She pursed her lips and inched closer. "Don't try to distract me with pie and party plans. I'm worried about you. You've gotten involved in murder cases before, and you always wind up hurt. I hate it, and this case is escalating. I keep worrying about what will happen next, and it's giving me hives." She extended her arm as if to display her proof.

"I don't see hives."

"Well, they aren't there now, but they were," she said.

I offered an apologetic smile. "I'm sorry. I don't mean to worry you, and I don't plan to get hurt this time. Promise," I said, hating the fear and sadness in her big blue eyes.

"You can't know you'll be safe,"

"You can't know I won't." I raised my brows in challenge.

She tossed her hands up, exasperated.

I doubled down. "You can't sit around worrying about things that haven't happened yet. Things that might never happen. Worrying won't change the outcome either way, but it will give you premature wrinkles and added stress weight."

Something told me I could take my own advice and apply it to the question of my family curse, but I chose to ignore that. As all enthusiastic advisors usually do.

Another customer made his way to the register, and Denise went to ring him up.

Meanwhile, I scrambled to think of a way to change the subject and cheer her up. Thankfully, it didn't take long to think of something. I smiled as she returned to me. "We haven't discussed your good news yet."

She frowned. "What?"

"You're buying a house!"

Her expression melted into surprise, then quickly turned to excitement. "I'm buying a house!" Denise made a squeaky sound, then hugged me.

It was a big reason to celebrate.

Finding the perfect home and landing a mortgage was monumental for anyone, anywhere, but doing those things on the island, where real estate was a hot, coveted commodity was practically impossible. It was one of the reasons our community was so tight-knit. There was only so much space. Only so many homes. And those who purchased here usually stayed, so availability was always scarce.

My phone buzzed, and I released Denise to check the message. "Grady," I said in explanation. "Looks like he's sending an attachment."

"What is it?" she asked.

I moaned as the image loaded. A pile of small fish, coins, and seaweed appeared on my screen. The obvious threat had been tossed on the ground outside his truck, the tips of his boots visible in the frame. A new text popped into existence beneath the photo while I gaped.

Looks like I'm getting your gifts now

Denise gasped, and a horde of baby spiders danced down my spine.

Grady wrote again. Apparently the person who threatened you took offense to my response

My phone buzzed and I adjusted the screen for Denise to read along.

This investigation will go much faster now

Denise groaned. "The two of you are made for one another," she said. "This stuff makes me sweat and want to hide. You two run straight toward it." She grabbed a pile of napkins from the counter and fanned herself.

"Toward what?"

"Trouble."

I wanted to argue, but I wasn't sure I could. Running toward trouble was practically in Grady's job description. And it was definitely in my blood.

"How can you stay calm?" Denise asked. "Anyone you meet could be the one who's been threatening you. They could pop up anywhere. Anytime."

"Well, that doesn't help." I leaned against the closed refrigerator door, feeling the wind leave my sails.

Grady had pulled the killer's attention away from me, and he was happy about it.

I hated it. Now he was in danger, and Denise was right. The killer's actions were escalating. The fish were a new and ominous touch that made my skin crawl. "I wish this threat didn't involve dead things." I zoomed in on the photo, looking for additional clues.

A smear of white on the road in the background stalled my breaths, and I tried to get a clearer look. A white vehicle driving past as Grady snapped the shot; it was barely more than a blur, but I couldn't help thinking of the white SUV I'd seen outside the realty office and Northrop Manor. Was it actually one and the same? And if so, what did that mean?

Another text arrived, interrupting my mental spiral, and I stilled to read it to Denise. "Grady says the fish are likely from a bait shop. He'll start there and keep me posted."

I tapped a thank you message while Denise watched.

She wrinkled her nose when I put my phone away. "It's like you two share the same brain. He's not even here, and you're both thinking about the fish. You do that kind of thing a lot. I mean this with love, but it's weird."

I smiled. "I kind of like it."

She laughed. "Good, because you're about to have that man in your head until you die."

My smile widened, loving the idea. I just needed to help him find Susan's killer before the threats escalated any further.

The seashell wind chimes jingled, and Faye walked in.

"I've got this one," I told Denise. "Welcome to Sun, Sand, and Tea." I waved and smiled.

Faye hurried to the counter and set her purse on top. "Hello!" Her smart blue dress slacks and coral blouse gave the impression she was on her lunch hour from work. "May I sit here?"

"Of course." I made a mental note to talk quickly. If I was right, she likely wouldn't have much time. "Sit anywhere you'd like."

She climbed onto the stool, and I set a napkin in front of her.

I pulled a clean tea jar from the drying rack and loaded it with ice. "What can I get you to drink?"

Her gaze rose to the giant chalkboard mounted on the wall behind me.

The daily menu and specials were scripted in pretty summer colors. Twenty iced teas to choose from, five meal options, and plenty of sweets.

"I think I'll have the lemon and rosemary iced tea today," she said. "And a slice of piña colada pie. That sounds like positively delectable."

Denise moved to the fridge to grab a pie. "On it."

"Thanks." I filled the jar with tea, then set the beverage on her napkin, barely able to contain myself as the opportunity for more Susan-related questions arose.

Faye glanced over her shoulder at the other guests, then leaned in my direction, cradling the drink between her palms. "I know you didn't ask me to do this," she said. "But I couldn't help myself."

I tensed, unsure how I felt about that statement and wary of whatever she might say next.

Denise delivered a plate, fork, and slice of pie to Faye, then slipped away, busying herself with unnecessary tasks behind the counter. Obviously listening in.

Faye waited for Denise to turn her back before she continued. "I dug around a little in the historical society records, and I found newspaper articles on microfilm featuring several men in your family line. I'm not sure what you had Susan looking into specifically, but she had notes on her calendar with your last name and locations like our town records and the historical society. So I guessed she was looking into your family history, and I gave it a try as well. I was surprised to learn many of your ancestors never married. Quite uncommon for women in history, but I suppose the island is only so big, and there likely weren't enough men to go around. Otherwise, there wasn't anything unusual there." She sipped her tea, and I immediately thought of the people in my town, calling themselves Sippers and watching my life as if it was a reality television show instead of, well, my life.

She set the tea aside with a pleased exhale. "I also learned Charm didn't have electricity until the 1950s," she said. "Can you believe that? Some towns had it in the 1930s, but not this one. It took Charm another two decades. How's that for remote and quirky?" She grinned. "I guess this place has always lived up to its reputation of being a little unusual. It's no wonder your family thrives here."

I frowned. This encounter wasn't going the way I'd anticipated. I'd expected to come up with some brilliant follow-up inquiries about Susan's final days and blow the case wide open while Grady chased dead fish sales. Instead, I was struggling with how I felt about Faye's prying where she wasn't invited. And how Charmers had made it into 1950 without electricity. Yikes.

Faye cleared her throat, possibly noticing my troubled expression. "Anyway," she continued. "It was dark by dinner in the fall and winter. A lot of accidents happened, taking the lives of numerous farmers and fishermen throughout the island. Really, the Swan curse people always whisper about would apply to most families living here back then. Life was rough, and Swans have survived it all. You're from a pretty hardy stock."

She opened her big leather purse and liberated a stack of printed pages, then set them beside her tea. "These are for you. I'm not sure if they're what you wanted, but I rather enjoyed the research." She lifted her fork and dug into her pie.

I went around the counter and hugged her. My feelings of privacy invasion were long gone after hearing her explanation of lost farmers and fishermen. Grady had said as much last night, but hearing it again, from someone without a pony in the ring, made it easier to see the number of pinholes in our alleged family curse. Maybe the whole thing boiled down to superstitions based on general happenstance.

Faye patted me awkwardly, and I stepped back.

"Sorry." I laughed. "It was really nice of you to do this for me, and I appreciate it very much."

Faye averted her eyes, embarrassed. "It wasn't any trouble."

I perused the paperwork while she ate, and I stopped on an article about the dwarf lemon trees on our family property. Lemons weren't an easy thing to grow in Charm, but our grove had been established long ago, and it had apparently gotten some attention from the local paper at one time.

I thought again of Evangeline Everly Swan, of her long marriage, her beautiful gown, and her somewhat miraculous lemons. I might not have been intentionally named after her, but I definitely felt a connection.

Faye worked her way through the dessert, watching me and glancing at the articles as I skimmed them and set them aside. "Swans have always had a way with plants," she said, pointing to the lemon tree article with her fork. "And baking." She redirected the tines to the final bite on her plate and hummed her approval. "You've done this tradition a great justice."

I smiled. "Thanks."

"How's everything else going?" she asked. "Need any help on that other matter?"

I raised my eyes to hers and chewed my lip a moment, unsure how to answer. I didn't want to unintentionally bring the killer's attention, or ire, onto anyone else, but curiosity plucked at my skin. "All this history talk has me thinking of an old story I hadn't heard since childhood but came up again this week," I said, as casually as possible.

Faye dotted the corners of her mouth with a napkin, then set it aside, giving me her full attention. "What is it?"

"There was an accident at Northrop Manor that killed some construction workers nearly forty years ago. Everyone says it was awful. Susan posted about it on her social media a few times in the weeks before she died. Did she ever mention it to you?"

Faye frowned. "I'm afraid not."

"Do you remember the accident?"

She nodded. "I do, but I was a new mom and recent bride then. I barely left the house or had time to do anything else. The adjustment was all-encompassing," she said, a look of remembered exhaustion on her brow. When her eyes met mine once more, she smiled. "Well, you'll know all about that soon enough."

My cheeks heated with a nonsensical blush at her words, and I warmed instantly with a rush of pleasant vibes. The memory of my conversation about having children with Grady lifted my lips into a smile.

And suddenly I couldn't wait to finish my workday so I could get back to clearing out my third floor and making room for my new husband and beautiful stepson.

∿

It was after ten before I took a break from cleaning the massive storage space that was my third floor. I'd set my phone to play my favorite tunes and kept my mind on the future as I'd worked, thinking only of creating a place Denver would feel at home and happy. I'd carried all my family's keepsakes and heirlooms downstairs, to be returned to the homestead. And gathered piles of donations into bins as well.

The bigger problem was a collection of things previous owners had simply left behind. I'd marked several boxes with sticky notes, then sent emails to various historical societies and museums identifying the contents. There were a number of old books, trunks of clothing, handmade quilts, and furniture from every era since the home was built, along with a lifetime of dust to go with them.

I'd scrubbed the floors, walls, and ceilings as I went, clearing a path through the open floor plan.

I didn't stop until Maggie appeared, threading her way between old chests that looked as if they could've been on the *Titanic* before it sank.

"Hello," I said, sitting back to wipe my brow, not at all surprised to see her seemingly appear out of nowhere. "What do you think of the progress?"

She rubbed her face against my outstretched hand and purred.

I crossed my legs before me and stroked her fluffy fur. "I know you like your freedom," I said. "But I hope you'll stick around more after Denver moves in. Your presence would be a great comfort to him, and you'd make wonderful friends. This floor is all going to be his space, so you wouldn't be cramped sharing."

Maggie tilted her head, luminous green eyes flashing as I spoke.

"Think it over," I said. "There's still time to decide. Meanwhile, maybe you can settle a debate I'm having with myself. Am I bonkers to think Grady, Denver, and I can be a happy family, despite a centuries-old possible-curse? Or am I bonkers to think an entire bloodline can be cursed? Because I don't know what I believe half the time anymore, and most days I just feel a little, you know." I spread the fingers on both hands and moved them around my head in wonky circles.

Maggie stood, turned her back to me, and walked away.

I didn't blame her.

I sighed. "At least stay for some tuna tarts," I said, rising to my feet and tracking her with my eyes.

She looked back at me over her shoulder. "Merowl." She took a few more steps, then looked back once more.

I watched, realizing I thought she might actually disappear and wondering about my sanity once more.

Maggie ducked under an old sewing machine built into a wooden table, then around a plastic Christmas tree.

I followed, stepping over boxes and dodging a myriad of ancient home decor. No one was watching. I could wonder whatever I wanted.

If she didn't blink away in a puff of white fur and smoke, maybe I'd finally see the place where she got in and out of the house.

She stopped at an old hatbox on the floor behind a hundred other things, invisible from anywhere else in the crowded portion of space.

I waited.

Maggie looked at me, then at the box. When I didn't move, she began to paw the hatbox repeatedly, sliding her claws down its short sides and leaving small scratches in the thick, aged cardboard.

"You want to sit in the box?" I asked.

"Merowl."

I laughed. "That is a very specific box to want to sit in. Can you pick something easier for me to reach?"

She turned back and clawed the box some more.

Thump. Thump. Thump. Thump.

"Wow. Okay." I shook my head. "Excuse me. Weirdo."

I stretched and bent over a steamer trunk between us, then hefted the hatbox off the floor. I carried the cat's treasure to a spot I'd just cleaned and searched for my spray and rag.

Maggie trotted eagerly to my side and waited while I removed a thick padding of dust.

"If there's a dead mouse in here," I warned, "or a dead bird. Anything dead, I will be so mad." I gripped the lid with both hands, reminding myself that anything trapped inside the box would be little more than bones by now.

Maggie circled me while I worked the lid free, apparently too excited to be still.

Thankfully, there wasn't anything dead inside. There also wasn't a hat. Only a very old book.

"What's this?" I asked, lifting the tome with gentle hands and gale-force curiosity.

Maggie leaped into the empty box and curled up. Her puffy white fur mashed and flattened against her as she got comfortable in the ancient space.

I opened the leather bound cover and marveled at the six simple words inside.

This book belongs to Magnolia Bane

My heart rate rose as I traced a fingertip over the delicate script. "Was this Magnolia's journal?" I asked Maggie. A tiny voice in my head wondered, *Was it* your *journal?*

She cleaned her paws and ignored my question, so I moved on, eager to see what else was written inside the book.

I rested the book reverently on my crossed legs while I deliberated. I wanted to read every word inside, to know her better, and to understand her legendary plight. But I didn't want to breach her privacy.

Was it a breach of privacy after the person was dead? Was there a time limit on bad manners? She'd been gone 170 years. Was it still too soon?

I fanned through the pages, enjoying the dry, ashy scent of old paper and attempting to see how much of the book was written in, without reading the words just yet.

The same scrolling, loopy letters from the first page adorned all the others. Faded ink tattoos of a forgotten life and time.

I recognized the format on several pages near the book's center as I fanned. "Recipes," I whispered, suddenly feeling inexplicably less alone. I looked at Maggie, then around the room, twisting on an old floorboard that creaked with my movement.

A loose leaf of deeply yellowed paper fluttered free from the back cover.

I lifted it carefully, eyes gliding over the narrow, tilted script. A recipe.

I tapped a finger against the book's spine.

Reading recipes isn't like reading personal thoughts and feelings, I told myself. Recipes were meant to be shared. There were plenty of journals in the family archives. I'd been reading those all my life. Except those books were donated by their authors. They weren't hidden, then found and pilfered.

My meandering thoughts halted as two words on the fallen page came into focus.

Lemon cake.

The air left my lungs. Magnolia had the recipe too.

I set the book down and concentrated on the loose page between my fingertips. The name at the top was Evangeline Everly Swan.

"You just keep coming up this week," I said to the now-familiar name.

The fine hairs on my arms and the back of my neck rose to attention, and I turned slowly toward the empty hatbox.

Maggie was gone.

"Okay, this is really not weird, and nothing about this chain of events is incredibly creepy at all," I told myself, rubbing my free hand over the gooseflesh on one arm.

I read the recipe, which had been hidden in Magnolia's journal, and written in Evangeline's hand. How many Swan women had made this cake? How many would bake it in generations to come? I tingled with a deep sense of connection to my lineage. To the ancestors of my past and the descendants of my future.

Then my gaze dropped to the subscript. *To bolster a hero's heart.*

Had Magnolia feared for Lou the way I feared for Grady? Is that why she had the recipe?

Lou had lived to be an old man, but Maggie had died.

Did she make the cake for him before ending her life? Was that the reason he'd lived?

I opened the diary with a whispered apology, and I began to read.

The pages were covered in love notes and poems, declarations of her clear and unending devotion to the married man who'd stolen her heart. I'd once read his letters to her as well. The couple had been as deeply in love as any two people could possibly be. But they were separated by a marriage his parents had arranged to ensure the family dynasty would persevere. Magnolia had never been an option for him. She was poor, from a family of farmers and rumored witches with a curse. So Lou had obeyed his parents and loved her in silence, behind closed doors and away from the public's scrutinizing eyes.

And she had baked him lemon cake because she believed it would protect him.

It was after midnight when I closed the book and held it to my chest.

I thought of the way the cake had become so important to me, and how significant the cake had become to me *and* Grady. Then I thought of all the times Grady had nearly been killed since our first kiss, and how I'd been feeding him my family's lemon cake for many months before.

My skin tingled again, and I pulled in my first truly deep breath in a very long time.

The lemon cake had saved him. The precious, delicious, Swan-original recipe was the key to everything!

Adrenaline spiked in my veins and I shot to my feet. My heart soared and the future I'd always wanted became impossibly, miraculously attainable.

I loved Grady Hays, and now I knew how to protect him.

The door to my living quarters opened downstairs, and Grady's familiar footfalls crossed the wooden floor below.

"Everly?" he called. "Your lights are all on. Are you still up?"

"Yes!" I called, racing down the steps to greet him. I lunged for him with open arms, Magnolia's book secure in my steel grip.

His chest rumbled against mine as I crashed into him, wrapping myself around his strong form. "I could get used to being greeted this way," he said. "I guess it's okay I used my key?"

"Always," I said, releasing him with a smile.

He looked into my wild eyes and pushed a hank of hair behind my ear. "You okay? Cause you look a little crazed."

"I'm better than all right," I said, in a rush. "I don't care about the curse anymore. I'm not sure I ever believed it. I just didn't want to take any risk with your life in case I was wrong. But none of that matters now, because I know how to protect you." The words rushed out in a jumble, falling over themselves as I whirled into my kitchen for glasses and plates. "We can get married and you'll be okay. We can live happily ever after like two characters in some novel where things are written perfectly just for them."

"Okay." He dragged the word into syllables as he climbed onto one of the stools at my island. "What happened?"

I turned back with the pitcher of tea from my fridge. "I found the answer in a journal upstairs. Maggie showed it to me while I was cleaning."

"The cat?" Grady glanced down the hall toward the steps to my third floor, then turned amused eyes and a goofy smile on me. "How long were you working in that attic? I think the cleaning chemicals and close quarters might be making you loopy."

"I'm not loopy. I'm elated, and I'm relieved." I set the book on the counter and tapped the cover, unable to curb the joy flooding from my heart. "You can't imagine how relieved."

"I'm glad you're happy," he said, still smiling, but looking at me as if I had two heads.

I kissed his cheek.

"Not so fast." He snaked strong arms around my middle and hauled me in close, fitting me between his knees on the stool. He kissed me long and slow until my mind was fuzzy and my limbs were jelly. "The cat showed you something in a journal that says I'm protected from your family's curse?" he asked. "Is the cat magical?"

"No." I set my palms against his cheeks as I looked into his eyes. "But I think my lemon cake is."

CHAPTER

EIGHTEEN

I invited my aunts and Denise to breakfast at nine the next day. I served a simple buffet of croissants and fruit, yogurt, and cheese. What I really wanted was the chance to tell them about Magnolia's journal and the recipe tucked inside.

They listened with rapt attention as I spoke, eyes widening and jaws dropping at all the most interesting spots.

There was silence when I finished.

The women looked at one another, then back to me.

Denise lifted a finger. "And the cat just appeared from nowhere, led you to the box, then vanished."

I nodded. "Basically, yes."

Aunt Fran smiled warmly. "She's trying to help you."

"The cat?" Denise asked, no judgment in her tone. Just a question of clarity.

"No," Aunt Fran said. "Magnolia."

"Ooh," Denise said. "Got it."

Aunt Clara lowered her fingers from where they'd

jumped to cover her mouth, then pressed them to her collarbone. "So it's the lemon cake."

"I think so," I said. "Grady doesn't believe it, of course, but we agreed that he doesn't have to, as long as he keeps eating the cake."

Denise snorted a laugh, then quickly pressed her lips and shook her head. "Sorry."

Aunt Fran looked from me to her sister. "This certainly is a game changer."

"It could be," Aunt Clara said. "I hate to think of poor Grady as a guinea pig."

I waved a hand. "There's more."

I shared everything with them that I'd learned about the men in our family. The things Grady had told me, and the information from Faye, including some of the Swan men's ages and causes of deaths, then the lengths of their marriages.

My aunts were especially interested in the story about their grandparents. They'd known their grandpa had died in his forties, but they'd had no idea he and their grandma had been married all those years before the accident.

"More than twenty years," Aunt Fran said, mystified. "Mama certainly failed to include that particular detail."

Aunt Clara patted Aunt Fran's arm.

I saw the hope in their eyes as they conferred with one another. Heard the hitch in their voices as they made plans to do some archival digging when they got home tonight after work.

Aunt Clara pushed her empty coffee cup aside and

steepled her fingers. "If lemon cake strengthens our loved ones against the curse, I wonder if all the other recipes do."

Aunt Fran sat back, lips parting in interest. "An excellent question."

I chewed my lip, considering. "Most of the archived recipes I've seen have subscripts, especially the older ones and original versions. If they're anything like the lemon cake, they state their purpose right on them. I just never knew what it meant."

"Fascinating," Aunt Fran said. "I could use something to help with my arthritis when it rains."

"I'd like a full night's sleep," Aunt Clara said.

Denise smiled dreamily. "I'd like to meet my soul mate."

The seashell wind chimes rang, and Wyatt appeared.

My aunts chuckled softly, elbowing one another as I welcomed Wyatt inside.

He cast my aunts an odd look as he approached the table, planting a kiss on each of their cheeks. "I'm not sure how I feel about this welcome. Seems like you ladies are up to something."

We all looked at Denise, and her cheeks went scarlet.

Wyatt and Denise had developed a strong friendship, dated briefly, then broke up. Anyone with eyes could see the flame burned as bright as ever on each side. But sometimes it took folks a while to pull their heads out of the sand.

"I changed my mind," Aunt Clara said. "I want a million dollars."

I broke into laughter alongside my aunts.

And the wind chimes jingled once more, but no one came inside.

Denise was speaking softly to Wyatt, so I went to see who'd wandered into our breakfast party.

"Welcome to Sun, Sand, and Tea," I said sweetly as I crossed into the foyer. "We don't open for another…" I stopped short at the sight of Alexander Lehman examining a collage of boardwalk photos on the wall.

"Hello," he said. "These are lovely. How old are they?"

"Um." I moved closer and glanced at the images. "The oldest was taken around the turn of the last century. Most are Great Depression-era." I turned back to him with a furrowed brow. "What are you doing here?" The way he loitered in my foyer, not looking for the café, told me he hadn't come for food or tea.

He smiled kindly. "You mentioned you worked here, and I was on the boardwalk when I saw the sign." He motioned to the world outside my front door. His bald head was sunburned, along with most of his visible skin. A red polo shirt enhanced the pink glow on his neck, face, and arms as well. Maybe folks in Chicago had something against sunblock. Or they didn't see the sun often enough to need it. "I wondered if I could have a few minutes of your time."

"Probably," I said, thankful Wyatt was only a few feet away and that I'd recently brushed up my escape-and-run skills, in case this man was dangerous after all. "What can I do for you?"

"I'm in town on business," he said. "I've stopped by Blessed Bee several times this week, but the owners are never at work, and the women behind the counter refuse to give me any details on where I can find them. You, on the other hand, offered to help, and I'm hoping the offer still stands." He removed a business card from his pocket and passed it to me.

"Alexander Lehman, Founder, Holistic Hands," I said, reading the tidy script on high-end ivory linen cardstock.

He smiled. "I'm primarily an investor, but I started Holistic Hands about thirty years ago to bring awareness to our earth's natural healing properties, including the American Honeybee. I saw a documentary on the Bee Loved YouTube channel featuring a set of sisters from this town, and I knew instantly I needed to speak with them. I'm always on the lookout for like-minded companies, products, and people to invest in. I think they can help me, and together we can make a major impact on the honeybee population and our bank accounts."

The soft rustle of movement and whispers drew our attention to the café behind me.

My family and friends were obviously eavesdropping, and there wasn't any reason not to make introductions.

I smiled at Alexander. "Why don't you come on in," I said. "I'm not officially open until eleven, but I'd love to introduce you to a few people."

He greeted everyone with a handshake as I made introductions and passed one of his cards to each of my aunts. "If you have a few minutes, I'd like to tell you about my company and perhaps convince you both to become the face of my brand."

My jaw dropped, and my aunts grew still and pale.

Wyatt cleared his throat. "I think you've got their undivided attention," he said, motioning to Aunt Clara and Aunt Fran. "Please, go on."

We listened intently as Alexander bragged, rightfully, about his amazing company and all the good it did for the earth, the environment, and the bees. He pitched himself with humbled grace and gushed about his love for my aunts' store, products, and position on small footprint living. All things he'd learned from their documentary filmed by Bee Loved. He wanted my aunts to appear on his large-media marketing, billboards and signage, as well as on a selection of his product labels, and he wanted to take them to Chicago to see his facilities. He didn't offer them a million dollars, like Aunt Clara had asked the cosmos, but he had offered an amount they couldn't completely refuse. So they'd agreed to visit the facilities and consider his offer.

We broke into group hugs and high fives when Alexander left.

Several moments of silence passed after that.

"I've never left the island," Aunt Clara said, officially beginning to process.

Aunt Fran crossed her legs beneath a long, gauzy black skirt, then arranged the material over her bouncing foot. "I took road trips with friends when I was young, but I was never gone long, and I've always wanted to ride in a plane."

"Planes are the best," Denise said. "Especially if you're in a hurry or just impatient like me."

Aunt Fran looked at me, then her sister. "Everly will be married soon. Grady will be here to look after her."

I rolled my eyes. "I'm thirty. Not thirteen. I don't need to be looked after."

A quiet round of chuckles ruffled my feathers, but I let it go. None of the other people in the room had been threatened four times this week.

Something passed between my aunts as they looked into one another's eyes.

I wished, not for the first time, that I could read minds.

"We wouldn't have to be gone long," Aunt Fran said. "We can fly to Chicago and back in a matter of hours. Maybe stay just a night or two."

Aunt Clara kneaded her hands, eyes bright and color rising on her cheeks. "We've never had a trip together. It would be very nice."

"And," Denise said softly, "if the love curse isn't real, maybe the travel curse isn't either."

The alleged travel curse suggests Swan women should never leave the island, lest something bad occur. Plenty of us have left over the years, but most come home following something unpleasant. A breakup. An illness. The loss of a spouse. And like the love curse, all those who've been hurt stand as evidence, cautioning other Swans against the urge to venture too far.

Aunt Clara slid her delighted eyes to me. "Sounds like we need a recipe for safe travels."

And just like that, the final bind that had plagued my family for centuries loosened, and we shared a long collective breath.

∾

I spent the next few hours near the register, making party plans and ringing up customers while Denise waited tables. I'd soon perfected the menu for Amelia and Ryan's sendoff and started a similar set of notes for my aunts' big news, assuming they would eventually, officially, accept Alexander's offer to become the face of his products.

By the time my aunts and Wyatt left, Aunt Clara had reasoned that even if they didn't find a recipe to protect their travels, and even if the curse about not leaving Charm was real, it couldn't be too terrible for them to take a short trip. Just a day or two.

I'd heartily agreed, and more than that, I'd reveled in the liberation I'd seen in her. Aunt Clara was a lifelong rule follower who, in seventy odd years, had never considered testing fate by deliberately snubbing the lore. So she'd stayed here without argument, and I'd never realized how much that submission had cost her until today.

Their decision to go, even for a few days, felt worthy of a major celebration.

Change was afoot all around me. My heart barely knew where to begin with its joy and anticipation. I considered fabricating a "safe travels" recipe to help my aunts feel at peace on the journey. Anything to be sure they didn't stop themselves from having this adventure together. I wouldn't, of course, because it felt deceitful, but I couldn't help wondering if that was exactly what all the other recipes were. Talismans of a sort. Written works of hope.

The Corkers arrived in a riot of brightly patterned clothing and laughter, interrupting my new train of thought. The bulk of the ladies moved to the rear windows, selecting a set of tables overlooking the sea.

Pearl and Margie Marie approached the counter.

Each woman wore a halo of curls around her head, Pearl's curls were white and Margie Marie's, red. Pearl's polka-dotted blouse was tucked into green elastic-waisted pants, and she had socks and Birkenstocks on her feet. Margie Marie wore black capris and a smart red top that matched her lips and nails.

I glanced at my cutoff shorts and logoed T-shirt, feeling instantly underdressed.

"Hey!" I said brightly. "You're just the ladies I'd hoped to see."

"We heard," Pearl said, climbing onto a stool with her friend's help. "Clara and Fran are walking on sunshine about that Chicago investor. And we hear you're in the market for a shop keep."

"I am," I said, gaze darting to Margie Marie. "Know anyone who'd want to hang out here ten or twelve hours a week?"

Margie Marie took the seat beside Pearl and grinned. "Say no more. I'm in. I'm excellent with people, and I know my way around a kitchen. I waited tables for seventeen years when I was younger and managed a successful restaurant for six after that. We can institute M&M Mondays and feature something from your menu as endorsed by me, M&M. Then, I can really push that dish to customers."

I laughed. "A woman with a plan. I love it. Thank you!"

She smiled and pointed one red nail at my open notebook. "Before you get too far with your party plans, you should know we're throwing Clara and Fran a party at Crooked Oaks. You don't need to do a thing. I've already reserved the bingo room. You can relax and celebrate with your family. Leave the rest to us."

Pearl nodded. "It's true. We're excellent party planners. If you need any help with your wedding, let us know."

Immediate appreciation flooded me. I was so accustomed to throwing the parties, I hadn't considered asking for help with my aunts' event so I could be present in the moment. Knowing the Corkers had already started the ball rolling, because they loved Aunt Clara and Aunt Fran too, was indescribably wonderful. "Thank you."

An outburst of laughter rose from the tables near the window, where the other Corkers had set up shop. They waved their hands overhead, motioning the ladies before me to join them.

Margie Marie waved them off and turned back to me. "Put me on the schedule here whenever you're ready. Denise can train me so you can focus on your wedding. Then I can cover shifts here whenever you want. It's the beauty of retirement. All I have is free time. Here's my number." She passed me a hot pink card with her name in shimmery silver script. A phone number was centered beneath. "I'll be waiting for that call," she said. "I miss the hustle of a busy café."

Pearl huffed and hollered across the room to their beckoning friends. "Hold your pants on. We're coming!"

"Before you go…" I said, the accident at Northrop Manor popping into my thoughts once more. The story hadn't been far from my mind all week, and while I'd yet to learn many specifics, I couldn't stop myself from asking these ladies about it too.

Their expressions turned sullen as I spoke.

Pearl's lips thinned into a heartbreaking grimace. "I remember that day well. It was the worst thing to happen on this island in all my days."

Margie Marie nodded, and the grief in both women's expressions was as genuine as if the loss had happened last week instead of forty years ago. Then again, I supposed grief was like that. Never weaker, just less often in mind.

Pearl rubbed dimpled hands over her forearms, apparently fighting a chill. "My neighbor, Tamara Wills, lost her husband that day. Her boys lost their father. They all lost their protector and source of income. They were forced to move in with her family on the mainland. None of them were ever the same. Broken hearts change us," she said. "Losing a spouse is tough. Losing a parent is something else entirely."

I knew that was true. I didn't remember my parents, but their loss had left two distinct holes in my heart. Grandma, Aunt Clara, and Aunt Fran had done their best to mend and heal the wounds, but Pearl was right, the loss was real and lasting.

I made a mental note to look for Tamara Wills online

later and see if she was reachable, though I didn't know what I would ask if I found her.

"Welcome to Sun, Sand, and Tea," Denise called, turning my head toward the doorway. I hadn't even heard the wind chimes.

Mary Grace moseyed to the counter, waving at the other guests before giving Pearl and Margie Marie each a hug.

The older women cooed and smiled in response, apparently under some kind of spell.

I couldn't remember if I was supposed to throw salt over my shoulder to ward off evil or form a cross with my fingers. Then, I remembered Mary Grace and I were on the verge of an unprecedented truce, and I forced a tight smile.

She fixed cautious eyes on me. "I heard there's piña colada pie," she said. "I'd love to try a slice and bring one home to my husband, if you haven't sold out."

Pearl's brows reached for her hairline. "Piña colada pie? Why didn't you lead with that?"

I pointed over my shoulder to the large white and yellow chalk drawing of the pie and fat red letters announcing its availability.

"Oh." She frowned. "Well, we'll take two. One for now, and one to go."

"Pieces or pies?" I asked, sure I knew that answer.

"Pies," Pearl and Margie Marie answered together, then laughed.

I moved a slice of pie onto a plate for Mary Grace, then stacked a pair of pies in boxes on the counter for Pearl and Margie Marie.

Pearl lifted the pies and climbed off the stool, followed by her cohort, presumably headed for the table with their friends.

Mary Grace eyeballed me. "Still looking into Susan's death?"

The older women widened their eyes and came back to their stools.

Pearl set the pies on my counter. "I think we'll each have a slice here before we join the group," she said.

I delivered a pair of plates and forks for Pearl and Margie Marie, along with a server, while keeping one eye on Mary Grace. "Maybe," I said, answering her question. "Why?"

She raised her fork to the pie. "I just thought I'd let you know I'm available if you need any help. I don't think you believed me the last time I said it."

"Us too," Margie Marie said, motioning from herself to Pearl with her thumb. "We're clever and no one ever suspects old ladies."

"It's true," Pearl said brightly. "Tap us in."

I exhaled a long breath. "Grady really wants me to stay out of this."

Margie Marie grinned. "I saw the way he threatened that killer on the *Town Charmer* last night. The bad guy said, I'm coming for Everly Swan. Then your man said—" She cleared her throat and made an angry face, presumably preparing to imitate my fiancé. "Oh, no you are not putting one finger on my lady. You'll have to come through me to reach her, and nobody gets through me."

I smiled. It wasn't a bad imitation, and her interpretation wasn't far off either.

Pearl set her fork aside and fixed her eyes on me. "Does the old construction accident have something to do with Susan's death?"

"I'm not sure," I said. "I think it might, but it's just a hunch."

Mary Grace took a dainty bite of pie, considering my words. "It's possible Susan was looking into that ceiling collapse for a reason. Maybe someone hired her."

My jaw dropped. Why hadn't I thought of that? "Someone at the historical society?" I asked.

Mary Grace shrugged. "Maybe. All I know is she was paid to research, and she was really good at it. I'm honestly not sure why she even asked for my help with those sales documents. She could've found those on her own."

"Maybe she didn't have time?" Pearl suggested.

"Or she didn't want any record of her requesting the documents," I said.

Pearl took another bit of pie. "Maybe someone wanted to file a lawsuit. Is it too late for that? If new evidence arose?"

I pulled my lips to one side. "I'm not sure what kind of evidence you mean or what the statute of limitations on something like that is." Was a suit even possible now?

Mary Grace licked the crumbs from her glossy lips. "Maybe someone just wants the truth. The same way you always chase killers, just needing the facts."

I sensed judgement in her tone, but her words were valid. Given the toll those deaths had taken on families, it seemed possible someone might be seeking answers, even after all these years. "I will have to look into that," I said as unenthusiastically as possible, hoping not to inspire the women before me to help. "Thank you."

Mary Grace fought a small smile as she sank her fork back into the pie. "You're welcome."

Miraculously, a bit more of the tension I'd held in her presence for the past twenty or so years faded a smidge.

I stayed busy at the register throughout the afternoon and made mental plans to revisit the law office again soon. With a little luck, someone there could confirm or dismiss the possibility Susan had been researching for a lawsuit. Even if Faye or the attorneys couldn't legally share client names, assuming the suit existed at all, just knowing Susan was working on this would point me in a new direction.

All in all, my life was shining up nicely. My family curses were falling apart. My aunts had an incredible opportunity to travel. I would soon marry Grady Hays.

And my investigation had a new lead!

CHAPTER
❧
NINETEEN

I made a trip to the law office first thing the next morning. Blue and Dharma had been returned to me as Grady promised, and I'd decided the car was my safest option for transport.

The day was beautiful and warm as I motored through town toward Lighthouse Road. I'd left the convertible top down and released my wild, wavy hair from its usual ponytail. The beating southern sun and balmy sea air were an intoxicating cocktail for my soul. And hope had lifted gooseflesh on my arms.

Before bed, I'd found Pearl's friend, Tamara Wills, on Facebook and sent her a message immediately. I'd explained clearly who I was and what I wanted to know. Then I apologized for bringing up such a tragic event from her past, and for bothering her if she wasn't the Tamara Wills I thought she was. There was room for error in research, but the woman I'd messaged was in the right age range, had references to life in the Outer Banks on a number of occasions, and three sons as friends on her pages. So I'd sent the message with hope and a prayer.

It had taken slightly longer for me to decide to ask Faye for her help with the case. I needed her to check whatever records the law firm kept about current cases. If I could confirm a lawsuit was underway, related to the construction accident all those years ago, the information would be a game changer. On the other hand, if Faye could provide assurance there wasn't a pending suit, then I would talk to Grady about taking a look through the files in Susan's office at the manor. Mary Grace was right. Susan took plenty of jobs outside the law firm. My search for family details was a perfect example of that. It was possible she took a research job about the accident, independently from her work at Krebs and Chesterfield.

I cruised into an open spot outside the law office and shifted into park. A white SUV with a volleyball decal in the window sat at the far end of the lot, nearer the beach than the law firm, under the thready shade of a small land-scaping tree.

Music and laughter rose from the nearby beach, and the scent of coconut sunblock mixed with summer flowers on the breeze.

I hopped out and marched up the steps to the office's glass door, then let myself inside.

A young woman in dark-framed glasses and a messy blond bun smiled from behind the desk. "Hello! Welcome to Krebs and Chesterfield. Do you have an appointment?"

I scanned the quiet room, gaze catching on the closed

door marked with Attorney Krebs's name. A pair of men's voices rumbled behind the barrier, and I wondered if Casey Winters was in there with him. And if so, what were they arguing about?

"Miss?" the woman asked. "Do you have an appointment?" she repeated, more slowly.

"I'm Everly Swan," I said, returning my focus to her. The previously cluttered desk where she sat was currently spotless, and the file room light was off. "I'd hoped to talk with Faye," I said. "Is she here today?"

The young woman wrinkled her nose. "It's just me today, aside from…" She pointed a pencil over her shoulder at the closed doors behind her. "It's my first time in this office. I'm from the temp service."

I nodded. It made sense the attorneys would have to replace Susan, but I hated that I'd missed Faye.

"Do you know who he's arguing with?" I asked, not needing to explain myself further. The voices had grown slightly in decibel since I'd arrived.

"No clue."

I released a sigh, torn between waiting to see who emerged from the room and leaving to make better use of my time before work. Ultimately, I decided to say goodbye. I didn't have time to waste today. Not when Grady was joining me for lunch in an hour. "If you see Faye, will you let her know Everly stopped by?"

"Absolutely." She scripted the message neatly on a sticky note and smiled. "Have a great day!"

I set my hands on the door to leave, then turned briefly

back. "Do you know if the white SUV out front belongs to Attorney Krebs?"

She pursed her lips a moment before answering, apparently reluctant to tell me what her new boss drove. "Everyone who works here parks in the small employee lot out back."

"Thanks."

I climbed back into Dharma wondering if the number of times I'd seen the white SUV since my first trip to the law firm was sheer coincidence, like wanting to get a puppy or have a baby, then noticing puppies and babies everywhere, or if there was something more to it. I hoped the former was true because the latter meant I was possibly being followed, maybe by Susan's killer, who was likely Casey Winters.

I'd seen the vehicle outside the realty office minutes after I was attacked and outside Northrop Manor on the day I first spoke with Casey about Susan. Then, there was the white blur in the background of Grady's fish threat.

I checked my watch and chewed my lip, deciding how to spend the hour I had before meeting Grady. He'd come over with Denver and a large pizza last night. We'd walked the beach and watched a movie until it was past everyone's bedtime. I'd been so distracted searching for Tamara Wills I'd forgotten to take a closer look at Casey Winters and his ex-wife. I still hadn't crossed the young attorney off my suspect list.

As an upside to collapsing into bed fuzzy-headed and exhausted, I'd slept more peacefully than I had in days, and

I'd woken ready to move mountains. Unfortunately, the only mountain holding my interest was the Susan Thames murder case. I needed to know who'd killed her and who was threatening Grady now. If Susan's ex-husband and his current girlfriend weren't to blame, as Grady said, then who?

Casey Winters was the only one who came to mind. Casey was still visibly upset about the role Susan had played in his awful divorce, and he represented the party trying to stake a claim to the contents of the well where Susan had died.

I pulled the phone from my purse before leaving the parking space. A quick search returned Casey Winters's name and the number to his law practice on Sandpiper Drive. I dialed the number with figurative crossed fingers, hoping I could catch him this morning. Or confirm he'd been the one arguing with Krebs. The firm's receptionist informed me Mr. Winters wasn't in the office, understandably refused to tell me where he was, and added that he had no time to speak with me later due to numerous appointments throughout his day.

"Any chance Mr. Winters drives a white SUV with a volleyball decal in the window?" I asked, before she disconnected the call.

The receptionist surprised me with a bark of laughter. "Don't tell me he's playing hooky again."

"No," I answered, taking her response as a yes. "I just thought I saw him when I was out earlier. Thanks again."

I puffed my cheeks as I pressed End on my phone screen,

then released a gust of air. The SUV belonged to Casey Winters, and I could only think of one reason he would been following me all those other times. And I wasn't a fan.

Traffic was light on my way back to the café, and my mind raced with unanswered questions. I stared into the distance at the top of Northrop Manor, its high-peaked roof visible against the backdrop of the sound. I wondered what it would take to talk Grady into giving me another look at Susan's office, specifically at her files. And if I could convince him during our lunch date.

My phone buzzed and Grady's number appeared.

I smiled, loving the cosmic timing.

I coasted onto the berm to check the message, surprised to see I'd missed the turn to my house. Apparently, my subconscious was already leading me to Northrop Manor.

Rain check on lunch?

I slumped a bit in unexpected relief, thankful nothing bad had happened.

Sure. What's up?

Duty called.

I rolled my eyes. He never canceled on me without good reason, and given the fact we were in the middle of an investigation and he hated giving me details when he suspected I might try to get involved, it was easy to read the subtext.

Something new happened on the Susan Thames case. Specifically, something he thought I'd want in on— something imperative enough it couldn't wait until after lunch.

A jolt of excitement pushed my thumbs across the keyboard as I texted back. Specifics?

I gnawed at my bottom lip while I waited, flinching when I got too carried away. "Come on," I urged the silent phone. "Give me details!"

The fish left outside my truck came from Thames Boating and Fishing.

My jaw dropped. Burt Thames was the killer? I waited for the thought to sound true, but it didn't. And if it was true, had Grady only told me Burt was innocent to keep me from pursuing him all this time? Had Grady known or was this a turn of events for him too? If he had known, I wasn't sure if I was impressed or upset by the subterfuge. Probably upset.

And did all the white SUV sightings mean nothing? Even when the vehicle's owner had a major beef with the victim?

I shifted back into drive when no further messages appeared. I didn't want to muck up his process by driving to Thames's business and distracting him, so I decided to move forward with my plan to visit Northrop.

Thames or not, the killer was still on the loose, and anyone can purchase bait from a boating store. It wasn't too late for me to find something significant to prove I was right about Casey Winters and seal the case.

I just had to find a way into Susan's office.

I pressed the gas pedal with more purpose as I neared my destination, then eased onto the lane outside the manor, rolling past the guard gate where tickets would soon be sold for major onsite events. I parked in the lot and climbed out with hope for my impromptu stop. Aunt Clara's car wasn't present. She'd mentioned the manor was still closed to visitors and guests. Hopefully, at least one person inside would be a sympathizer when I pled my case for entering Susan's office. *Not a sympathizer,* I thought wryly. *I needed a Sipper.*

I hurried up the walk to the front door, smiling at the grounds crew on their stand-up industrial mowers. They returned my greeting with waves as they cut the plush emerald lawn in perfect crisscrosses at full speed.

A trio of men with tool belts and wheelbarrows of brick headed for the distant well.

My heart ached at the flash of memory. Susan's unseeing face. The thick tangle of seaweed on her skin and in her hair.

I tugged open the massive, ornate front door with gusto and stepped into the foyer, immediately disappointed at Oscar's empty desk and stool. I craned my neck, peeking down the hallways, looking for signs of his return.

Distant sounds of vacuums, footfalls, and muffled voices told me plenty was happening inside the manor, despite the empty foyer.

My eyes rose to the arched cathedral ceiling overhead, then lowered to the marble flooring beneath my feet. Four men had died where I stood, or very near, when the beautifully crafted ceiling above had given way. Flashes of what that scene must've looked like when help arrived erupted in my mind, followed closely by images of the moment the ceiling had collapsed. I shivered as I realized the men likely knew they were going to die. They'd probably heard the groan of bending beams or the snap of the wooden supports. I felt their panic, imagined their screams as they tried to warn the others and tried to run.

My stomach coiled, and I pressed a hand against my sternum, feeling the thunder of my heart. I stumbled to the antique desk where Oscar normally sat, then moved impulsively to the opposite side, scanning the sets of keys mounted to the wall. Each was marked by a number above a small hook where it hung. The numbers didn't correspond with anything I could think of, so I had no idea if one was Susan's. Or if they went to offices at all.

I snapped a photo of the keys and the board where they were mounted, then headed down the hall. The police tape had been removed from Susan's door, revealing a small letter and number beneath the nameplate. I reopened my camera app to check the photo.

If I found Oscar, I was sure I could convince him to give me a peek inside, now that the police tape was down. Maybe as a trade for some delicious, hand-delivered café cuisine.

I compared the letter and number combo on her door to those in the picture and puzzled over the results. A hook with a matching code was visible, but the key was already gone.

Had the Charm P.D. removed it from the premises to keep people from going inside? Was it kept somewhere else due to the ongoing investigation? Or was someone inside the office now?

I leaned closer, tilting my head and pressing my ear against the polished wood. When I didn't hear anything, I turned the knob.

The door swung open with a creak, and I held my breath as I sneaked inside.

I gasped when a figure came into view.

Faye stood before the bookshelves, eyes wide and mouth agape. "Heavens!" she whispered. Her body sagged in relief when our eyes met.

I closed the door quickly and leaned against it, trying to stay upright despite the shock. "What are you doing here?"

"I'm looking for clues about what Susan was up to when she died," Faye said, her whisper rising to something more fit for a stage than a small office. "You?"

"Same." I inched into the space, still hyper-organized from the Charm P.D.'s efforts.

Faye wore black slacks and a long-sleeved black blouse with black pumps and a pair of dark sunglasses perched on her nose. A massive leather tote hung from one shoulder. She looked like a character in a book about middle-aged spies. "You seemed so sure her death was related to something she'd been working on, I thought I'd dig around in here and see if I could find out what that was."

"Exactly what I was thinking," I said. I chewed my lip, wishing there was a polite way to tell her to leave, to stay out of this case and remain safe while I dug deeper. Especially since Grady was working a major lead. But she'd gotten here first, and I wasn't sure how to tell her to go now that I'd arrived. I wasn't her boss, and she had no reason to listen to me. I considered telling her about the threats Grady and I had received. The attacks on Blue, Dharma, and me.

Instead, I opened the filing cabinet and started snooping. The sooner we finished searching the office, the sooner we could leave. Hopefully, without being caught.

Faye thumbed through the stacks of folders on the bookshelves. "What are you looking for exactly?" she asked, her round face contorted by a frown. "I'm not sure where to start."

"Me either," I said, flipping through the hanging folders. "Do you see anything about the accident that happened here, killing that construction crew? Or something about Casey Winters?" I asked. "Susan seemed interested in the accident, and Casey seemed pretty upset about his divorce when I spoke to him. He might blame Susan for the unfavorable outcome."

"Dear," she said. "I didn't realize she worked on that case. It was awful. He lost everything."

"Yeah," I said. "He had good reason to be upset, but I got the feeling he was angrier with Susan for finding what she did than he was with his ex for taking it."

"If I recall correctly," Faye said, "Casey hid his money well, but Susan is very thorough." She rifled through the contents of another folder before neatly returning it to a pile on the bookshelf. "Am I looking for anything else, aside from Casey?"

Male voices outside the office window drew my attention to the masons headed away from the well with empty wheelbarrows.

I closed the drawer I'd been looking through and opened another. "If you see anything about the well, let me know," I said. "That could be important too. Apparently, whoever owns the mineral rights to this property thinks they also get dibs on whatever is at the bottom of the wishing well. The historical society says the contents of the well belong to them, and there was a squabble out here earlier this week on the matter."

She stilled a moment. "About the well?"

"Yeah." And Casey was at Krebs and Chesterfield, possibly arguing about the well contents at this moment. I raised my eyes to Faye, then spilled everything I knew. "Casey Winters is still angry with Susan for the role she played in his divorce. He lost his life savings thanks to her skilled research, and it cost his parents their retirement. Now, he's the lawyer in a legal dispute over the well's contents. What if one of the reasons he's working so hard to claim whatever is at the bottom of the well for his client is because he killed Susan and a clue fell down there with her? If it's something small, the rescue crew would've completely overlooked it, but anyone combing through every stone in search of items with value would wind up discovering proof of his guilt."

I thought of my discussion with him at that same location. Had he been revisiting the scene of his crime?

Faye made a small sound, drawing my attention. Her gaze was fixed on the contents of a manila folder.

My muscles tensed at the sight of her. A deep sense of foreboding swirled through the air and over my skin, raising goose bumps in its wake. "What did you find?"

She wet her lips, then looked to me with uncertainty. "I found a sketch of tunnels that says they're beneath the manor." She moved slowly to my side and offered me a sheet of paper from the file. "I think this is the well."

A rough pencil sketch of paths centered the page with markings along the edges. An X marked a room with what seemed to be three rows of short, cursive letter u's. Or a drawing meant to indicate water.

"Should we check this out?" Faye asked. "Are there really tunnels under this place? That lead all the way to the well?"

I closed the filing cabinet door, fixated on the drawing and wondering if this was the clue I'd been waiting for. The moment felt significant and charged as Faye and I turned our attention out the window to the distant wishing well. No crime scene was void of proof, and this was my chance.

Visions of Indiana Jones leapt to mind, and a thrill pushed me into motion.

"Let's go," I said, pulling the door open at my side.

And we hurried into the hall.

CHAPTER
TWENTY

We crept along the quiet hall, listening to the distant sounds of voices, hoping not to be caught where we didn't belong. I hadn't brought anything from my café, so I couldn't explain my presence as a meal delivery in progress, or even a friendly family visit, because Aunt Clara's car hadn't been in the lot.

All I could do was hope to uncover an irrefutable clue that would support Grady's new lead and pray I didn't run into Susan's killer in the process.

I checked my phone to be sure I hadn't missed an update from Grady. I was dying to know what he was up to and if he'd intentionally deceived me by saying Burt Thames was innocent.

No new messages.

My heart raced as Oscar came into view, seated at his desk.

Faye motioned me in a new direction and I followed.

She turned the sketch over in her shaky hands, trying to

determine our relative position. Her dark ensemble blended into the shadows, working in her favor, unlike my white sneakers, which seemed to glow like tiny beacons against the maroon and gold floral carpet runner. Security lighting illuminated rooms and halls beyond the main section of the home, where we moved steadily toward the back.

"We're looking for a basement door," she whispered, holding the map up for my view. "It's practically impossible to read in this terrible lighting."

We stopped at the next intersection of hallways and listened before continuing on our way.

My phone dinged, and I cringed in response. The single chime seemed to echo and linger in the air. I looked to Faye in horror.

She pulled me into a dark room, eyes wide.

A row of motion-censored lights flashed on, and I groaned.

Faye put a finger to her lips, then shooed me with her hands, hurrying me away from the door. She rushed me to the opposite side of a thick bookcase pressed against the wall, then moved to stand beside me, making us invisible from the doorway.

I switched off the volume on my phone before it made any other sounds and did my best to settle my panicked breathing.

A fresh thrill ran through me as I viewed the notification. "Wait," I told Faye. "I was waiting for this."

"What is it?" she asked softly.

I moved the phone between us, giving her a better view

of the message I'd sent to Tamara Wills, and her newly received response.

Yes. I lost my husband in the Northrop Manor ceiling collapse. He was my world. I've tried to put it behind me for decades, but my sons continue to struggle with the reports made that day. My youngest believes his father's boss was negligent, therefore responsible. And because that man was never punished, Billy recently made a trip to the island to look into things further. My heart breaks with the knowledge another life has possibly been taken over this. I truly hope the two are unrelated.

I lifted my eyes to Faye.

Color seemed to leach from her cheeks. Her eyes darted up to meet mine. "The statute of limitations on wrongful death is only two years in North Carolina," she said. "Three for negligence, which could go hand in hand with what she's saying, but the time for a proper lawsuit is over. What could this man have hoped to accomplish?"

Spoken like someone who works at a law firm, I thought with a frown. "I'm sure her son just wants closure."

Faye nodded, brows furrowed. "What does this mean?"

"I'm not sure," I said, as a row of bouncing dots appeared, indicating Tamara was typing once more.

"Then we should probably get out of here before we're found," Faye said. "According to the map, access to the tunnels is up ahead on the right."

I followed her to a dead end.

A tall, narrow table sat against the wall, topped with an array of pretty things. A vase filled with flowers, an elaborate antique clock with a pearl face, and an ornate brass lamp with a Tiffany shade. A large painting of a wishing well laden in blooms hung above the table in a chunky gilded frame.

Faye ignited her phone's flashlight app, then peered around the clock, examining the wall behind the table. "It's a door!"

I hurried to see for myself.

From several steps away, the simple glass doorknob was hidden by the strategically placed décor, and the wide golden frame of the oversized painting discreetly covered the door's outline.

"Well, what do you know?" I said, smiling. "Old island houses and their secrets."

We gently moved the table enough to access the door, then open it and walk through.

I used my phone's flashlight app for a better view of the wooden basement steps before us and scanned the walls for signs of a modern electricity switch.

"No electricity when the home was built," Faye said with a sigh. "Maybe there's a bulb on a pull string somewhere if wires were run later." The beam of her light bobbed steadily ahead, stopping only when she reached the basement floor.

The dry, ashy scent of dust and old wood assaulted my nostrils as I descended, one creaky stair at a time, feeling much more unsure than I had moments before. Without electricity, how could we navigate a series of underground tunnels? Our flashlights were limited, and depending on current battery charge, not long to this world.

My phone vibrated silently, drawing my attention to the new message from Tamara Wills.

Billy wouldn't hurt Susan. They became friends after she took his case. She wanted to find the truth about what happened to those men as much as Billy. They were looking into the property owner from the time of the accident. You should go to that man for answers about her death. Not Billy.

My heart kicked into a sprint as I read her words, and I responded quickly, before potentially losing signal underground.

Who? What was the man's name?

"Everything okay?" Faye asked, struggling to orient herself with the map once more.

"Yeah. Tamara wrote again," I said, stepping onto solid ground at her side. "She says her son wouldn't have hurt Susan."

"Of course a mother would think that," Faye said, beginning to move confidently through the open space, toward an archway at the back. "But if she's right, I suppose that leaves us with Casey Winters and whoever he represents in the fight against the historical society over the well's contents." She strode easily through the dark, unfamiliar space while I shuffled nervously along behind her. "Can it be a coincidence Casey was connected to Susan in two ways? Through his divorce and also through his client and the well?"

"Maybe," I said, senses straining against the dark and unknown. "It's a small island, and there are only a handful of law offices to choose from."

A narrow tunnel stretched out on the other side of the archway, and the flat ground beneath our feet angled steadily downward. The air grew cooler and more moist with each step. A nagging voice in my head screamed for me to turn back, but unanswered questions were my kryptonite. I'd never know where the map led, or what lay at the end, if I walked away now. "How much further?" I asked, mouth dry and skin prickling.

"I don't know," she said, turning left into a tunnel still invisible to me in the dark.

I swept the beam of my light over dirty floors, stone walls, and a low, cobweb-covered ceiling. *What if we get lost and can't find our way out? What if we unintentionally walk into a trap or stumble upon the killer?* "What do you think Susan was looking for down here?" I asked, following Faye around the corner. "Do you think the contents of the well are really valuable enough to kill over?" It seemed to me that, regardless of monetary worth, taking the equivalent of other people's wishes for personal gain would result in some seriously bad karma. It had to be bad luck or manners to take anything found in a wishing well.

"I suppose we'll have a better idea soon," Faye said.

A shaft of light pulled our attention to a small doorway on our right, and we stepped eagerly into the space. I breathed immediately easier. The dank darkness of the confining tunnel opened into a cavernous expanse, arching skyward and bowing in each direction, as if a giant ball had been inflated here once and the earth formed around it. A circle of light shone down from above, effectively lighting the area. A rope and bucket hung at its center.

A pool of glistening water centered the room. I stepped

closer, curious and awed. My sneakers sank slightly in the soft ground. I'd seen underground lakes in travel magazines and on television, but never in person. It was oddly shaped and no larger than the average in-ground swimming pool.

"Is this the wishing well?" Faye asked, creeping toward the water's edge.

"I think so."

I'd never given any thought to what was at the bottom of a well, but I'd supposed the cylinder of bricks, visible above ground, continued below the water's surface, appearing exactly as it did at the top. Instead, the circle of light overhead looked like an enormous blowhole, and I was in the belly of a whale.

Moss and duckweed grew along the shallow depths, collecting and feeding on light from above. The room had probably been filled with water at one time, maybe for centuries, before drying out. The tunnels had been made much later, searching for the reason their well was dry. The remaining water reached lazily toward the earthen walls, coming up incredibly short.

A wave of grief and remorse swept over me at the realization this was where Susan had died.

I baby-stepped closer to the water's edge, drawn by the flicker of sunlight on old coins and treasures glinting beneath the surface. Did the police know this place was accessible from the manor? They hadn't seemed to on the night Susan died. An officer had rappelled down to recover her body, and they'd raised her out the way he'd gone in. Had he seen something of significant value while he was here?

My phone buzzed again, and I jerked my attention to the screen, prepared to confess my nosiness to Grady and get him down here ASAP.

The message was from Tamara.

This is the guy

"I can't believe you get reception at the bottom of a well," Faye said, moving carefully to my side. Her pumps made squishy, sticking sounds with every step.

"I think the blowhole helps," I said, motioning to the ceiling above. "Tamara's sending an attachment." I extended my arm toward the shaft of light, hoping to strengthen the cell signal.

An image appeared, and the headline befuddled my anxious mind.

The man in the faded photo onscreen was Attorney Krebs. He was significantly younger, but it was him without question. He stood at a podium outside Northrop Manor making a statement to the press. Was there a civil suit at the time of the accident? Had he represented the families or the property's owner? Was he even old enough to be a lawyer in this photo?

My eyes dropped to the text below, and I read. "'Local entrepreneur, Milton Krebs, makes a donation in the names of the workers lost last weekend. Krebs, a lifelong area resident and current law student, pledges to investigate the possibilities of faulty scaffolding and bring justice for this heinous tragedy.'"

The phone flew from my hand so suddenly, I wasn't sure what had happened.

I watched in confusion as it plunged into the shallow lake, clouding the waters with disturbed sand and sediment.

I spun to look at Faye.

She dropped her phone into her giant shoulder bag. Her expression was wary but resolved. "Sorry," she said. "None of this was supposed to happen, but you know how it is. Islanders learn to adapt and move forward." She folded her hands before her, eyes scanning the underground room.

"What are you talking about?" I flicked my gaze to the water where she'd obviously knocked my phone from my hands. "Is this about the article?"

My addled mind scrambled to make sense of her actions and her drastic mood change following the mention of Attorney Krebs all those years ago. He'd made a donation to the families who'd lost workers. He'd gone on to use his law degree to look for a way to pursue justice for them. What was the problem with any of that?

Faye shook her head, kneading her clasped hands and looking remarkably tired. "Milton purchased this property with the last of our savings," she said. "He had big dreams and even bigger aspirations."

"That's good," I said. And it took another moment for my mind to catch up. "Your savings?" I asked. "Attorney Krebs is your husband?"

I thought back to the day I'd first met Faye at the law office. No one had been there except her. I'd assumed she worked there. But obviously she was more than that.

"You were covering Susan's absence on the day we met, working from her desk until someone from the temp agency could fill in," I said. All those files about Northrop Manor had been part of Susan's research.

"I tried to redirect you," Faye said. "But you just wouldn't be swayed."

"That's why you were so eager to help me," I said, feeling the weight of my naivete in my core. "You were keeping me close so you'd know how I was doing on Susan's case."

She set a hand on her hip and nodded. "I spent a lot of time looking into your family. Trying to give you better things to do with your time. A fat lot of good it did me. Here we are, doing this anyway, despite my best efforts to avoid it."

"Doing what?" I asked, fearing I already knew the answer.

Faye's husband had hired the crew who'd died here. And I suddenly understood why she cared that I knew. "Those deaths were Krebs's fault somehow. Weren't they?" I asked. "The two of you have been covering that up for nearly forty years, and Susan found out."

Faye's frown deepened and my eyes widened.

I was right.

"This could've been completely avoided if I'd found some way to remove those mentions of the accident from Susan's social media," Faye said. "Why must everyone post everything online? It's a sickness."

I stepped away from her, contemplating the best way back upstairs without my phone as a light.

"What happened to the workers?" I asked, hoping to distract her. Had Krebs cut corners? Pushed long hours?

Offered too few breaks? "He caused their deaths, then promised to avenge them?" My stomach twisted and threatened a revolt.

What kind of person could do that?

Faye's placid expression turned to a snarl. "He did not cause their deaths. It was an accident," she snapped. "Do you have any idea what it costs to flip a house this big? One this historically significant? No? How about law school? Any clue how much that costs?"

I inched further away.

"Milton spent all our money buying this place, because he was so sure we could fix it up cheap and turn a huge profit," she said. "He didn't realize the extent of repairs required to sell at the price he wanted, so he did what he could within the budget. He paid the workers well, and what happened wasn't anyone's fault." Her gaze turned distant, eyes unfocused, perhaps seeing something in her past I couldn't. "Milton was a young father putting himself through college. He couldn't afford to do more than he did for those men. The foreman wanted OSHA guidelines followed, but we just couldn't. If he'd paid to make the changes, he wouldn't have had enough money left to finish the job. So he paid them each as much as possible to just get the job done."

I tried to keep the horror from my expression. The Occupational Safety and Health Administration had rules to protect workers for good reason. And Milton Krebs had ignored them. Worse, he'd been touted a hero for his donations and promises to get justice for workers whose deaths he'd apparently caused. Or at least contributed to. Then, he'd gone on to be one of the island's most successful attorneys and a respected part of our community. "How do you live with yourselves?"

"It wasn't easy," Faye said, remorse changing her features. "Raising our son alongside the children of those workers was tough. We had to smile, shake their mothers' hands, and pretend as if we hadn't known there were questions about their safety before the ceiling fell."

My nose wrinkled in distaste. "What a bummer for you," I said coolly, wishing I could call Grady and send him straight to Krebs's office with cuffs. Then I recalled what she'd said earlier. "Is it truly too late for those families to sue now?" I asked. "Are you going to get away with those deaths because you managed to cover it up for so long?"

"Yes."

"Gross," I said. "I hope you're wrong."

"So judgmental," she said, clicking her tongue. "As if you're perfect. The island's little princess. You've never made a mistake?"

I barked a laugh. She really didn't know me at all. "I make daily mistakes. But when I realize it, I confess and apologize. I don't hide like a coward and pretend those things didn't happen. I face my wrongs. I try to be honorable and live a life I can be proud of." *One my grandma and aunts can be proud of.* "What you did was selfish and horrible. You got to raise your son, and he got to have a father."

Faye turned her face upward, peering into the light overhead and fully ignoring my rebuff. "Today you're going to make the irreversible mistake of leaning too far over the wishing well. The new mortar hasn't had time to set, so you'll fall in, just like Susan, mashing your head on a rock at the bottom of an unforgivingly shallow lake." She lifted a hand, revealing a large, muddy rock.

I gasped and stumbled back. "Tamara's son hired Susan to find the truth about what happened to his father and those men because he wanted closure. Susan figured it out, so you murdered her too." I gave her my most disgusted face. "What's one more death on your hands, I guess. Now that I know, you plan to kill me too."

"Susan's death was an accident," Faye said softly, determinedly. "All of the deaths were accidents. The ceiling collapsed because we didn't have another ten thousand dollars to reinforce it as they worked. Susan fell because she wouldn't listen."

"You're the reason she was at the well in the dark during the fish fry," I said, putting the last piece of the puzzle together. "You lured her out there to throw her in."

"I asked her to meet me," she corrected. "She'd agreed to hear me out, but when I tried to make her understand, she refused to listen. She tried to walk away, so I grabbed her. I wasn't finished talking, but she yanked free and fell. I didn't throw her in."

I guffawed. "You sure didn't stick around or try to get help for her. And now, you're telling me you plan to kill me with a rock and your bare hands. You keep crying accident, but maybe it's time you took a look at what you really are," I said, the heat of indignation rising in my core.

Faye's eyes narrowed and she stepped forward, driving me back toward the bumpy stone wall.

Faye Krebs was a killer, and she stood between me and the door.

CHAPTER

TWENTY-ONE

Faye prowled closer, raising the rock as if she planned to smash it against my head.

I wasn't sure how good her aim was, but the shrinking space between us would only improve her odds. "You don't want to do this," I said. "You think you do, because you've been in cover-up mode for most of your life, but you need to stop. You're making it worse now."

I watched intently, gauging her steps and expression, imagining how I might maneuver around her and into the hallway beyond. Preferably without getting a significant dent in my skull for the effort.

My words seemed to hit a nerve; she paused, so I went on, buying time to make a plan. "Now that I think about it, I can see your husband didn't murder those men. He was just dishonest—and a terrible boss. He was young and lacked life experience." *Not to mention common sense, scruples, a backbone, and heart,* I thought. I doubted saying any of that would help my case though, so I kept it to myself.

"He's a good man," she said, swiping away a falling tear with her free hand. "He's not a killer."

"And neither are you," I said. "You didn't push Susan into the well. Or decide to take her life just to stop her from telling your story."

"Exactly," she agreed, moving forward again. "It was an accident."

Her chunky two-inch pumps sank in the soft ground as I worked my way along the wall toward the water.

The ceiling angled sharply, and I was suddenly out of space. To escape, I'd have to either tackle Faye or cut across the water. If I tackled her, she might drop the rock. If so, I was sure I'd beat her in a footrace once we were upright again.

But if she held me against her, or saw my attack coming, she'd have time to hit back. The rock in her grasp was large and heavy enough to break bones. I considered grabbing a weapon of my own, but couldn't afford to take my eyes off of her long enough to find one. And I wasn't convinced I could bring myself to hurt her, even if I was armed.

Running through the shallow lake, on the other hand, was the ultimate shortcut. And if I made a big enough splash with my steps, she might stay back to avoid the dirt and lake water that would become evidence during her trial if I didn't survive.

I wet my lips and shored my nerve. "So far, there have only been two terrible accidents," I recapped. "You and your husband aren't murderers. But you will be if you do what you brought me down here to do." I shot a pointed look at her raised arm. "Did you even find that map in

Susan's office today? Or was that a ruse too?" She'd navigated the darkened tunnels like someone who'd made the trip before. Maybe in search of evidence from the night of Susan's unfortunate fall.

I struggled not to roll my eyes at my naivete. I'd stumbled on her searching Susan's office for the evidence against Krebs, and she'd seized the opportunity to lead me down here and make sure I didn't come back up.

Her eyes narrowed, either realizing I'd formed a plan, or shoring up her aim. "You've got nowhere to run," she said. "And I can't let you leave here misrepresenting our actions. Milton and I are good people. You'll ruin our names and our legacy. You'll wreck our son's life too, and I can't have that. So be a good pet and hold still."

I launched myself toward the water.

The stone smacked against the place where my head had been seconds before, then exploded into a thousand bits of compacted earth and sediment.

I screamed at the sound, trying not to imagine what the same hit would've done to my skull. My feet sank into the mucky lake bottom, and the icy water rose above my knees. I said a silent prayer of protection against poisonous snakes or other hidden cave-dwelling creatures as I tromped through their possible home.

Faye walked parallel to me on dry land, halting me in the water. She smirked, a new rock in hand. "Perfect. It won't be difficult to sell my story if I kill you in the lake." She raised satisfied eyes to the well above. "Seems like you took that fall after all."

I splashed her.

"Ah!" She jumped back, mouth agape and fire in her eyes. She chucked the new stone with fervor and a hearty grunt.

The resulting splash sent water over my clothes and onto my nose and cheeks.

We bent in unison. I cupped my hands while she selected another stone. With a sweep of my arms, I sent a mini tidal wave to collide with her face. "How do you plan to explain that?" I screamed, giving in to my panic. "You're soaking wet with water from this well, and Grady will be able to prove you were here. Are you going to tell them you dove in after me and magically lived?"

She gaped, wide-eyed and considering.

I splashed her again and she cried, "Stop that!"

A familiar screech echoed down the well as a grand, bird-shaped shadow swooped over the water around me.

"Help!" I screamed. "Help!"

Faye's arm whipped and pain reverberated through my body as the projectile collided with my sternum, momentarily crushing the air from my lungs.

I stumbled back, gasping for breath, the thick muck tugging one shoe from my foot. My body left the ledge I hadn't realized I was standing on, and I plunged underwater when a drop-off took me by surprise. I kicked instinctually, propelling myself back to the surface, desperate for air.

Another rock crashed into the water beside me, only inches away, and another wail burst from my burning lungs.

The next stone was small but fast, crashing into my face

before I'd even seen it thrown. Streaks of light flashed in my eyes as pain exploded in my cheek and nose. Warm blood poured over my lips.

Faye crouched to lift another, larger rock with both hands, and she hoisted it over her head.

I dove deep, suddenly thankful for a lifetime spent in the water and the ability to hide a few moments in the murky depths. I kicked away from where I'd been with a frantic fan of my legs. The rock connected with my ankle and sent a tsunami of pain through my body.

I returned to the surface with a scream, desperate to curl up and quit. My latent fight-or-flight response demanded I keep moving.

"Squawk!" The circling bird cried, his great shadow spinning over the water. "Squawk! Squawk! Squawk!"

Faye turned her eyes skyward, and I scrambled to the water's opposite edge.

"Help!" I choked and pleaded between pants, pulling myself onto land like a seal.

Faye rushed for another big rock.

I worked onto my knees, blood dripping over my hands and the muddy ground. I threw handfuls of sand and sediment into her eyes before pushing onto my good foot and making a wild hop through the door.

She released a slew of startling curses, temporarily blind and raging at both me and the soggy ground.

I hoped the thick muck near the lake had pulled the pumps from her feet. Maybe that would buy me a few extra moments while she decided if the shoes were worth saving or if the risk of being caught was too big to leave them behind.

I placed my hands on the cool stone wall and concentrated on moving forward, toward the stairs to the manor and away from my attacker. Pain radiated through my ankle and up my leg in nauseating waves, making me certain I would collapse before I made it back to where we'd begun. How could I beat her up the stairs without the use of my right foot? How could I even make it that far?

At least if she caught me and managed to finish what she started, she'd have to drag my body back to the lake, and it would be impossible to cover a crime scene that big. She would undoubtedly be caught and punished.

Still, I couldn't let things come to that.

I squinted in the darkness, trying uselessly to adjust my eyes to the absence of light. Without my phone, it was impossible to see. I followed the gentle incline blindly, my panting breaths and soft whimpers of pain audible beacons to my position. "Grady." I whispered his name like a prayer. *Help*. I forced the plea from my mind and into the ether, willing him to somehow sense my fear and pain. He always seemed to know what I needed before I did. He could find me in a crowd without effort. We were linked by fate the moment our paths had crossed, maybe even before. And I needed that connection now more than ever. *Help*, I repeated silently, daring a backward glance as I felt the wall shift into a corner.

My first turn.

A spray of light entered the space behind me as I took

the next tunnel. I watched in horror as the beam swept along, growing brighter and larger as Faye erased the distance between us.

She wasn't injured, and she hadn't lost her light like I had. She was moving twice as quickly and would reach her first turn, and me, very soon.

I pressed the toes of my injured foot onto the ground and bit back the blinding pain. Then I pushed off once more, applying enough pressure to propel myself quickly down the hallway ahead. Fear attempted to seize me as I hurried awkwardly along, tightening my chest and throat, and causing my eyes to burn. My thoughts waffled between desperation and self-berating.

I'd never suspected Faye. Not for a single minute.

I was completely blinded and bamboozled by her declaration of being my fan. How utterly gullible could I be? And now my life was on the line because of it.

I'd been so caught up in solving the case I'd missed the truth until it heaved a rock at me.

Muffled thuds registered overhead, rattling the ceiling and shaking dust into my sopping hair. I hoped it was my rescue squad. That Grady had impossibly heard my prayer.

A low chuckle echoed behind me. "There you are," Faye taunted. "I see you now."

I spun in the direction of her voice.

No one was there.

"You're leaving a trail," she said. "Like a big wet slug."

Unbidden tears gushed from my eyes, racing over my cheeks and mixing with the blood from my nose. I cursed my wetness, my likely broken ankle, and my idiocy for not seeing through the thick veneer of over-friendliness worn by the monster behind me.

Disorientation overtook me in the face of immeasurable pain and fear. I no longer knew where I was in the maze of paths below the manor, or which way was up. When the wall I'd been using to guide me vanished, I swung my arms wildly, searching for something else to hold onto. Had I taken a wrong turn? Wound up in another underground chamber like the one with the lake? What did this room hold?

Did it also only have one way in and out?

A beam of light swept the space, sending my shadow out before me, where it stopped at the base of the stairs.

And I began to hop. "Help!"

My head jerked back as Faye fisted one hand in my hair, stopping me short. "Oh, no you don't."

The pounding overhead returned once more, and my eyes darted to the top of the stairs. "Grady's here," I whispered, knowing it was true without seeing him. "He came to save me."

"No one knows you're missing," she said, tugging me backward.

I dug my good foot into the solid floor, arms pinwheeling as I fought for balance. "He's here," I repeated. "It's your last chance to leave me alone and make a run for it."

"No one knows you're—"

"Everly!" Grady's voice boomed though the air, cutting her off.

In the next heartbeat, he appeared on the stairs. A flood of light from the manor behind him caused me to blink and flinch against the knives of pain shooting through my head.

"Here!" I cried.

He jogged down the steps, eyes hot with anger as he scanned me, then going cold at what he found. "Let her go," he growled.

I could only imagine what he saw in my terrorized expression. I was wet and filthy from my dunk in the underground lake and from being hit with numerous stones. I'd lost a shoe and was balancing on one foot. My nose was likely broken, and blood coated my lips. The flow mixed with tears as it trickled over my chin, probably staining my soaking shirt.

"Let her go," he repeated, his tone a feral growl. "I know it was you who killed Susan Thames. The fish you left outside my truck were purchased at Thames Boating and Fishing. Your inept attempt to make me believe it was Burt or June. But the island has eyes, Faye. Cameras everywhere. On homes and businesses, tourists and locals. You bought those fish and headed straight to my truck. I can track your path with photos. I have witnesses who saw you at the fish fry before Susan's death, but not after. And tech traced the IP address of the person who sent the public threat against Everly to the *Town Charmer*. Your IP address. We have Susan's files on the accident your husband caused. She'd saved it all on her computer, which we removed from her office the night you shoved her down the well."

"Stay back," she said, staying carefully behind me, using my body as a shield.

Grady stalked forward, looking more dangerous than any criminal. "Get your hands off her. Now. Before I remove them for you."

The sweet, patient man I loved was nowhere to be seen, utterly swallowed by a lawman homing in on a killer. Anything she said or did now would become part of the case against her.

And I smiled despite the pain.

"Faye Krebs," Grady began. "You are under arrest for the murder of Susan Thames and the assault, abduction, and attempted murder of Everly Swan."

She released me suddenly, crouching quickly before standing once more.

I yelped and teetered, struggling to find balance in the moment between her moves.

Grady's hand landed on his sidearm.

Faye raised a rock to my temple, and she gripped my hair once more.

Grady curled his top lip in warning, then flicked free the safety strap on his holster, prepared to liberate his gun. "Put the rock down. There's no way out of this now."

Faye pulled my back to her chest, resting the rock against my head. "You'll hit her if you try to shoot me," she warned. "I know you won't take the risk. So here's what's really going to happen. You're going to let me leave, and your girlfriend is coming with me."

"Not a chance."

She mimed pounding the side of my face with the rock, and Grady removed his sidearm.

He slid his gaze to me, jaw locking, calculating his odds of stopping her from hurting me without accidentally hurting me himself. I could practically hear his frustrated thoughts. *Still think you don't need more self-defense classes?*

I grimaced against the pain and Faye's change of direction as she began nudging me toward the stairs instead. "I've got this," I told him, determined to gain the upper hand and prevent my unhinged captor from being shot. "Trust me."

Grady locked his eyes with mine, and I willed my thoughts to him.

Do not shoot her. I have a plan.

It took a long moment for the silent communication to pass between us, but he nodded when the message was received.

I sighed as he stepped back and raised his palms.

"Thank you," I whispered.

"Yes! Thank you," Faye said. "Don't come after us."

I inhaled deeply, still caught in Grady's stare. Then I clamped my hands over Faye's wrists and jerked them straight down, causing her to drop the rock. I tucked my head and rocked forward, using my center of gravity against her.

She flew over me with a startled wail. Her back connected with the ground on a heavy gust of breath. In the next heartbeat, she was silent.

I collapsed onto my knees with a bone-rattling thud. My ankle screamed and my head lightened until I was sure I'd black out.

Grady dove at us, flipping Faye onto her stomach and locking her limp arms behind her with shiny silver cuffs.

I curled into a ball and cried.

My body shook with an excess of adrenaline, and my chest ached with every sob.

Grady was with me in seconds, holding me carefully and promising things were going to be okay. Faye was out cold, but she was alive, not shot, and she would pay for the things she'd done. The courts would see to that.

He made phone calls and spoke in acronyms, calling for backup and two ambulances, then for assistance from Northrop security.

Oscar arrived with a look of bewilderment, mouth open and eyes wide as he took in the scene at the bottom of the stairs.

"Don't let her out of your sight," Grady told him, tipping his chin to indicate Faye, lying still on the floor at my side.

As I struggled for even breaths, working to ease my hysteria, Grady swung me into his arms and carried me up the steps. Sirens were audible in the distance as we moved down the halls and through the front door.

"Sorry I'm late," he whispered, lowering us to sit on the front steps and wait. He carefully positioned me on his lap.

"How did you find me?" I asked, drawing in his calming strength with each ragged breath.

He didn't answer for an impossibly long beat.

I tried to tip my face up for a look into his eyes, but he cradled me tighter to his chest.

"I had a bad feeling after we spoke," he said quietly. "I couldn't shake it, so I headed to the café after I finished tracing the fish purchase to Faye. You weren't there, and your seagull nearly took my hat off in one of his weird fits. Something just seemed wrong. And the possibility you were in danger set me back in motion. I called dispatch to see if anyone had eyes on you in the time frame since we talked, and that was negative. The officers hadn't been able to pick up Faye at her home or her husband's office, and I just knew."

I nodded against his shoulder.

"I'm not explaining it well," he said.

"You are," I said, knowing how surreal reality could often seem. For someone like Grady, who relied on facts and reasonable explanations for everything, accepting the stranger pieces of life was tough. "Sometimes you just know."

I thought of the familiar squawk I'd heard in the well, and the massive shadow of a bird circling overhead. Lou had somehow known I needed help too.

"When I tried to leave, the gull sat on my truck," Grady said, confirming my thought. "He looked so intensely at me, refusing to fly away, even after I'd started the engine... and it was as if a fist tightened in my chest. I tried to call you, and I got voicemail. I tried to track your phone, and I couldn't. I checked the GPS on your car radio and saw you were here. The bird was already here when I arrived. Your car was in the lot, but no one had seen you. Then Lou started throwing another fit at the well. I thought I heard you screaming." He shook his head, emotions breaking through his cool lawman façade. "I couldn't tell where your voice was coming from."

"We were in the well," I said, teeth starting to chatter as chills racked my body. "There are tunnels in the basement that go all the way to the well."

Grady gathered me closer, rubbing the gooseflesh on my arms with his large, warm palms. He pressed his lips to the crown of my head. "So a seagull led me across town to you because he somehow knew you were underground and in trouble."

I thought of how Lou had once attacked a killer trying to shove me off a cliff. And how my cat had led me to a hidden hatbox with my lemon cake recipe inside. Then I thought of how a close look at my family's curses had revealed that we might not be cursed after all. And really, anything seemed possible.

"Maybe."

Grady stroked my hair as the emergency vehicles arrived. "I can't think of a sane explanation for that," he said finally.

"We don't need one," I said. "You found me. That's all that matters. Well, that," I said, "and my one move."

He was still for a long beat before bursting into laughter and startling the pair of officers headed toward the manor.

Our friend and EMT, Matt, smiled broadly as he approached behind the officers. "Everly Swan. I should've known. I got a message about an injured female who'd faced off with a murder suspect. There's only one woman repeatedly doing that sort of thing around here."

I smiled, then winced at the pain.

"Let me guess," Matt said, scanning my bloody face with well-trained eyes. "I should see the other guy?"

Grady frowned. "She's out cold in the basement. I cuffed her and left her with Oscar until uniforms arrived."

"Good to know." Matt flashed a penlight over my eyes, then glanced at Grady. "Another ambulance is on the way."

He grunted.

Matt looked back to me as he pocketed his light. "The Sippers at dispatch are going to want to hear all about this."

I balked, then smiled again, cringing at the pain. "You know about the Sippers?"

"Sure." Matt fished into his uniform pocket and pulled out a round sticker with a cartoon jar of iced tea and the words Official Tea Tester written across it. "Get it?" he said. "Sipper? You want one?"

Grady took the sticker and pushed it into his pocket. "I think our dispatchers need a refresher on professional behavior."

Matt grinned, lifting my wrist in his hand, checking my pulse. "You know, Everly Swan, for an allegedly cursed woman, you are just about the luckiest human I have ever met."

I looked into Grady's steel gray eyes and felt another smile spread. "I agree."

CHAPTER
❧
TWENTY-TWO

The next two weeks passed in a blur of wedding preparations. I still had more than two months before the big day, but Amelia, my planner and coordinator extraordinaire, was leaving town soon. So I'd finalized all the details with her in the evenings and secretly arranged the specifics of her going-away party during the days.

Ryan and Grady had been incredible assets to both processes, and I appreciated them more than they could know.

My broken nose, bruised ribs, and fractured ankle had kept me in bed a day or two, then stopped me from doing more than waving my arm frantically to appease my bossy fitness bracelet for another week and a half. At fourteen days post-attack, the swelling in my face was minimal and the remnants of bruising was invisible under my carefully applied concealer. Makeup application had never been my strong suit, but I'd found a tutorial online to help. The trouble was worth it, because tonight was about Amelia, and I didn't want to distract guests with my faintly purple, green, and yellow face.

I decided to leave my wild hair down, letting it tumble over both shoulders in thick beachy waves. My sea green sundress fell loosely from thin straps into a flattering A-line design. The selection had been strategic, both party-appropriate and unconstricting, for the sake of my tender ribs. Overall, it was a good look, but there was little I could do about the chunky gray boot protecting my ankle as it healed. My non-booted foot had a pedicure with white polish to match the manicure on my hands.

Grady winked at me as he returned to the deck with two plates of hors d'oeuvres from the buffet on my café's counter.

Denise and Margie Marie were playing hostess while I stayed off my feet.

"You didn't have to serve me," I said. "I'm allowed to walk."

"But your job is to heal," he said, sliding the plates between us on the table. "Besides, I like serving you." His lips curved mischievously, and I laughed.

"How'd I get so lucky?" I asked, enjoying the freedom that came with the word lucky. My gaze swept over the beautiful seaside, my handsome fiancé, and the collection of beloved guests all around.

I was so much more than merely lucky.

Most of the town had come to show their support for Amelia, and my heart swelled with love for our community. Men and women smiled as they passed, some patting my arm or speaking their appreciation for the party. Others stopped to offer gentle hugs and handshakes.

Grady stiffened with every unexpected embrace of a Charmer. I struggled not to laugh but couldn't stop my smile. The standoffish cop I'd met three years ago had officially been accepted into the fold. Hugs came with that package. "Told you I could make them all love you," I teased.

Grady Hays made a fantastic Charmer.

Laughter and music poured through the open patio doors, and I shimmied my shoulders to a favorite oldie on my radio. The gentle crash of ocean waves behind me played the melody to my life.

My aunts and Mr. Butters had decorated the café, transforming it to party central while I'd concentrated on the food and drinks. Mr. Butters hung prints of the illustrations from Amelia's children's book, *The Mystery of the Missing Mustang*, on the walls and placed them in frames as centerpieces. Aunt Clara had hot glued tiny plastic ponies to brightly colored napkin rings. And Aunt Fran had attached black handles to a number of round glass serving plates, creating an array of large magnifying glasses. Ryan had arrived a little early to set up and hide a small projector that threw the text from Amelia's story onto the floor and walls.

Grady turned his eyes toward a peal of laughter rising from the beach below, where Denver rode on Wyatt's shoulders. "I was sure I'd never like that guy," he said, a smile tugging at his lips. "Now, look at him making Denver happy."

I smiled fondly at Wyatt, my first love and ex-boyfriend. The once selfish cowboy really had grown into a wonderful man, the kind I always knew he could be. "He's one of the good ones," I said. "Your son certainly loves him, and we both know Denver is an excellent judge of character."

Grady covered my hand with his on the table. His white button-up shirt enhanced his perfect tan and soulful eyes. "Denver is your son too," he whispered. "He adores you and cannot wait to call you Mama when you're ready."

Breath caught in my chest as I watched Grady's strong jaw lock and his eyes mist with emotion. He'd loved Amy with all he had. Her death had been absolutely tragic. Their son barely remembered her, and I could never take her place. I wouldn't dare try. But I was willing to do anything and everything to patch that hole in their hearts. I would gleefully be the balm and bandage. And I knew Amy would be happy they'd found someone to love and care for them. It's what any wife and mother would want if they were taken too soon.

"He doesn't have to wait to call me Mama," I said, flicking my eyes back to Denver, playing in the sand. "I've thought of him as my own for a very long time."

Grady's bottom lip trembled slightly, and he coughed into his fist before releasing a long, steady exhale.

"Daddy!" Denver called, racing back to the house with Wyatt on his heels. "We're going to make snow cones!"

Grady and I tracked the duo visually as they climbed the grassy bank to my home and into the café, where Denver wrapped Denise's hips in a hug.

Wyatt set his hand on her back to stop her from losing her balance, then pressed a smiling kiss against her cheek.

Her lids fluttered shut in response.

"When did that start again?" Grady asked, his voice steady once more.

"I'm not sure it ever stopped," I said. "I think he was so worried about messing things up between them that he pulled away before he could fail her." Wyatt and I had talked at length about it all, and there wasn't any mistaking his love for Denise. "I'm glad they're figuring things out."

"I approve," Grady said.

"High praise. I believe island life is softening your edges."

"You have softened my edges," he said.

I smiled. "I haven't even gotten started."

Grady snorted, then released my fingers in favor of pulling his phone from his pocket. He glanced at the screen, reading whatever message had appeared.

"What is it?"

He sighed. "One of the officers met with Milton Krebs today. He's claiming responsibility for his wife's behavior and blaming himself for the toll his actions took on her over the years."

"It was a heavy weight to carry," I said. "I couldn't have done it."

"You wouldn't have done it," Grady corrected. "There's a big difference. I'm trying to be glad the two are finally coming clean, but it hardly seems like enough in the face of the damage they've caused." His gaze skimmed my face and torso. "All those deaths before, then what she did to Susan and to you."

"Hey." I waited to catch his eyes before continuing. "I'm okay because you saved me, and at least the families of those workers will have some closure."

I couldn't think of a silver lining for Susan.

We'd learned specifics about the construction accident in the days since my attack. Krebs had bitten off more than he could chew, trying to flip Northrop Manor, just as Faye had said. Unable to pay the bills, buy groceries, diapers, and formula, he chose to skip the necessary safety measures in favor of expediting the work. So when the foreman warned him repeatedly about taking precautions, Krebs offered the team extra money to stay quiet and keep going.

Grady rolled mournful eyes back to meet mine, gazing at me from beneath thick lashes. "Those men took the extra cash and lost their lives. I've been trying to put myself in their shoes to make sense of it, but I can't imagine the pressure Krebs was under, or what the workers' situations must've been like."

I rubbed his forearm where it rested on the table, understanding his inner conflict. There were too many senseless deaths. "Will Krebs be punished? For willful negligence? Maybe something more?"

"I don't know. That's something for the lawyers to figure out," Grady said, covering my hand with his. "A lot of time has passed. The consequences of his actions were horrific, but they weren't intentional. I'm just thankful not to be a lawyer on this one."

I offered a small smile, seeing the struggle in his eyes. "People are complicated. We can't always understand why others make the choices they make, because we aren't them, and we don't know the options they had. And some things just defy reason."

As if on cue, a gust of warm ocean wind brought Lou to the railing opposite us. He ruffled his feathers before settling on the corner post.

"Faye is being charged with Susan's murder then?" I asked, pulling Grady's attention from the gull to me. "She wasn't able to get out of that like she'd planned?"

"No." He shook his head. "Susan had defensive wounds and Faye's DNA was found beneath her fingernails. She might not have intended to knock her into the well, but she had definitely been attempting to hurt her. That's another one the courts will have to decide. I'm just glad she confessed to everything where you were concerned. Your stories completely lined up, which means she will be punished for your abduction, assault, and attempted murder."

I swallowed hard, muscles tensing with the rush of unbidden memories.

"There's reason to believe the map she used to lead you through the tunnels belonged to her," he said. "According to the rescue team who retrieved Susan, the area appeared sealed while they were there. I think Faye went down after the fact, searching for evidence that fell in with Susan. A piece of Faye's jewelry or a thumb drive of Susan's. I'm not sure. But I think she knew exactly where she was leading you. She'd already found the well and opened the sealed archway days before you showed up asking questions."

Maggie prowled into view, distracting me from the horrific thoughts. Her long white fur glowed brilliantly under the bright southern sun, and she wound slowly, deliberately, around Grady's legs, then mine.

"Squawk!"

Maggie gave Lou a long, appraising look, then leaped onto the railing and sat a few feet from his side.

Grady watched the animals curiously. "The cat's been around a lot more lately. Have you noticed?"

"I asked her to," I said. "For Denver's sake. I thought he'd like having a cat."

Grady slid his eyes from me to the cat and back. "I'm not going to say any of the things I'm thinking, because part of me suspects she'll understand. And the fact I just said that confirms my final transition to cuckoo is complete."

I grinned. "Welcome to my world."

My aunts made their way through the open patio doors, each with a plate of desserts in hand.

"You know I made plenty of sweets, right?" I asked, eyeballing the selection of chocolates, cookies, and tarts. "You can start with the food this time, if you want."

Aunt Clara smiled sweetly. "We only live once, dear."

Aunt Fran cheerfully nibbled the corner of a pizzelle. The cinnamon-flavored recipe had come from one of the archive books and included a dash of allspice for luck.

The women had each worn their hair in a long braid and pulled it over one shoulder. Their simple lace and cotton tent dresses were significantly older than me, and as usual, they'd stuck to their personal color palettes. Aunt Clara in cream. Aunt Fran in dark gray. A perfect yin and yang in every way. Two unique halves of a whole, who managed to also be complete unto themselves.

I glanced at Grady, realizing I thought the same thing about us.

He rose to greet my aunts with quick hugs. "It's nice to see you both again. You look happy. Is it the anticipation of your first flights?"

Aunt Fran looked at her sister, then turned her smile back to Grady. "Alexander is flying us to Chicago, first class, then meeting us at the airport and showing us around the city before we join him at a board meeting. He'll introduce us to his team then, and we'll discuss the possibility of being part of his rebranding campaign."

"And," Aunt Clara added, "when I told him I wasn't ready to push our luck with an extended out-of-town stay, he agreed to fly us home the next night."

"He sounds like a considerate man," I said. "Any new details on the role you'll play in the rebranding?"

Aunt Fran tented her thin brows. "He wants to use our images," she said. "He liked our look and felt it was exactly the wise, earthy, healthy, holistic impression he needed to take his sales to the next level. The exposure and visual recognition will be fantastic for our products as well. We'll be famous in the crunchy community."

Grady frowned. "Crunchy?"

Aunt Clara nodded. "It's what we tree huggers are called. You know, like granola-eaters. We're…crunchy. And with the money being offered, we've decided to retire."

"What?" I asked, a bolt of shock and excitement zinging through me. "What do you mean?"

"We're well past a traditional retirement age," Aunt Fran said. "Being mayor has taken me almost completely away from the store and gardens. Clara's been carrying the weight of my absence, and it's a drain. Even with part-time help."

Aunt Clara gave a sad smile. "It's true, and I'd like to spend more time at the manor, recording and preserving the unwritten history of our town for prosperity. We can't live forever, I'm afraid, and there's still so much I'd like to do."

My heart both broke and leaped for them. They deserved to spend their time doing whatever made them happy, but I didn't like the reminder that they would be gone one day far too soon, light-years before I was ready to let them go.

Aunt Fran slid a free arm around her sister's back. "As a bonus, we won't have to travel any more than we want. Alexander purchased all the rights to the Bee Loved documentary, and he plans to use clips from that in his ads. For print work, he's sending a professional photographer to us as needed."

"We can't beat the deal," Aunt Clara said. "It's like a brand new beginning, and the possibilities that spring from this are endless."

I opened my arms and flicked my wrists, indicating I needed hugs.

My aunts easily obliged. They leaned over me, squeezing me gently to spare my tender ribs, but covering me in their love nonetheless.

"I'm so proud and excited for you both," I said. "I can't wait to hear all about your travels and to see what you do with your newfound freedom from the shop. Will you sell it?"

Aunt Clara planted a kiss on my cheek. "We're still noodling on that. We'll let you know."

"Okay." I felt the presence of more people waiting nearby.

When my aunts released me, Mary Grace and Chairman Vanders came into view.

Grady rose to shake the man's hand.

Mary Grace smiled at my aunts, then looked tentatively at me. "Hello."

"Hey."

Aunt Clara and Aunt Fran carried their plates to an empty table nearby.

"Your face is looking better," Mary Grace said, somewhat flatly and without any of her usual menace.

I flicked my attention to Grady, who was openly watching the awkward exchange.

"Thanks," I told her, equally unenthusiastically.

Grady smiled.

Vanders beamed.

"Your dress is nice," I said.

"Thanks." She chewed her lip and averted her gaze, looking slightly less confident than I was accustomed to seeing.

We turned to look at the men.

Grady motioned to the empty table on our left. "Would you like to pull up a couple chairs and join us?"

"No," Mary Grace answered quickly. "We just wanted to wish Amelia safe travels and thank you for hosting." She smoothed her sleek hair with one palm, then reached for her husband's hand.

I nodded. "It means a lot that you came out to support her. She's pretty amazing."

"She seems to be," Mary Grace said. "It's good to have friends." Her eyes caught and released mine once more, then she squared her shoulders and lifted her chin.

For the first time since my return to Charm, I wondered who Mary Grace's friends were. Or if she had any. Was it possible she was lonely? Vanders obviously loved her, and vice versa, but there was something about having female friends. My heart missed a beat at the thought of not having Amelia, Denise, and my aunts in my life.

"It's almost time to send those wedding invitations," I blurted, offering a more genuine smile than I'd ever given her.

"Oh, about that…" She cast a guilty look in Vanders's direction, then slid her eyes back to me. "You don't have to—"

"I can't wait for you to see them," I interrupted, infusing my tone with a little pep. "And we've been meaning to ask if you two wanted to bring the kids over one night for a fire on the beach and a night swim. Haven't we, Grady?"

Grady's gaze heated my cheek, but I couldn't look his way. "Absolutely," he answered smoothly, having my back, even in this impulsive lie.

Mary Grace's jaw dropped, and she snapped it shut.

Pressure built in my chest as I prepared for her snide retort and public rejection, but I knew it was never wrong to be kind. So I waited, trying not to fall off my chair in anticipation of her response.

"Maybe we can grill out," Grady said, his voice soothing my coiled nerves. "Do your kids like hot dogs?"

Vanders barked a laugh. "Do they? Do men like football?"

Grady's brow furrowed. "Yes?"

"Darn right." Vanders chortled. "We've got a pool out back, where the kids love to play. It's our hangout when M.G. needs a break. And I grill a mean fillet," he bragged. "M.G. bought me a World's Best Griller apron and everything. Didn't you, hon?"

She blinked at him with the same *what is happening* expression I was likely wearing. "Yeah."

I marveled at the image of Vanders playing with children and making dinner so his wife could take some much-needed time to herself. The thought made me happy for the entire family.

She grasped his elbow and tugged. "We should go. Thank you for a lovely afternoon." She looked curiously at me for another long moment before giving a small nod. "Thank you," she repeated quietly.

And the couple walked away.

"Change is in the air," Aunt Clara sang.

I swallowed an unexpected lump. "I guess so."

Grady raised his tea jar to me. "To new beginnings all around."

"Hear, hear," my aunts echoed.

Ryan and Amelia crossed the threshold onto the deck as I lifted my drink to Grady's. They held hands and made moon eyes at one another everywhere they went these days. I imagined I'd be attending their wedding next year, if not sooner. Assuming she didn't kill him on the cross-country road trip.

Maybe I was projecting.

"Enjoying the party?" I asked.

She beamed in response. "Yes. Everything is utterly amazing."

Ryan met Grady's gaze, then tipped his head, indicating he wanted to speak with him elsewhere.

Grady rose and kissed me chastely before strolling off to see what that was about.

"That was my doing," Amelia said, as if reading my mind. "Sorry. I didn't want to chase your fiancé away, but I'd hoped for a minute alone with you."

I smiled. "The really nice thing about him is that he always comes back."

She took Grady's vacated seat without bothering to laugh at my dorky joke, and she set her fidgeting hands on the table.

Worry punctured my heart. "What's wrong?"

She shook her head fiercely, but trouble brewed in her deep blue eyes and two fat tears slid over her cheeks.

I immediately wondered if Ryan could outrun me in my boot. "What did he do?"

"It's not him," she said, eyes widening as she wiped away her tears. "Ryan's amazing. I'm happy. Really."

"Then why are you crying?"

She sighed. "I've never been away for so long. I know I'll have breaks between regions, and I can come home more often than that if I want, but I won't live in Charm for a year. And when I do have time to come home, I'll only be visiting. That's really weird, and I'm not sure how to feel about it, other than homesick, and I haven't even left yet."

I tipped my head over one shoulder and returned her sad smile. "I'm going to miss you too."

Her tears flowed freely then. She rose to round the table and hug me. "I'm excited to go, but I also want to be here. It's confusing and I'm an emotional wreck."

I laughed against her wet cheeks. "You're a famous author on a national tour," I whispered. "Everything is perfect."

She pulled back, wiping her eyes and nodding.

"Amelia," I said, wonder infusing the word. "You're a famous author on a national tour."

Her answering grin warmed me through.

She laughed, then covered her mouth in both hands and squealed softly. "How is this even real?"

I laughed with her. "It's real because you are amazing and this trip will be too. I can't wait for every single detail, and I expect you to update your social media every day so I can see all the great things you're doing."

"Deal," she said, returning to her seat. "And I swear to you I will be here for your wedding. I don't care if the publicist books me on the national news that day. I will not miss my best friend's wedding."

"Deal," I echoed.

Ryan and Grady returned a moment later, hands in their pockets and small smiles on their lips. I was sure they were hiding something as Ryan led Amelia back to the party.

"He's going to propose to her while they're away. Isn't he?"

Grady grinned. "Maybe."

I laughed. "Is there some other reason you're smiling like that?"

He braced his hands on the arms of my chair and leaned in close enough to kiss me. "I'm smiling because you're going to be my wife."

EPILOGUE

I stood on the warm dry sand outside my home, waves rolling in before me, toes curling into the softness below. A painted wooden sign at my side announced Shoes Optional, and I'd kicked off my flip-flops upon sight of it.

Mr. Butters had painted the sign, then driven it securely into the ground several yards from where he stood now, laughing and chatting with Ryan and Wyatt as they arranged the final row of folding chairs.

My aunts had arrived early to weave long white strips of chiffon through the wooden beams of a newly erected pergola, fixed into place as the tide went down. The same gauzy fabric was tied in swoopy bows around the back of each chair. Garlands of white and coral-colored blooms from the family gardens would soon be added generously to everything in sight, creating the perfect pop against the neutral décor and glorious blue sea backdrop.

A black shepherd's hook stood at the end of each row, an antique lantern hanging in its care. The glass and metal containers swung gently with the breeze, a single pillar candle with a ring of flowers positioned inside, prepared to light my way into Grady's arms.

We would be married at sunset, in the presence of our closest family and friends. Which was why we'd changed our mind about the size of the guest list not long ago. Instead of twenty-two chairs, there were now nearly one hundred. Because when we thought of the people who'd impacted our lives for the better, twenty-two chairs weren't nearly enough to contain them.

Every invitation we'd sent had returned with a resounding yes!

"There she is," Amelia said, her voice carrying to me on the wind.

I turned to find her and Denise marching toward me through the sand, the skirts of their gauzy champagne-colored gowns clutched in fists at their sides. My aunts had altered the dresses from a local bridal shop to nearly match mine, minus the straps and with slightly less poof. The women looked phenomenal. They'd each pinned their blond hair up and tucked baby's breath into the elegant twists. Identical gowns and hairstyles, both blond with suntanned skin and dancing blue eyes. They looked like sisters or two versions of one person heading in my direction. Denise was several inches taller and more athletically built than petite and narrow Amelia, but their expressions were exact duplicates of joy and love.

The duo stopped before me, admiring the ceremony's setup.

"Beautiful," Denise whispered.

I couldn't have agreed more. "It's straight out of my dreams," I said. "It's as if I spoke it into existence when Amelia asked how I'd envisioned my wedding day." She'd taken my words and made them reality.

Amelia tipped her head and rolled her eyes. "The original version had about eighty less chairs."

I laughed. "True, but this is even better."

"Now, come on," she said, grabbing my wrist in a surprisingly viselike grip. "It's time to do your hair and makeup. Then you have to get dressed so we can invite the photographer up to take the girls-only pictures."

Denise collected my shoes from their place near the sign, and together, my friends towed me away.

I stole one last look over my shoulder at the sand and sea.

And in the split second before my eyes focused, I was sure my grandma and mother were standing near the surf, arms around one another, their loving smiles on me.

I sucked in a breath as the image blinked away. My grandma and mother might not be visible in the photos today, but they would absolutely be with me, ever-present in my heart.

"Do not start crying," Amelia said. "If you start, then I will too, and I just finished my makeup."

"I'm just so glad you're here," I said, voice cracking. "I'm unreasonably blessed by the most perfect family and friends."

"Stop," she warned.

"You've barely gotten any sleep since you got back," I said, needing her to know I saw the work and sacrifices she'd made for me. "And you have to leave again so soon, but you've still made every minute about me and my wedding."

Amelia had taken a red-eye to the nearest airport three days ago, where Grady and I picked her up. Her feet had barely hit the ground in town before she was off and running to confirm every detail for today. She'd even tricked me into attending a book club meeting that turned out to be a bridal shower, because she'd missed the one my aunts held last month. She was the first person here this morning, and she'd been the last to leave last night.

I loved her so much I was sure I could burst.

We climbed the steps to my front porch, already lined in flower garlands and planters filled with coral blooms and white bows.

"Hey." She tugged me to a stop outside the door while Denise went inside with my shoes. Her eyes shined bright with unshed tears.

"What is it?" I asked, taking both her hands in mine.

"Webflix loved the shows we taped, and their testing audience did too, so once I finish this book tour in the spring, I'll have more travel to do next fall. They want to tape additional shows based on my book's sequels. In Orlando."

I balked, then pulled her in for a tight hug. "That's amazing!"

She nodded wildly. "I know! I'm really excited, and I won't be gone nearly as long next time. I wanted to tell you before the news got out. I'll be flying back and forth a bit, but only for a week here and there."

I swung our joined hands and smiled crazily at her, absorbing and memorizing everything I could about the moment. Then I hugged her once more.

Tears rolled over her cheeks when we broke apart, and she looked suddenly, uncharacteristically stern. "I promise you I will never miss anything that is important to you. No matter what else is going on. I will always be here when you need me. Always."

"Promise accepted," I croaked. "And vow returned."

The front door swept open as we sniffled and wiped our eyes. My aunts appeared in the threshold. They exchanged a look before pulling us both inside, then up the steps to my living quarters, AKA bride central.

The deck door was open, allowing fresh salt air to blow in. My gown hung from a hanger on the thick bronze curtain rod. The soft chiffon skirt pillowed and floated on the breeze.

Three bouquets stood in vases on the island. White lilies for me. White and orange for my bridesmaids.

I thought of Amelia's news and how much could change in a single year. In a month. In a minute. I'd returned to Charm with a broken heart three years ago, certain I was meant to be forever unattached, romantically, like my aunts and grandma. I was sure I'd never see Wyatt again.

I believed I was cursed. But I met and fell head over heels in love with Grady in a matter of months, even if it had taken me a while to realize. And even longer to admit. Now, Wyatt was going to be in my wedding. He was one of my closest friends, and I was eternally grateful for him in my life. So much had changed. Everything had changed.

It had taken less than a year for Grady to adjust to island life, to embrace my admittedly quirky community, and to heal from his unthinkable loss.

Amelia had spent a year getting her book published. A year from now, she'd be finishing up a second set of Webflix shows.

And I would be celebrating my first wedding anniversary with Grady.

I turned in a small circle, taking in the tidy, open space and wondering what my life would look like when that milestone came around. I imagined two sets of dusty cowboy boots by the door, two hats hanging on hooks in the hall. Grady's toothbrush in our bathroom. Denver's toys on the floor. Tiny stains on the rug and furniture from late night movie marathons and ice cream parties with a half-dozen little cowboys.

Would my heart still feel this full?

Aunt Clara popped into view, her bottom lip caught between her teeth. She'd applied blush and light lipstick. Possibly a swipe or two of mascara as well. "I can see you're having a moment," she said softly, "but we have something for you."

Aunt Fran moved to her side, having apparently undergone a similar makeup routine.

They'd both chosen wide-legged jumpers in the palest shades of blue and gray, and wound their long hair into small, tight buns.

"What's up?" I asked, looking from one aunt to the next. "Everything okay?"

Aunt Clara produced a long, narrow velvet box. "This was your mother's," she said. "Hazel gave it to her on her wedding day, and we think they would want us to give it to you on yours." She opened the lid to reveal a delicate gold chain with a crescent moon charm and a single blue teardrop stone. "Aquamarine was both their birthstones."

My chest tightened as Aunt Fran raised the necklace from the box and secured it around my neck. Grandma had given it to my mother, and now it was mine. "Thank you," I whispered, not quite finding my voice.

She returned to Aunt Clara's side with a small, proud smile. "Something old, something blue," she said. "And technically, you borrowed the dress, so there's that."

"All she needs now is something new," Denise said, popping into view behind them and moving to sling an arm around Aunt Clara's shoulders.

"My whole life is about to be new," I said. "New husband. New son. New hope. No curse." I chuckled through another slap of joy. "New emotions," I said, head bobbing. "I was never this emotional."

"To new beginnings," Amelia said, ferrying a tray with five champagne flutes to our circle.

"New beginnings," we toasted.

"And long histories," Aunt Clara added.

We agreed and sipped once more before they went to work on my hair and makeup, turning me into an unrecognizable beauty. I marveled at the girl who lived in cutoff shorts and flip-flops staring back at me through lightly lined and shadowed eyes. My petal pink lips matched my manicure and pedicure. The glow on my cheeks was more joy than blusher. And my endless dark curls had been piled expertly into a complicated style that kept the focus on my face and mostly exposed neck. Select tendrils of hair fell against my shoulders in loose spirals.

The long chiffon of my gown plumed and fanned with each sweep of ocean air through my patio doors, making me feel impossibly light. For the first time in years, I didn't care how many dress sizes I'd gained since leaving home. And I didn't care how many steps I took today, as long as some of them were down that sandy aisle to Grady's side.

I crept to the patio doors and peeked carefully around the curtain, looking past the deck to the beach, where guests had begun to take their seats. My aunts were mingling, and my bridesmaids were on their way to deliver gifts from me to Grady and Denver. I'd placed a smooth black stone into a box for my new son, and included a card. *To Denver, Love Mama.* He'd found the stone at the homestead while visiting the bees with my aunts, and he'd carried it with him until it was time to leave. Then, he'd set it down, because Wyatt had taught him the concept of not leaving a trace. People should enjoy nature without changing it, which meant not bringing tokens home or leaving anything behind. I'd put the stone in my pocket for this moment. Grady's box contained a photo of my pretty yellow lemon cake, on a fancy white platter, seated on my bed. My lacy wedding-night ensemble might've played a role in the arrangement as well, alongside a ready server.

A soft knock spun me toward my door, and I felt heat climb into my cheeks, caught in a pre-wedding night fantasy. I scanned the gathering crowd outside, easily tracking all the people I knew well enough to climb my private staircase and expect to see me only minutes before the wedding began.

Curiosity winning as usual, I released the curtain and a steady breath, then hiked up my full, beautiful skirt and hurried to the door. "Coming," I called, pausing to unlock and open up.

The staircase was empty, save for a small white box on the top step. A thick crimson bow was tied neatly on top.

I smiled, wondering if the gift was from Grady. But if that was the case, why had his messenger run away? I crouched to collect the box and remove the tag tucked beneath the ribbon. My name was written on the front in an elegant curling script.

Not Grady's handwriting at all.

I closed the door and returned to my rear window, glancing again at the guests filling chairs below. Then I slid the bow away and lifted the lid.

A square of embossed ivory cardstock lay inside. The message it carried was made in the same lovely hand.

Everly,
I wanted to give you something unique and
special on your wedding day. Something to
feed your relentlessly nosy nature. A secret
you can never speak of to anyone, except your
bossy husband, who already knows anyway.
I'm trusting you with this, so please keep it close.

A little flame kindled in my core as I greedily devoured the words. A secret on my wedding day? I wanted to hug the sender and Grady for this most perfect surprise. My gaze darted quickly to the next words, separated from the rest by a wide margin of space.

I am the Town Charmer

"What!" I exclaimed, clamping my free hand over my mouth.

Best. Gift. Ever.

I read the signature below on a gasp. A bark of laughter rumbled through me and burst from my lips as I stared again at the name. I pressed the card to my chest and peeled back the curtain once more, peeking at my seated guests outside. Careful to hide my dress, I stepped closer still, revealing only my face to anyone who might notice me spying or have heard my exclamation moments before. And I searched for the Charmer.

Mary Grace turned knowing eyes instantly to meet mine, and I nodded in awe and gratitude.

"Of course it was you," I whispered, a wide smile splitting my face.

I ducked back as Grady made his way to the altar, and soft music began to play.

"It's time!" Amelia cried, crashing into the room and nearly scaring the tea out of me. "Are you ready? Are you nervous, because I am nervous. It just hit me, and I might need a minute to sit down."

I turned to see her, bewildered expression, half-frantic in my living room as she rubbed her palms against the skirt of her gown.

"You were a theatre major," I reminded her. "You love being in the spotlight."

"Then why do I feel as if I need to puff into a paper bag?" she asked.

I laughed. "That would make for fun photos." I crossed to her and squeezed her biceps, then lifted the bouquets from the vases on my island. "For you and Denise," I said, passing the bunches of lilies into her hands.

"Thanks. Hey, what's that?" she asked, staring quizzically at the open box and satin ribbon on my couch.

"A gift." I smiled, then tucked the small note beneath the books on my bookshelf. Later, I would move it to the hidden alcove, where it would be safe from all eyes but mine and Grady's.

For now, I had a cowboy to marry.

"Let's go."

My aunts met me at the bottom of the stairs and linked their arms with mine, leading me toward my future.

"I love you," I whispered, as we watched Denise and Amelia take their measured stroll before us.

Each aunt hugged me tight. For one long, private moment, they covered me in their flawless, unyielding love.

Then the music changed. And my heart stopped as Grady looked up.

In that moment, trapped in his gaze, surrounded by a community of loved ones and held by my aunts, it was impossible to imagine any of us could have ever believed we were cursed.

But just in case, there was lemon cake.

EPILOGUE

DENVER

"Have you seen my slingshot?" I asked Maggie, the white cat stretched out on my bed.

She blinked at me, then rolled onto her back and stretched a paw toward my closet.

"Thanks."

Maggie was the best cat. She rarely left my side, which was nice when I was bored or lonely, but I wasn't either of those things right now. Right now I was getting my things together because Evie was on her way. Once she got here, Denise and Wyatt were taking me camping. Four days of hiking, fishing, and kayaking. I couldn't wait. Hopefully, Maggie wouldn't miss me too much.

I found my slingshot on the closet floor and stuffed it into my backpack along with another pair of socks. I hated wet socks, especially when I hiked.

"Denver?" Dad called up the steps. "Ready?"

"Almost," I said. "I need my pocketknife and my first aid kit."

"Top desk drawer," Mama called. "With your comics."

"Thank you!" I smiled as I glanced to my desk.

Everly had only officially been my mama for a year, but she was really good at it. Maybe even better than Denise, who'd taken care of me for much longer, but always felt more like a really old sister than a parent. Everly made me go to bed at nine on school nights and get up for breakfast on weekends. She made me taste a bite of everything she made for meals, even if it was green and I spit it out, and I always had to do my homework before I could play. And Dad liked to kiss her a lot, even when he said she never listened to him.

"Hey, cowboy?" Mama called. "Hurry a little, okay?"

"Okay."

Maggie leapt from the bed and sat beside me on the floor. She bumped her head against my arm, begging for pets, as I moved candy from the nightstand to my bookbag.

Maggie liked to remind me it was okay to miss my first mama sometimes, and that it was okay to love both mamas as much as I wanted. Because loving them both didn't mean I loved either of them less.

She purred when I scratched under her chin.

"Did you know Evie is a family name?" I asked. "That means other people in the family have that name too. I was named after Grandma and Grandpa Denver. Evie is short for Evangeline. She's named after someone I don't know and her great-grandma. We should show her all the best hiding places in this big house and how to make a good sandcastle."

"Denver!" Dad called.

"Coming!" I jerked my backpack off the floor and all my stuff fell out.

Dang it! I didn't pull the zipper.

It took a few seconds to force everything back inside and grab my pocketknife from the desk drawer. Then I made a run for the steps with my bag. "Bye, Maggie! Love you!"

Dad met me at the bottom of the stairs, his cell phone at his ear. It looked like he was pulling his hair with the other hand. "Just get here," he whispered into the phone, before putting it in his pocket.

He made a fake smile for me. "Hey, buddy. Do you have everything you need? I think Denise is right around the corner, and Uncle Matt is on his way too."

"Uncle Matt?" I repeated, consumed, but excited. "Is he bringing the ambulance?" I ran toward the stairs in our living room, slipping both arms into the straps of my backpack. "Maybe he'll let me play with the lights. This is the best day ever! Sirens and camping!"

Mama leaned against the wall near the door, trying blindly to slip on her shoes. She'd stopped being able to see her toes during the summer.

"I'll help," I said, pushing the flip-flops onto her feet.

"Thank you." She sighed, giving me the same fake smile as Dad. "Help me down the steps?"

"I've got you," Dad said, leaving their bedroom with two duffel bags, a pillow, a small fan, and bag of books. He caught my eye and nodded to the stairs. "Matt and Denise are outside. Run and let them in."

I braced my arms on the walls in the stairwell and jumped four steps at a time. My record was five, but that took longer and more concentration.

I opened the front door and let our company inside.

Somewhere behind us, Mama growled.

Uncle Matt laughed as he stepped into the foyer. "Hey, Denver. Sounds like Everly didn't tell your dad to take her to the hospital when it was time."

"Dad says she never listens," I reported. "Grandma says she's stubborn, and one time she hit Grandpa with a rock."

"I remember," Uncle Matt said, laughing a little louder this time.

Denise pulled me against her side and kissed my head. Everyone loved when I told that story.

When Mama and Dad reached the foyer, Mama's face was really red.

Uncle Matt put his hands on his hips and shook his head at her. "Were you hoping to see me today? Or do you just like riding in my ambulance?"

"Shut up," she said between puffs of air. "Also, thank you."

"Anytime." Matt helped Dad lead her onto the porch. "How far apart are the contractions?"

"About four minutes."

Dad cussed while he locked up behind us. "She went to

bed before Denver last night," he said. "Her back hurt. I didn't realize she was in labor until a little while ago."

Denise made a stunned face. "She's been in labor for what? Twenty-hours?"

"I've told her to call her doctor a dozen times," Dad said. "And she told me to fly a kite."

"I was waiting for Amelia," Mama said in a scary-movie voice. Then, she gritted her teeth and closed her eyes.

"I'm here!" Aunt Amelia called, running to the porch and reaching for Mama. "I couldn't get a flight when you called, so we drove all night. Ryan and Dad are on the way to pick up your aunts, and they're meeting us at the hospital."

Mama blew out a long breath and hugged her friend. She looked at me and Denise, then Matt and Dad. "Now, I can have this baby," she said. "Let's go."

EPILOGUE

GRADY

There weren't supposed to be complications.

Her pregnancy had been textbook, aside from a little extra weight gain and long-lasting nausea. But her doctors had assured her everything was fine. So why was I sitting in a waiting area fearing the worst? For her. For the baby. For my heart and family.

Why was everyone buzzing around me, chatting normally, as if my entire world wasn't in the hands of a team of physicians who looked half my age?

I hated hospitals.

Hated waiting. Hated not being in the know.

She wasn't due for another couple of weeks. The baby was early. And we'd arrived late.

Everly had dragged her feet, and I'd let her, knowing she was setting things in order for the baby's arrival. Maybe if

I'd pushed, we would've been here in time to change whatever was happening now.

I gripped and kneaded my hands, wishing for an outlet as the brewing energy inside me turned into a storm.

Everly worried her family curse was at play, the way she always did in extreme moments like this. We'd been over it a thousand times since the day I'd proposed, and despite our pure happiness together in the twenty-two years since we said our wedding vows, the fear had lingered in her. I supposed old habits die hard. Even when she didn't come out and tell me she was worried, the lemon cake would appear.

I'd gained six pounds in lemon cake alone since this pregnancy announcement. But feeding me gave her peace, so I ate the damned cake and loosened my belt.

A familiar lump rose in my throat, choking my breaths and stinging my eyes. I slumped forward on the miserable waiting room chair, resting my elbows on my knees and covering my face with my hands. I had to be strong. There wasn't a single other useful thing I could do for her right now. So I would at least do that. I'd sit here and keep it together no matter what happened. And when she looked at me, Everly wouldn't see her fears reflected. She'd see confidence, assurance, and love.

Our baby was having a baby. Our family had beaten her imagined odds, and this too was going to be okay.

A shuffle of feet caused me to press the heels of my hands against my eyes and take a steadying breath before sitting up straight. Showtime.

Amelia and Ryan fell into the chairs beside me. Denise and Wyatt were close behind.

"How is she?" Amelia asked, breathless but hopeful. "Did I miss it?"

I shook my head, thankful for the woman before me. The definition of a best friend. She'd promised Everly never to miss anything important to her, and in all the years I'd known her, she'd kept that vow. I owed her everything for the way her presence calmed my wife.

I cleared my throat, making sure my voice was stable before attempting to speak. "She's being prepped for surgery now. Emergency C-section." It wasn't the way she wanted to deliver, but it had stopped being about personal preferences the moment the baby's life became at risk.

Denise and Wyatt took turns patting my shoulders before taking their seats as well.

Both of these couples had been with Everly and me from the beginning. We'd been in both their weddings. None of us were blood related, but we were undeniably family, and I couldn't imagine sitting here in this moment without them.

"I'm glad you're here," I said, a little too gravelly. "It means a lot."

Amelia tipped her head, love and sympathy in her gaze. "Where else would we be?"

Behind her, a sea of blue and green scrubs crisscrossed the hallways, attention fixed to tablets and charts.

My mind raced with things I could've or should've done differently. Better.

All I came up with were images of a blessed life. Every

moment. The ups and the downs. The joy and the pain. Even our weirdo little town and all its nonsensical ways. This life had healed me, and it had healed Denver. But we'd lost plenty along the way as well.

And I'd said goodbye at this hospital more times than I cared to count.

I would not say goodbye to anyone else today.

A tear fell and I suppressed a frustrated growl as I rubbed it quickly away.

Matt strode into view with a smile and a tray of disposable cups in one hand. A large bag with the Sun, Sand, and Tea logo hung from his opposite fingers. Everly had convinced him to make a run to the café for lemon cake. Her personal form of magic. Our family talisman.

"How is she?" he asked, passing out drinks to our friends.

"They're prepping Evie for surgery," Amelia explained, when I couldn't find the words.

"Ah." Matt set the bag on a low table covered in tattered magazines and crouched before me until I met his eyes. "She's going to be okay," he said. "I stopped at the desk, and it sounds as if the level of emergency is low. The C-section is an extreme abundance of caution. Have faith. And eat your cake." He winked before stretching to his feet.

"How's Everly doing?" I asked, grateful for his hospital connections and love for my family.

"Here!" she called, hustling toward our little crowd. She bent to hug each of our friends before shooing Ryan out of his seat so she could sit beside me and take my hands. "Sorry. I spotted Denver in the lot and waited for him to park."

"Denver's here?" My heart thundered as I looked up, searching for our son. He and his wife moved to the mainland to be closer to her parents, and we didn't see them as often as I liked. I hadn't expected to see him until tomorrow, or at least much later tonight.

I launched toward him the moment he came into view. He wrapped me in a bear hug and I wondered for the thousandth time how my first baby had gotten taller and broader than me. How he'd become the kind of man I aspired to be in only a few years' time. Thirty-one to be exact.

Hell, that never seemed right. It couldn't be, otherwise Everly and I would be over fifty and that was more than I could get my head around. But it was true nonetheless.

We pulled apart and Everly was there with us, having followed me, the way she always did. Some days I thought our souls were tethered to the same wire. I felt sorry for anyone who didn't know what that was like.

"How are Sophie and the kids?" she asked. "Are they here? Can you stay a few days? There's plenty of room at the house. You're all welcome to stay with us at the homestead, but you'll have more privacy at the house, and I know the kids love the beach. Plus, Evie and the baby will be with us once she's released from the hospital."

"Soph and the kids will be here after Hope's ballet class," Denver answered. "How long is Brad on leave?"

"Not long enough," Everly said. "Never long enough."

Evie's husband was a military man who came home at every opportunity, but the opportunities were sometimes few and far between. Everly had made sure our daughter and her baby would be comfortable with us until Brad was home again, or until Evie was ready to return to their apartment on base.

I slid my arm around Everly's back, appreciating the dogged determination she applied to everything and everyone she loved. Some days, just watching her was exhausting. But today I tapped into her strength.

She melted against me at the touch.

I stroked her wild hair, thankful for every streak of gray and moment I'd gotten to spend with her. After twenty-two years as her husband, I prayed for twenty-two more, and then some. "She's going to be okay," I whispered. "Evie's tough like her mama. Don't underestimate her."

"Mr. and Mrs. Hays-Swan?" a woman's voice called, turning us in her direction.

Our troop of friends and family were on their feet and at our back before the woman with a white coat and clipboard could reach us.

She smiled. "I'm Dr. Yang. I know we promised to give you a moment before taking Evie in for surgery, but added fetal distress caused a change of plans. We took her straight back and got right to it."

Everly gripped my arm. "She's okay?"

My muscles tensed to the point of pain, and my heart seemed to seize as I waited. The seconds felt like millennia before she spoke again.

"Yes. They're all doing well. Evie and the babies are in recovery now. Brad's with her, but you'll be able to see them all very soon."

A cheer rose up around us as air returned to my lungs. "Thank you," I whispered. "Thank you for protecting my baby." The tears fell then, an unstoppable flood of relief. Over my cheeks and through my beard. I didn't care enough to wipe them away. "Thank you for saving my grandbaby."

"Babies," she said with a grin.

"What?" Everly asked. "More than one baby?"

Dr. Yang nodded, rocking onto her toes. "Evie insisted I keep the details a secret throughout her pregnancy, even from her. She figured it out a while ago, when both babies began to stretch at once. She thought she might be having an octopus."

Everly laughed and hugged me tight. "Wait until I see her! I can't believe she kept this from her mother."

"Thank you," I repeated, voice going hoarse once more.

"It was my pleasure," Dr. Yang assured. "They all did great."

Denver moved in on my opposite side, clapping a hand on my shoulder. "Are the girls in the nursery? How soon can we see them?"

The doctor frowned. "I never said she was having two girls."

"It's kind of a family tradition," he said. "So, I assumed."

The rowdy little crowd behind us went still, listening for whatever the answer might be.

Dr. Yang's lips tipped into a smile. She looked over each shoulder, then dragged her gaze across our friends. "Come with me."

We followed her down the hall to the nursery,

attempting to look inconspicuous despite the fact there were eight of us.

The wing was still and bright. A round window on one side filled the space with natural light and a beautiful view of the sea.

"Don't stay long," she said when we arrived at the viewing area. "Evie will want to see you when she wakes up. She'll be in room 2014."

I nodded my goodbye, unable to take my eyes off the bassinets lined up on the other side of the glass. Two beautiful, dark-haired cherubs snoozed peacefully before me. A name tag had been attached to each tiny bed.

Clara and Fran.

A faint sob broke on Everly's lips, and I pulled her back to my chest, feeling the heady mix of emotions run through her. Evie had chosen a beautiful tribute to the women who'd raised my precious, tenacious wife. A profound reminder of their absence in our world.

"How lovely," Amelia whispered behind us.

"They would've loved this," I said gently. "I'm sure wherever they are, they're honored."

Everly stepped back, face wet with tears. She pressed a palm over her heart and the necklace she'd worn since our wedding day. "They're right here," she said. "Always."

Outside the window beside us, a seagull landed.

Piña Colada Pie

Kick off the summer in true Swan style with the family classic!

Serves: 8–10 | Total Time: 40 minutes + chill time

Crust:
1½ cups graham cracker crumbs
⅓ cup confectioners' sugar
8 tablespoons butter, melted

Garnish:
1 cup heavy cream
½ cup confectioners' sugar
1 teaspoon vanilla extract
Toasted coconut
Maraschino cherries, with or without stems

Filling:

8 oz cream cheese, softened

¼ cup sugar

1½ teaspoons rum extract OR 1–2 tablespoons Malibu
    Coconut Rum

1 teaspoon vanilla extract

½ cup Coco Lopez Coconut Cream

1 (20-ounce) can crushed pineapple, well drained

Prepare the Crust:

Preheat the oven to 350°F.

Combine the graham cracker crumbs and confectioners' sugar in a medium bowl.

Add the melted butter and stir until fully mixed.

Press firmly onto the bottom and up the sides of a
9-inch pie plate.

Bake for 10–12 minutes until it smells toasty and the
edges are just beginning to brown.

Remove from the oven and cool completely before filling.

Prepare the Garnish (Step 1):

Beat the heavy cream in a mixing bowl until stiff.

Transfer to another bowl and store in the refrigerator
while preparing the filling.

Prepare the Filling:

Beat the cream cheese and sugar until smooth.

Add the rum extract/Malibu Coconut Rum and vanilla
extract to the cream cheese mixture.

CHAPTER
ONE

I smiled at the sound of seashell wind chimes jangling over my front door. "Welcome to Sun, Sand, and Tea!" I called, waving to the café's newcomers from my position behind the cash register. It was nearly seven o'clock, closing time, and the final rush of folks were arriving to pick up to-go orders and after-dinner sweets.

I handed my current customer her change, then lifted my eyes to welcome the next in line.

My seaside iced tea shop was a favorite of locals at any hour, but I'd noticed a definite pattern in the two years since I'd opened. Folks liked to have lunch on the decks of my historic Victorian home, and in the dining room overlooking the sea. I'd done my best to play up the fantastic location and majestic views by showcasing the abundance of windows and carrying the beachy color scheme inside. The efforts were a hit, and the place stayed busy through the afternoon most days. But after five, the bulk of my regulars purchased snacks and drinks to-go, then peppered the beach and boardwalk outside, enjoying my culinary handiwork along with the balmy ocean breeze.

"Hey, Mrs. Waters," I said, recognizing the general store owner's wife and my former babysitter's mom. "I've got your cookies right here." I plucked her bag from a lineup of ready orders, then passed the treats her way. "One dozen Colonial Cutouts and a bag of Her Majesty's Munch Mix." I scanned the receipt, then lifted a finger. "And…" I turned briefly to retrieve a chilled container of my best selling brew from the refrigerator. "One quart of Grandma's Old-Fashioned Sweet Tea."

"Bless you," she said, extending a stack of cash in my direction, eyes glued to the bag of goodies before her. "I'm addicted to these cookies. Please tell me they aren't going away after opening night."

I grinned. I'd started to learn a thing or two about sales since opening my shop, and one of those was that people loved themed and limited-time items. Especially when those items had adorable names. My cutouts and munch mix were two more in a long line of examples. Both were named in honor of *The Lost Colony*, a historical outdoor drama preparing for its eighty-fourth season. The Roanoke Historical Society organized the massive annual production, which required more than one hundred people to fill roles from actors to stage crew. The show's popularity made both recipes impossible to keep on the shelves.

"Mr. Waters and I have season tickets, you know," she said, looking immediately younger and wistful. "He took me to opening night on our first date, and we've been together ever since. Haven't missed one in forty-three years."

"I love that," I said, passing her change and receipt. "I'm taking some refreshments to the cast and crew after I close."

She beamed. "Lovely. Oh, how lucky they are. I'd better not keep you."

The Lost Colony was a big deal for locals of Charm and all the other little towns sprinkled along the barrier islands of North Carolina, known to many as the Outer Banks. The play depicted the story of the lost colony at Roanoke, where more than one hundred English men, women, and children landed in the sixteenth century, established an English settlement, then vanished without a trace soon after. The settlers' disappearance was a four-hundred-and-fifty-year-old mystery that still baffled today. Some folks considered the show the heart of the islands. I didn't disagree. Who could resist a good mystery?

ACKNOWLEDGMENTS

I can't believe this is the last time I get to join Everly and her friends on a new adventure, but I am deeply humbled and thankful for the seven precious stories that brought me here. And for the incredible support team that made those stories possible. Anna Michels and Jenna Jankowski at Sourcebooks; my agent, Jill Marsal; my critique partners, Danielle Haas and Jennifer Anderson; and my amazing readers and friends. I have an extra-special shout-out to my Cozy Queens reader group on Facebook, a group that lets me field all sorts of wacky questions and scenarios as my stories take shape. And to one of those Queens in particular, the delightful Melissa Kidd, for her delicious piña colada pie recipe. I'm pretty sure it only serves one, at least when I make it. And last but never least, thank you to my family. You are absolutely everything.

ABOUT THE AUTHOR

 Bree Baker is a mystery-loving daydreamer who got into the storytelling business at a very young age, much to the dismay of her parents and teachers. Today, she is an award-winning and bestselling author. When she's not writing the stories that keep her up at night, Bree stays busy in Kent, Ohio, with her patient husband and three amazing kids. Today, she hopes to make someone smile. One day, she plans to change the world. You can learn more about Bree and her books at breebaker.com.